"I told you—I'm here t

Garth's eyes took on a smoldering tint that caused her heart to thud. Without looking away, he leaned closer.

"You have," he whispered. "And I'm going to kiss you."

Fully unprepared, Bridgette had no response.

Allowing that to happen was a huge risk, but the moment his lips touched hers, she knew it was the right decision. An expansive thrill raced through her system and she looped her arms around his neck.

Her lips parted at the first flick of his tongue and the battle was on—her tongue against his, and it was the most dedicated fight they'd ever had. He went on until they were both winded, and their lips separated by some mutual consent.

However, as their eyes met, their lips met again. The first kiss had immediately become an exploration of unfamiliar ground, but this time it was a gentle journey of territory already discovered and appreciated. She'd known him for years, yet hadn't experienced the depth of that until now. And just as she'd imagined, kissing him was utterly amazing.

Author Note

The orphan trains that distributed children across the plains for over seventy-five years have always intrigued me, and I was excited to finally create a story involving this piece of history. From the moment I started plotting this book, I knew the hero and heroine had traveled west together as children. They hadn't been childhood sweethearts as much as they'd been the anchor that each of them had needed. Then as I started writing the story, the characters took over, changing the plot I'd originally created because, although they'd "gone their separate ways," they both still craved the one person who'd made a difference in their lives—each other, but neither of them was ready to admit it.

I hope you enjoy Garth and Bridgette's story as much as I enjoyed creating it.

LAURI ROBINSON

—

The Cowboy's Orphan Bride

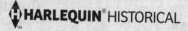

Recycling programs
for this product may
not exist in your area.

ISBN-13: 978-0-373-29923-2

The Cowboy's Orphan Bride

www.Harlequin.com

Printed in U.S.A.

A lover of fairy tales and cowboy boots, **Lauri Robinson** can't imagine a better profession than penning happily-ever-after stories about men—and women—who pull on a pair of boots before riding off into the sunset...or kick them off for other reasons. Lauri and her husband raised three sons in their rural Minnesota home, and are now getting their just rewards by spoiling their grandchildren.

Visit her at laurirobinson.blogspot.com, Facebook.com/lauri.robinson1 or Twitter.com/LauriR.

Books by Lauri Robinson

Harlequin Historical

Daughters of the Roaring Twenties

The Runaway Daughter (Undone!)
The Bootlegger's Daughter
The Rebel Daughter
The Forgotten Daughter

Stand-Alone Novels

The Major's Wife
The Wrong Cowboy
A Fortune for the Outlaw's Daughter
Saving Marina
Western Spring Weddings
"When a Cowboy Says I Do"
Her Cheyenne Warrior
Unwrapping the Rancher's Secret
The Cowboy's Orphan Bride

Harlequin Historical *Undone!* ebooks

Rescued by the Ranger
Snowbound with the Sheriff
Never Tempt a Lawman

Visit the Author Profile page
at Harlequin.com for more titles.

To my critique partner, Paty Jager.
Thanks for always being there to bounce ideas off!

Chapter One

Central Kansas, 1877

"Those damn cowboys!"

Bridgette Banks tightened every muscle against the way she'd flinched at Cecil Chaney's outburst and how he slammed the door. Neither was unusual, she just hadn't expected him to be home so soon. He'd barely been gone an hour, probably less. Which should not have surprised her. He had to be the laziest man she'd ever encountered.

"I'll shoot the lot of them if a single one steps foot on my property!"

She dried her hands with her apron before turning away from the boards nailed to the wall to form the crude counter barely large enough to hold the dishpan. "A cattle drive is near?"

"Of course a cattle drive is near," Cecil barked. "I just said as much, didn't I?"

"No, you said you'd shoot every cowboy." She didn't point out there wasn't a reason anyone would *want* to step on his property.

The chair creaked as Cecil dropped his heavy frame on the seat. "Same thing."

"No, it's not," Bridgette insisted. Arguing, especially with Cecil, got her nowhere, but she'd quit caring about that. His constant complaining had frazzled her nerves since the moment she'd arrived. He complained when it was hot. Complained when it was cold. Complained when it rained. Complained when it didn't. His attitude was exhausting. As had been living in his house the past six weeks. Keeping her voice hushed, she said, "You may want to see if they have a cow you can buy. One nursing a calf. The milk is needed, as is the butter and cream."

"Where am I supposed to get the money to buy a cow?" he snarled.

She bit her tongue to keep from saying he could forgo a few bottles of the hooch he bought from Graham Linkletter and kept stashed behind the barn. Turning around, she picked up the water basin. "Perhaps you could make some sort of bargain with them." Walking to the door, she added, "Emma Sue could use the nourishment, even more once the baby arrives."

"I've used up all my bargaining on you."

Bridgette ignored the disgust lacing his words. Telling him she could leave at any moment would be the most wonderful thing ever. Except for Emma Sue. Goodness, what that woman saw in Cecil, how she'd ever lain with him, become pregnant, took more imagination than Bridgette had. She'd rather bed down in a den of snakes than next to Cecil Chaney. His breath alone was enough to make her eyes water.

"That's what you're here for." Cecil's shout followed her out of the door. "To make sure Emma Sue has nourishment. Meals and rest so she can pop out that baby alive this time. Doctor's orders."

The desire to slap him made Bridgette's hands shake. The fool had no idea how lucky he was to be married with a baby on the way. To have a family. Knowing she couldn't slap him, at least shouldn't, she pitched the water out of the basin with such force dirt splattered across the bottom of her skirt. That increased her ire. There was more than enough to do around here and washing clothes more often than necessary was not a welcomed chore. Reminders of her duties were not necessary, either. Being farmed out to women nearing their delivery time had been her job for over six years. Ever since she'd turned twelve. Others on the Orphan Train had said she was lucky to be adopted by a doctor and his wife. They wouldn't think so now.

"Where is she?"

Containing her thoughts, Bridgette held her attention on wiping the inside of the basin with her apron as she walked back into the two-room shanty made of square blocks of sod. She'd seen many houses just like this one since being taken in by Dr. Rodgers and his wife. Those who lived in homes made out of wood usually had their own help, or other family members, when someone was ailing. That's what she'd have someday, a house made of wood, not dirt. And a family all of her own.

"Your wife is resting," Bridgette said. Emphasizing exactly who she was here to help was a waste of breath, but so would telling him to be quiet. It wouldn't have done any good when he'd stormed into the house and it wouldn't now.

"Already? We just ate breakfast." He harrumphed. "She slept all night. Better than me."

His pouting increased Bridgette's ire. He was big and

homely with black hair so greasy lice couldn't catch enough footing to live in it. And no one had gotten any sleep last night except him. Half the town of Hosford probably heard his snoring, and that was four miles away.

Keeping those thoughts to herself, she removed her apron and switched it out for the other one hanging on the nail. "Creating a new life is hard work on a woman's body."

"It's been happening since the beginning of time, girlie."

"And women have been dying from it for just as long," she answered, walking out the door.

"Where are you going?"

"Someone needs to water the garden," she shouted over her shoulder. Then for her own ears only, muttered, "Lord knows those weeds won't grow on their own." There were pitiful gardens, and then there were pathetic gardens. To call this one merely pathetic would have been a compliment.

The entire acreage of the Chaney place could be described as pathetic. It didn't have to be that way, but Cecil had the ambition of a slug. Emma Sue didn't, which could explain why she'd lost two babies already. Last year and the year before. Both times Cecil had refused Dr. Rodgers's suggestion of help so Emma Sue could rest. Bridgette wondered if Emma Sue's father, who managed the land office in town, had been the one to pony up the extra cost of her staying at the Chaney place. There was no love lost between Douglas Phalen and Cecil, but Douglas must still love his daughter.

Love. Bridgette sighed heavily. Sometimes, the older a person got, the more love they needed. She fully understood that, and hoped someone loved Emma Sue.

She was sweet and kind. Quiet and gentle. The exact opposite of her husband in every way. While Emma Sue was tiny and delicate, Cecil had the shape and co-ordination of a drunken bull.

Bridgette smiled at her own wit. Of course bulls didn't drink, but if one did, it would look exactly like Cecil. Smell about the same, too.

Stopping as she rounded the corner of the house, Bridgette lifted her face to the sky. The summer sun blazed down enough arid heat to make plants curl their leaves. She didn't mind. It was hot, but the brightness and fresh air were a wonderful reprieve from dark and gloomy dankness inside the sod shanty.

She closed her eyes and let the sunshine fill her. Cleanse her. A thud inside the house made her open her eyes and sigh. Feeling fresher and lighter, she pinched her lips as a silly image formed. That of the chair collapsing under Cecil. Smiling, she made her way to the garden.

A short time later, sweat trickled down her back as she drew water from the well and carried bucket after bucket to the tiny fenced-in area behind the house. Careful not to waste a drop, she watered only the vegetables, plucking out weeds as she made her way up and down the meager rows. The only thing producing were the bean plants. She'd have to pick them again today.

She should be happy about that. Six weeks ago, critters were eating anything that popped out of the ground. The fence had done wonders. No thanks to Cecil. He'd merely pointed out where there was some old lumber. Mr. Phalen had brought out the wire when coming to visit Emma Sue one day.

Too bad he hadn't brought out jars. She wanted to can the beans so Emma Sue would have a few more reserves come snowfall. Mrs. Winters had taught her how to can practically anything several years ago when she'd stayed with the Winters family for an entire fall, but asking Mr. Phalen to provide jars was out of the question. Emma Sue refused to ask her father for things. Said Cecil didn't approve of her doing so.

Therefore, despite Cecil's complaint that he didn't like green beans, there would be more on the table for lunch, and supper.

Bridgette had no idea what made her stand up and gaze southward, beyond Cecil's scrawny and scraggly field of wheat. An irrigation ditch from the creek that flowed freely not too far past the line of barbed wire Cecil had erected to keep others off his property could turn that wheat into strong, flourishing stalks. Emma Sue said no one owned that land, but diverting the water would be too much work for Cecil.

To hear Cecil talk, walking was too much work for him. Bridgette hadn't mentioned that to Emma Sue, or that the land next door was the piece Cecil should have bought, but she'd thought it. That creek flowed from the river and would provide plenty of water for people, animals and crops.

That's what she wanted, and would have. Someday. A piece of land with plenty of water and good, fertile soil, and a solid house made of wood, with floors and windows and a real cookstove complete with an oven. And it would all be hers. Truly hers. A place to plant roots. She'd be the one having babies then, children she'd welcome and love with all her heart and never, ever, let out of her sight.

Bridgette continued to scan the horizon. The land was so flat a person could watch a bird fly away for days. New York hadn't been like that, what she could remember of it, and the land between here and there had been decorated with rolling hills and trees. And houses, big ones surrounded by flowers and fences.

Her house would be surrounded by trees. Big leafy ones that would provide shade from the summer sun and protection from the cold winter winds.

She grinned at the thought, and how memories started to form. Those of playing games with the other children on the train, each guessing what they might see next.

Her heart fluttered slightly when she recalled how Garth had predicted he'd see an elephant. Everyone had laughed, but minutes later, they'd pulled into a train station, and sure enough, there, on another train, had stood an elephant.

She rarely thought of the other orphans who'd been shipped West with her all those years ago, except for one. A day hardly passed, even after all these years, when she didn't think of him.

"Garth McCain," she whispered. "Whatever happened to you? Do you even remember the promises we made?"

Bridgette let her mind roam and wondered if she'd recognize him when she did see him again. Not if. When. Garth would find her. He had to. Otherwise all her years of waiting, all their promises would be for naught, and she refused to believe that. His hair would surely still be brown, and his eyes. He'd be taller, but she couldn't imagine he'd have grown fat. Not like Cecil.

She shook aside a shiver at comparing Garth to Cecil, and her gaze settled on a spot on the horizon. There was nothing distinguishable, but the gray haze said something was there. The cattle drive Cecil had mentioned, most likely. They traveled through this region each summer, on their way to Dodge City.

Unlike Cecil, the small town of Hosford welcomed the cattle drives. Dodge was still twenty miles north, and though the cowboys rarely entered town, the trail bosses often did, restocking supplies for the last leg of the long trip they'd embarked upon months before down in Texas.

She'd never been to Dodge, but she'd heard it was a wicked and wild town. Where soiled doves ran naked in the streets and men chased them, whooping and hollering when they caught one of the women.

It wasn't for her to say if that was true or not, but she'd like to see if it was. Dr. Rodgers and his wife, Sofia, whom, even after nine years, Bridgette still referred to as Mrs. Rodgers, would be horrified to know she wondered about such things, therefore she never mentioned her curiosity. Not to anyone.

In the nine years since she'd left the Orphan Train, there hadn't been anyone to share secrets with, not like she had Garth. He'd known all her secrets, and she'd known his.

Staring at the gray haze rising from the ground to faintly obscure the blueness of the sky, she sighed. "It's been a long time, Garth," she whispered. "And I'm getting tired of looking for rainbows."

"Are you done out there?"

Bridgette breathed through the spine-crawling sensation of Cecil's shout before grabbing the empty water bucket. Leaving the garden, she swiped aside the hair that had escaped her bun to tickle her cheek. "Baby Chaney," she mumbled, "if you want to meet your father, you best hurry up. He's getting close to being whacked by a frying pan."

Chapter Two

"Mr. McCain!"

Garth twisted in his saddle to watch a cowboy ride through the haze of dust. The herd was anxious to get moving this morning, butting into one another as they found their place to start marching north. Churned up by thousands of hooves, the dirt stung his eyes as it swirled in the wind. He used the back of one hand to wipe his lips before asking, "What?"

One of the drovers, Martie, Brad Martie, who should be riding drag, rode up beside him, and shifted the reins from his left hand to his right and back again.

Twisting the tension in his neck, Garth cursed beneath his breath. He hated men who fidgeted almost as much as he hated whiners. Calling Brad a man was stretching it. The red fuzz on Brad's chin said he wasn't much more than a kid. Having just completed a ride from the rear to the head of the herd, doing a final check before heading out, Garth had already eaten enough dust. He gestured for Brad to follow him a short distance away from the cattle before he repeated, "What?"

"A heifer let loose."

Garth tipped back his hat and wiped away a band of

sweat before it dripped into his eyes. The sun was hot today, and the cattle would need water come evening. Hence their excitement to get going. A cow could smell water miles away. "Which one?" he asked.

Switching hands on the reins again, Brad answered, "The big white-faced one."

Garth cursed beneath his breath. He was hoping that one would make it to Dodge. In truth, he hoped they all would make it to Dodge. They couldn't be more than four, maybe five days out. That heifer was a fine specimen and her calf would have brought good money. He'd hauled a calf in the chuck wagon before, for a day or two. Five was too long. The separation would be too much on the cow, and the calf could never keep up on its own. Not only would it slow down its mother, they both would easily become trampled by the others. He felt the loss of every cow, and didn't like it, but there were plenty of things about a drive that weren't easy. The loss of any life was the worst, but he couldn't jeopardize the herd or a man's life over one calf. His stomach clenched, but still he ordered, "Shoot the calf."

The revulsion that rippled across the young man's face pulled Garth's jaw so tight his back teeth clenched.

"Couldn't we find a sodbuster and give it to them like we did down south?" Brad asked, with a goodly portion of hope lacing his young voice.

"No," Garth said. "I don't have time to roam the countryside searching for sodbusters." The sorrow on Brad's face reminded him of years ago, when he'd been fourteen and shipped West with a trainload of sad-eyed, snot-nosed kids. They hadn't all been snot-nosed. Not Bridgette Banks. She'd been the one wiping everyone else's noses. Taking care of everyone else. That had been her. And of all the things he'd tried to forget about his life back then, she was still the hardest. For all his efforts, he just couldn't erase her from his mind.

It had been years, but he'd bet his best horse she was still as cute as she'd been back then. He'd yet to see a pair of eyes as blue as hers. He'd bet, too, that her feathery blond hair would still catch in the corner of her mouth when she spouted off over some infraction or another. Though she'd looked sweet and angelic, she'd had the mouth of a New York orphan. He'd appreciated that. Others hadn't. Especially not Mrs. Killgrove.

He hoped the family that had adopted her had treated her well over the years. She deserved that. That's all she'd ever wanted. A family. A home. A place she could call her own and people to love. She'd still been on the train when he'd been sold. That's what it had been. An auction not so unlike the old slavery traditions, except there was no money exchanged for the boys, only promises of providing food and shelter by bidders who didn't want a child, but a worker. One they didn't have to pay.

Pulled back to the present by mooing cows, Garth looked at Brad while gesturing toward the cattle. "See that herd? They haven't had water in two days. That's my job today, to find water, not sodbusters. If I don't find water, none of us will sleep tonight. We'll all be riding guard, hoping they don't stampede."

Brad nodded, but didn't look convinced.

Garth held his temper in order to say, "We gave those calves down south to Indians so they'd let us pass through their territory without any issues. A sodbuster would need to have a cow that would let that calf nurse, and that's not easy." Cows didn't take to orphans any better than humans did. Flustered by having to give a drover a school lesson, Garth spun his horse around. "Shoot it."

He kneed his horse into a run, and didn't let it slow until the dust was well behind them. The thought of ordering Brad to put down that calf reminded him of his first drive. He'd been fifteen, and had been assigned to ride drag the entire trip. Afterward he'd sworn that would be the last time. He'd taken it upon himself to learn what it took to be a trail boss, the good and the bad. Putting down that calf was the bad, as was doing the work of two men when he was a man short. That, being a man short, unfortunately, had happened more often than he'd liked over the years. There were just too many men out there who had signed on thinking a trail drive was little more than a stroll to church on Sunday. He'd never regretted a one that had left his employ. If you couldn't do what had to be done, you'd never amount to anything. That was his motto. Being in a saddle for sixteen hours a day wasn't unreasonable, and he let go any man who thought otherwise.

Not a one of the men he'd fired had stolen from him. Other trail bosses sometimes discovered men had taken off with a horse from the outfit's remuda after being fired. He didn't. He laid down the law on exactly how a thief would be dealt with from the day he hired a man, as well as plenty of other expectations. He lived by the rules he set as strongly as he laid them out.

Despite what some liar in New York had said all those years ago, he'd been honest his entire life, and expected as much from others.

There were fifteen men in his outfit, not counting himself, JoJo—the best trail cook God ever gave a frying pan to—and Bat, JoJo's helper. While riding alongside the herd, even as his thoughts roamed, Garth counted heads. Human ones. He hadn't lost a single hand on this trip, and was more than relieved about that.

He was pleased, too, and would be the first to admit it took a lot to please him.

Satisfied with the number of men he'd counted and confident the cattle were moving at a solid pace, Garth forced himself to put the calf out of his mind and rode past the point riders to catch up with JoJo.

The chuck wagon always traveled a few miles ahead of the herd, and as Garth rode, the calf crossed his mind again. Even if he found a sodbuster to take it, the calf wouldn't have much of a chance. Orphans as a whole didn't stand much of a chance. He was reminded of that every time he traveled north into Kansas.

If the orphanage hadn't taught him that, the farmer who'd taken him off the train had. He'd spent over a month with Orson Reins before deciding he'd had enough. Orson had said from the moment Garth had arrived at his farm that you could take a boy off the street, but the only way to take the street out of the boy was with a whip. When Orson had broken out his whip again, something had snapped inside Garth and he'd wrestled the whip out of Orson's hands and left.

He'd carried that whip with him for five years, until one night when he'd burned it, concluding his past was well and gone. He was never going back, so there was no need to hold on to any reminders of his past.

"Heading out, Boss?" JoJo shouted above the rattling of his chuck wagon.

Garth caught up with the wagon, and then reined in his horse next to where JoJo sat on the wagon seat. "I remember some water being a short distance ahead."

"Still figure we're about five days out?" JoJo asked.

"Four if we're lucky."

"You're lucky all right," JoJo answered with a laugh.

"This trail is working out for us. You know I had my reservations."

"You liked the Chisholm," Garth answered. On his way south last year, he'd veered west to explore the Great Western Trail. Some swore by it, others claimed it was cursed. The same was true for the Chisholm.

"Was used to the Chisholm," JoJo said. "Knew every hill and water hole on that trail. So did you."

"We did," Garth admitted. He'd chosen the Great Western this year because these were *his* cattle being driven north. After spending all winter acquiring and paying room and board for the whole lot of four-footed beasts, he needed to get top dollar.

"But Dodge is paying more than Wichita right now, so we took this one," JoJo supplied, rubbing his scruffy gray beard with one hand.

Garth nodded. "You're smarter than you look. Guess you do have a brain under that bald scalp." Though Wichita was still accepting cattle, the days of the big drives were limited. The farmers were putting up too much of a fuss and the townspeople were agreeing with them, laying down more and more rules for the cattle-men to follow.

JoJo pointed a finger. "And your mug is uglier than you think."

Garth laughed. "I never claimed to be handsome, but can't say I've had any complaints, either."

JoJo chortled, and rubbed his beard a bit more when he asked, "What you gonna do with all that money you're gonna make on this trip? Got yourself a woman holed up somewhere?"

Garth laughed. A woman was the last thing he wanted. "If I did, I sure wouldn't tell you about it. You'd try stealing her."

JoJo laughed so hard he coughed. With watery eyes, he said, "Not me, but Bat might."

"Uh-uh," Bat said, shaking his head. "I don't want no woman telling me what to do."

Bat was the youngest on the drive. Too young really, maybe ten or twelve, but JoJo wouldn't leave Texas without the kid he'd found somewhere over the winter. Knowing the options for an orphan too well, Garth had agreed the boy could join them. He wasn't sorry, either. Bat was a good little worker and certainly earned his wage.

The boy was an added bonus, to Garth's way of thinking. Bat was the reason JoJo had been willing to leave the outfit he'd been with for the past several years. JoJo never said Evans wouldn't let a kid join his drive, hadn't needed to. Bottom line was Evans's loss had been Garth's gain. An outfit needed a good cook, and JoJo was one of the best. Even though he was a bit cantankerous at times, and full of himself.

"Now that's smart thinking if I ever heard it," Garth said to Bat.

The boy grinned and sat a bit taller on the wagon seat.

"Malcolm sure was sad to see you leave," JoJo said.

Malcolm Johansson, the man who'd hired him when he'd been as green as grass, was still a trusted friend and a man Garth was thankful to have met. Malcolm was a hard man, but an honest one, and had taught Garth a lot about life. "I told him my plan the day he hired me." A plan he was still working on. That's how he did things, thought each detail out thoroughly before putting them in place, and then followed them through to the end. That had been the one lesson he'd learned back at the orphanage that he'd held on to. Not thinking things through made for a tough life.

"I heard as much," JoJo said. "But Malcolm was still sad to see you leave his employ."

"Sam Taylor will serve Malcolm well," Garth told JoJo the same thing he'd told many others when they'd questioned him leaving Johansson's employ. "He's been driving cows to Wichita for years."

"Yeah, he will," JoJo said. "But Sam Taylor ain't no Garth McCain."

Coming from JoJo, that was a compliment like no other, and Garth figured it was a good place to end the conversation. "I'll be back in time for the evening meal," he said, tapping his heels against his horse.

"Don't forget my supplies!" JoJo shouted.

Garth waved a hand to signal that he'd heard while urging the horse into a gallop.

They had to be around forty miles south of Dodge City. He could almost smell the town. Every stinking inch of it. Dodge smelled of cattle, booze, cigar smoke and women. Not a single one of those things was offensive to him.

This would be the first time he'd dealt with the stockyards there. All his other drives had ended in Wichita. That's where he'd made his way to after leaving Orson's place, and where he'd run into Malcolm. At the Wichita stockyards. The man had told him if he ever made it down to Texas to look him up. He was always in need of cowboys.

That was exactly what Garth had done, followed Malcolm all the way south, and along the way, told Malcolm his plan. That he'd work for him, until it was time for him to go out on his own. That had been nine years ago, and last fall, after returning to Texas, he'd told Malcolm it was time. It had taken him years to save up enough money to assure all would turn out just as he'd imagined. A good sale this year would guarantee he'd been right.

Malcolm hadn't tried to talk him out of going out on his own. Instead he'd offered a place to pasture the cattle Garth had bought and rounded up throughout the winter—at a price of course. Garth hadn't expected any less.

That's how life should be. Fair. Honest. That had been an issue for him. People's dishonesty. Malcolm claimed Garth had driven away more cowhands than any man he'd ever known. Garth had retorted by saying Malcolm should be happy about that. No one wants a dishonest man in their employ. Or foolish or impulsive ones. That's how mistakes were made.

Malcolm had agreed, but had also warned him to be careful about expectations. Said sometimes a man doesn't know what he wants until he sees it.

Garth laughed at the memory. He knew what he wanted. Right now, that was water, so he settled his attention on the lay of the land, looking for telltale signs. In this country, that meant trees.

Glancing in both directions, and straight ahead again, Garth drew a deep breath and let it out. He'd settle for one. One tree. That's all he needed. Just one.

Once he found a water spot for the cattle to rest for the night, he'd ride on into Hosford and pick up some coffee and bacon. JoJo had said this morning there wasn't quite enough to get them to Dodge. The cook had offered to ration the portions if needed, but Garth had said no. His men earned their wages every day, and their fodder. He'd never told a cowhand he couldn't eat his fill, and he wasn't about to start now.

The other reason he needed to go to Hosford was to send a telegram to Dodge, to make sure the stockyard was ready to receive his cattle.

He held up a hand to shield the glare of the sun as he scanned the horizon. One of the downfalls of being the first drive of the year was not having a clear path to follow. The trail had been well-worn last fall when he'd taken it south. Now a new growth of grass covered the prairie. What he'd followed last fall could be a few miles either east or west. He didn't think so, but had to admit it was possible. Cattle needed grass to eat along the way, which meant drives didn't follow an exact trail. Rather, the route was spread out east and west for miles. Hence, why some called the Great Western trail cursed. Water, the other thing cattle needed, could be elusive. Might be only a mile away, yet never found.

The same was true for the Chisholm, and he'd been the first on that trail more than once over the years. Trusting his gut, he angled his horse slightly northwest. This land was so flat, so barren, a tree should stand out like a red petticoat, but dang if he could see one right now.

He clearly remembered a creek crossing the trail around these parts. An offshoot of the larger river farther east. He'd camped near that creek. Alone last fall, he'd traveled much faster than he could with a drive of over twenty-five hundred head of cattle, but considering they'd stayed near the Big Basin two nights ago, that creek had to be close. Hosford couldn't be more than five or six miles north of here.

Scanning the area again, he pinpointed his gaze. A dot on the horizon could be a tree, or it could be a house. There was only one way to find out.

Chapter Three

"These green beans are so delicious, Bridgette," Emma Sue said with a voice that was little more than a whisper. "How did you make them?"

"I fried them in the bacon grease left from this morning," Bridgette answered while gently covering the dough she'd just rolled out and cut into strips. Squaring the corners of the cloth to make sure dust or insects didn't settle upon her egg noodles as they dried, she continued, "I also added a few onions I found growing west of the house."

"I think that's where the former owners had their garden," Emma Sue said. "Cecil didn't want it that far away from the house. Said it was too far for me to carry water."

Bridgette chomped her teeth together to keep from making a comment about Cecil carrying the water and pretended to be focused on securing the edges of the cloth with a couple of spoons.

"I'm sure Cecil will like green beans prepared like this. He claims he doesn't like them, but he must, because he never brings home any other seeds." Smiling, Emma Sue chewed another small forkful of beans before speaking again. "I got some carrot and turnip seeds, and a few others from my father, but I'm afraid Cecil forgot to water them when I first took ill."

"He didn't forget," Bridgette mumbled as she crossed the room to add salt to the pot of water holding the rabbit she'd shot after tending to the garden this morning. Cecil may be too lazy to see Emma Sue got the proper nourishment, but she wasn't.

"What? I'm afraid I didn't hear you."

Bridgette covered the pot and pulled up a smile before she turned about. "Nothing, just talking to myself."

"Cecil's not always this grumpy," Emma Sue said. "He's just frustrated because…" Her cheeks turned pink as she laid a hand on her protruding stomach. "Because with me so far along we can't…"

Bridgette held up a hand, hoping to stop Emma Sue before she finished her sentence, but it was too late.

"Well, you know, be husband and wife."

Bridgette stifled a groan. She'd known what Emma Sue had been referring to, and hadn't needed to hear it. If she let that image into her head, she might never be able to sleep again.

Moving and using her hand to gesture toward the table, Bridgette said, "There's more bread and the beans are on the stove for when Cecil returns. I set the rabbit to simmer while I'm gone, and there's nothing you need to do with it or the noodles." She'd hoped to have left long before now—sincerely wished she had—but Emma Sue hadn't wanted lunch prepared until Cecil arrived home. Not willing to wait any longer, Bridgette had overridden that notion, explaining there were other tasks that needed to be completed yet today.

"Will you teach me how you made those noodles?" Emma Sue asked, gesturing toward the cloth. "Cecil really enjoyed them when you made them last week with the pheasant he shot."

Bridgette had to bite her tongue to keep from pointing out that *she'd* shot the pheasant—another skill she'd been taught while being a nursemaid to yet another family. Once the urge passed, she said, "You just beat a couple eggs with enough flour to make a sticky dough and then fold in enough flour until you can roll it thin and slice it into strips." Pulling the apron over her head, she crossed the room to hang it on its nail. "I'll be back as soon as possible, and add the noodles to the pot then, so don't worry about that. They'll only need to cook a few minutes and supper will be ready."

"I don't know what I would have done without you these past few weeks." Emma Sue sighed. "Walking all the way to Hosford and back to sell the eggs would have been too much for me."

"Yes, it would have been," Bridgette agreed. Suggesting Cecil could easily make the trip, considering the money they made from selling eggs was about their only income, crossed her mind, but there was no need in pointing out the obvious. "You'll rest while I'm gone?" she asked Emma Sue pointedly.

"Yes. I might sew, but I'll do that in my bed."

"Good, that's what I needed to hear." Bridgette took down her bonnet from the nail in the corner where her personal belongings were folded and stacked, including the blankets she spread out on the floor to sleep upon each night. Twisting the bonnet ties into a bow beneath her chin, she said, "I already have the rabbit fur soaking. Once I've tanned it, you'll be able to make something for the baby. Maybe a warm hat for this winter."

"Oh, that is so nice of you." Emma Sue shook her

head. "You are so smart. How did you learn about so many things?"

"I've been a nursemaid for many families over the years," Bridgette answered. "And have learned something from each one of them. Opal Andrest showed me how to make the egg noodles and Ted Wilkenson taught me how to tan a rabbit hide."

"Oh, what are you learning from us?"

How I don't want to live. Not able to say that, she smiled. "I'm not sure yet, but I'll tell you as soon as I do." Since that didn't sound very flattering, she added, "Someday we'll have time for you to teach me some of your embroidery stitches. You are very good at that."

Emma Sue beamed. "Oh, yes, I will teach you." Her smile faded. "But I'll need to get some more thread and—"

"Don't worry about that now," Bridgette said. "We have time." Picking up the two baskets of eggs, she added, "But I don't. I must hurry. Don't want Mr. Haskell closing his store before I get these eggs delivered."

"Please remember Cecil's plug of tobacco."

Bridgette nodded and walked out the open doorway. If she kept biting it, she wouldn't have a tongue left by the time Emma Sue delivered that baby. Leaving the door open for some air circulation, she started down the pathway that would eventually lead her to the road to Hosford.

She couldn't seem to walk fast enough. It was as if she was escaping, running away. That wouldn't happen. She was only taking the eggs to town to sell them. However, that in itself was an escape. A welcome one. Even though it wouldn't be more than a couple of hours.

She couldn't be gone any longer than that. Emma Sue's time was near.

A shiver rippled Bridgette's spine. "No," she said aloud, forcing her mind not to bring up any images. Not to remember Emma Sue's statement. She knew what husbands and wives did to produce babies. She'd helped with numerous deliveries and had performed several alone when Dr. Rodgers hadn't arrived in time.

Every birth made her think of her own life. Her future. Babies of her own. It felt as if she'd been waiting forever for that to happen. Waiting to start living the life she dreamed about each night. Waiting for her husband.

She sighed at that thought. Garth wasn't really her husband. It hadn't been a real marriage. She'd been seven and just learned the truth about her parents, that they'd died and would never be coming back to get her from the orphanage. She'd told Garth she didn't want to be an orphan and he'd said he'd be her family, then neither of them would be orphans. When she'd said two people couldn't just become family, he'd said they could if they got married. So he'd married her. It had been a pretend ceremony, in the backyard of the orphanage under the same big tree she'd fallen out of— and broken her arm in the process. But she'd never felt like an orphan, never felt alone, after that make-believe ceremony.

An outsider yes. That she'd been since being taken off the train. Living with people who would never be her family.

"Hold up there!"

Frustration shattered her thoughts. Letting out a long sigh, she turned about and watched Cecil riding his big plow horse along his barbed wire fence. She squinted as he rode closer, trying to figure out what he had on his lap.

Curiosity won out, and she made her way toward the hole he'd made in the fence. A gate would have been too much work for Cecil. "What do you have?" she asked.

"You told me to get a cow," Cecil shouted. "I did better than that! Got a calf!"

Sure enough, it was a calf. She recognized that now that he'd pointed it out. "How on earth do you expect to keep a calf alive?"

He rode past her, toward the barn that was in serious need of repair. "I ain't gonna keep it alive. We's gonna eat it."

Momentarily stunned, Bridgette shook her head, questioning her hearing. It only took a moment for her to realize she'd heard right. This was Cecil, and that's just how he'd think. "Oh, no, you're not!" she shouted, running after him. She'd carefully packed straw around the six dozen eggs in the baskets to prevent breakage, but at this moment, she didn't care if every egg broke.

When the horse stopped near the barn door hanging on one hinge, she set down both baskets and marched forward. "A calf's not better. Emma Sue needs milk, cream and butter. That you would have gotten from the calf's mother. Whom that calf needs. Where is she? Where's this calf's mother?"

"Back with the rest of the herd," Cecil said. "And I am too gonna kill this here calf. That's what that cowboy was gonna do."

"What cowboy?" she asked, rubbing the calf's nose. It was adorable. Red-brown with the cutest little white face and big brown eyes. The poor thing couldn't be more than a few hours old.

"One of the cowboys with the cattle drive," Cecil

said. "The trail boss told him to shoot the calf. Lucky for me I rode up when I did." Curling one edge of his upper lip, he chortled. "He didn't want to shoot it. Tried, but didn't have the guts to pull the trigger. I watched him."

Infuriated, Bridgette slapped his leg. "Get down."

"Let me hand you the calf."

"No," she snapped. "Leave the calf where it is. Just get off that horse."

"I cain't get off with it on my lap."

She grabbed a handful of his pant leg and pulled. "Yes, you can. Now get down. Hurry up."

"Why?"

Holding back a scream that tore at her neck muscles, she growled, "You either get off that horse, or I'll leave. I'll go to Hosford and you'll be out here alone, taking care of Emma Sue, and the baby that'll be born any day now."

"You cain't do that."

"Oh, yes, I can." As a second thought, she added, "And I'll tell Emma Sue's father you wouldn't listen to me. That I couldn't tolerate being in your presence any longer."

He scooted back in the saddle and swung a leg over the horse's rump. "You don't gotta get snippy about it. I thought you'd be happy. I did what you said."

As soon as he was out of the way, she gathered her skirt with one hand and stuck a foot in the stirrup. "No you didn't," she said once she'd swung into the saddle. "I told you to get a cow."

"Well, whaddya call that?" Cecil frowned. "Where you going?"

Once she had her skirt positioned so she could sit comfortably, she scooted forward, easing the calf onto her lap. "To get its mother."

"They won't give you its mother," Cecil said. "They wanted it dead so they could take the mother to Dodge."

What she'd told Emma Sue had been the truth. She'd learned a lot from the other families she'd been farmed out to as a nursemaid. The things she'd learned came in useful every day. Including today. "Give me those egg baskets."

"What for?"

Huffing out a sigh at his ignorance, she explained, "Because I'm going to trade them to the cattle drive cook for the calf's mother."

"Eggs for a cow." He guffawed. "You're addlebrained."

"No, I'm not." Unable to hold it back, she said, "You are. Eggs are a luxury to the men on a cattle drive." More than once she'd seen people trade eggs and vegetables for beef when the drives came through. "Go in the house and get me that bucket of beans, and my apron."

"What ya need the calf for if'n your trading the eggs for its momma?"

She closed her eyes in order to gather her temper. "Because there will be hundreds of cows out there. I'll need the baby so the mother will sniff it out, and that will tell me which cow is its mother."

Cecil frowned. "Well, what—"

"Just go get the beans and my apron, and hurry up! This calf isn't going to live long hanging over this saddle."

He spun around. Bridgette knew it wasn't because of her. Emma Sue had shouted his name from the doorway. Loud enough it had startled her. She breathed easy though, seeing Emma Sue standing in the doorway with the bucket of beans and her apron.

"Go get them," Bridgette said. "Don't make her walk out here."

She waited until he'd taken the items from his wife before she said, "Emma Sue, you go lie down now. We don't want that baby coming any earlier than necessary." For the baby's sake. If it was up to her, the baby would have come shortly after she'd arrived so she could get out of this place and never lay eyes on Cecil again.

Emma Sue waved and stepped back inside the house.

"What are you gonna do with this stuff?" Cecil asked while handing her the bucket and apron.

"Just get me the eggs." After hooking the bucket handle over one arm, she used the calf as a table. Laying out the apron, she folded the skirt in half, tucked the edges around each other and used the ties to form a makeshift bag. She then dumped in the beans.

Handing the bucket to Cecil, she hooked the strap around her neck and then took the egg baskets from him. One at a time set the baskets in the bag, trying not to smash the beans or jostle the eggs too much. They were now worth more than if she'd taken them to town and sold them to Haskell's store. Once satisfied the bag would hold, she eased the apron around her side. "Help me," she told Cecil while holding onto the neck strap that was tightening against her throat with one hand. "Place the bottom of the bag on the swell of the saddle. Right in the middle. Use the beans to level it so it won't bounce about too much."

"Use the beans?"

"Yes, they are in the bottom. Be careful, but separate the bottom of the bag enough so some beans are inside the saddle swell and some are on the outside."

He did as she instructed. "I'll be. That works pretty well." He stepped back then. "But it's a long ride to where I got that calf."

It couldn't be that far. He never traveled too far.

"We'll make it," she told the calf, not Cecil, and then nudged the horse forward.

"Don't you want directions?" Cecil asked.

If he'd found it, she'd find it. "No," she answered. "I'll just head toward the dust in the air."

"That's what I did," Cecil said, walking beside the horse.

"You don't say." She nudged the horse again, desperate to pick up enough speed to leave Cecil behind.

"If'n you don't come back, I ain't coming to look for you," Cecil shouted as the horse gained ground on him.

"Thank you," she shouted in return. He most likely wouldn't grasp the insult, but she did, and that made her smile.

"You best be back in time for supper!"

She opened her mouth to tell him there was food on the stove, but chose against it. The shout could startle the horse or the calf, and neither deserved that. The calf was newly born, and the horse had to be as uncomfortable as her. The saddle was made for a riding horse, so the tree was too narrow for the plow horse's wide back, making it ride high on the horse's sides, and knowing Cecil, she couldn't imagine he'd had much concern for the animal in tightening the cinch.

Letting the horse amble along, she petted the soft fur of the calf. "Don't worry, little one. We'll find your momma. That we'll do." The notion the trail boss might not be interested in making a trade for eggs and beans crossed her mind, but she sent it packing. There was no sense in worrying about something until it happened.

Chapter Four

$\backsim\!\!\!\!\!\curvearrowright\!\!\!\!\!\sim$

By the time Garth rode into camp, one of his eyes was swollen shut and the other wasn't far behind. Despite the mud he'd caked on, the side of his face was on fire. JoJo had found the marker he'd left and already had a fire going, thankfully. Unable to see much, he'd relied on his nose to lead him to the campsite. There was no doubt the men had settled the herd in for the night a mile or so away, as usual, and today he appreciated their competency more than ever.

"What happened to you, Boss?"

"My horse stepped on a hornet nest," he told Bat while swinging out of the saddle. "Unsaddle her and put her up for me."

"That looks sore," Bat said.

"It is." Garth tried harder to see out the eye that hadn't been stung, but it was watering profusely, and that forced him to leave the things he'd picked up in town for Bat to collect as well. "Both packs are full of supplies."

"Got it," Bat said. "You need help?"

"No." Garth spun about to make his way to the camp, but paused. "Who's that?" Things were too blurry to

make out much other than the chuck wagon and a large
plow horse. Strangers of any kind visiting the camp
singed his nerves almost as sharply as the hornets had
stung his face. Cattle drives held no room for social
gatherings. Most folks respected that.

"She brought us some eggs," Bat said.

"This here gal needs to talk to you, Boss," JoJo
shouted the same time as Bat had spoken. "I done said
it's a fair deal, but that ain't my call. No siree, it ain't
my call. Even if'n I'm thinking it's a fair deal. A mighty
fair deal."

Dang near blind, one foot snagged on a rock or lump
on the ground of some sort. Garth caught his balance
before going down, but his frustration tripled.

"What the hell happened to you?" JoJo asked.

"Hornet nest."

"You fall on it?"

"No, I didn't fall on it," Garth answered. "I put the
mud on to cool down the sting."

"You gotta tug out the stinger, not force it in further," JoJo supplied.

Garth's nerves had snapped awhile ago. "I couldn't
see the damn stinger," he growled.

"Well, I'll get it out for ya," JoJo said.

Having arrived near the wagon, Garth gestured toward the woman standing on the other side of the fire.
"In a minute," he said to JoJo. "What deal?" It probably
was a good thing he couldn't see. This country had a
way of making even the finest gal look beyond her years
in no time. The brim of this one's gray bonnet arched
from one side of her chin to the other and hid most of
her face. He didn't need to see it in order to imagine her
skin had been wrinkled and aged by the wind and sun.

She pointed toward two crates sitting on the ground.

He squinted, but it didn't help him make out much. The eggs Bat referred to most likely. The other crate had some kind of greens it. As water dripped out the corner of one eye, he turned his other eye back to the crate holding the eggs. His mouth practically watered. He'd considered buying eggs while in town, but there had only been half a dozen in the basket on the counter of the mercantile. Not nearly enough for eighteen hungry men. The cowboys had to be as hungry for something besides beans, biscuits and bacon as he was.

"Those for the calf and its mother," the woman said.

Disappointment that neither he nor anyone else would be eating eggs filtered in amongst his frustration at not being able to see. "We don't have any calves, ma'am." Another heifer had better not have let loose. That was about the last thing he needed this close to Dodge.

"Yes, you do," she said. "The one you ordered to have shot this morning."

The loss of that calf had hung in the back of his mind all day. Not only for the critter. He'd counted on getting the entire herd to the stockyards. The money every cow would bring in. Before leaving Texas, he'd calculated on giving a few head to the Indians; they expected it, and he'd gladly given them the beeves for allowing safe passage, but loosing another one, even a calf, was not in his plan. Furthermore, her snooty attitude settled about as well as the hornet sting had. "How do you know about that?"

Her entire frame, though it was no taller than JoJo when his rheumatism didn't have him stooped over, stiffened. "There's no need for cursing," she snapped. "Just as there is no need to kill an innocent calf. Such actions border on despicable."

"Border on—"

"Despicable," she repeated. "It means appalling. Disgraceful."

"I know what it means." Holding back a few choice words that she probably didn't know the meanings of, he glared at JoJo with one eye. "Where's the calf?"

"Brad is…" JoJo gestured with his chin. "Was looking for its momma. Looks like he found her."

Garth spun around and made out the blurry sight of a rider climbing off a horse. There was a cow behind the horse, and sure as hell, a calf beside the cow.

Sucking in air hot enough to blister his lungs, Garth walked past the woman, heading directly towards Brad. The young cowhand was probably shaking in his boots. As he should be.

"What part of my order didn't you hear this morning?" Garth asked as he strode forward.

"No part of it, Boss. I—I was ready to shoot it when this woman's husband—"

"He's not my husband," she interrupted.

Garth didn't bother looking over his shoulder. Feeling her following was enough.

"The boys ain't had eggs since we left Texas," JoJo said. "It sure would help their morale. The green beans, too."

Garth spun to glare at his cook. He had expected JoJo to stay behind. Cooking. That was his job. "I know how long it's been since we had eggs, and there's nothing wrong with the morale around here." They'd traveled dang near six hundred miles since heading out. Six hundred grueling miles of dust and dirt, and wind and rain, and sun hot enough to fry a man's brains in his head. Every man here knew that before they headed out. If any one of them was pissing and moaning about it now, it was their own fault, and they damn well better be keeping their complaints to themselves. His hornet-stung face was their first injury.

"If'n you say so, Boss," JoJo said. "It's your call, but it's a mighty fine deal. A mighty fine one. Eggs and green beans. A mighty fine deal."

"You've. Said. That," Garth growled, emphasizing each word. His head hurt, and what he wouldn't give to have two good eyes right now.

"I sure enough did," JoJo answered.

He didn't need to see JoJo, there was a grin in his tone. The old coot never questioned authority, because he knew in the grand scheme of things, he was the only one who could share his opinion without fear of re-percussion. Turning back to Brad, Garth asked, "Why didn't you shoot that calf?" He expected orders to be followed at all times, and the kid better have a good reason for not doing as told.

Brad shifted from foot to foot. Watching the move-ment made Garth's eye water more, and his temper flare.

"I—I was about to, Boss, but this man rode up and asked if he could have the calf." Still shifting from foot to foot, Brad continued, "I—I figured that was as good as shooting it. Knew it wouldn't live long without its momma."

"So you'd rather it suffered than putting it out of its misery?" Garth asked.

Brad took off his hat and then put it back on.

Garth balled one hand into a fist. Fidgeting was a sure sign of weakness, and he was close to losing his patience with this kid. He'd fired a man for fidgeting before, and probably should have again. He hadn't because he'd hoped Brad would grow up during the trip, and hadn't wanted to be wrong.

"I didn't think of it that way," Brad said. "I guess I thought the man had a cow it could nurse on."

Holding his temper was difficult. If the woman hadn't been there, he might not have kept it in control. That might not be true. If his face wasn't on fire and if he could see, he would have already lost his temper. Completely. As it was, it just boiled inside him. "I told you that's rare." Garth growled. "It takes a lot of work to make a cow take on a calf that's not her own, and that's hard on a calf. Smelling milk and not getting any."

Shifting again, Brad shook his head. "I didn't think of that, Boss. I didn't know that."

Garth wasn't sure what increased his irritation more. Brad's constant fidgeting and lack of knowledge, the pain throbbing in his head, or how the woman had stepped forward to pat the cowboy's arm consolingly.

As much as he didn't want to have to order it again, there was a lesson Brad needed to learn here for future reference. "Take that cow back to the herd," Garth ordered. "And then shoot the calf."

"He most certainly will not!" the woman bellowed as she stomped forward to put herself between Brad and him.

Damn, she was uppity. And full of herself. She had a lesson to learn, too. "Fine." He'd had enough and pulled out his pistol.

She launched forward, grabbing his arm. "You can't shoot it."

"Like hell I can't." Except he couldn't see the animal very well. Good thing he was a good shot.

"Like hell you will!"

She had gumption, and that reminded him of

Bridgette. They'd both been kids, but he'd never forgotten how she'd stepped up to his defense all those years ago. "I thought you didn't take to cursing," he pointed out.

Ignoring his statement, she tried pushing his arm down. "You will not be shooting this calf, nor will anyone else."

She was stronger than she looked, but not strong enough to move his arm or change his aim. "It's not going to survive without its mother," he said.

"I know that," she said. "That's why I brought the eggs and beans, to trade for the mother and the calf."

"The mother is worth a lot more than a few eggs and some green beans," he said.

"How much more?"

He wished he could see her better. She smelled clean. Like clothes did after being hung on the line. Though blurry, he could see her dress. It might smell clean, but was well-worn and the same dull gray as her bonnet. Even a poor man has scruples, so he didn't judge a person's character by their clothes, but he did use their appearance to judge the size of their pocketbook. Hers was empty. "You don't have enough money to buy that cow."

"What do you need besides money?"

When Brad had called the man who'd taken the calf her husband, she'd quickly pointed out that he wasn't her husband. But how then had she got the calf? Her uppity stance didn't fit with a loose woman, but Garth's instincts said if that man had been her brother or father, even an uncle, she'd have supplied that information. She hadn't. That left one thing. Aggravated, he twisted out of her hold. "Get on your horse and go home."

"No. Not until I get what I came for. What do you need for the cow and the calf, besides money?"

"Nothing." He pointed his pistol toward the calf. His stomach churned at the idea of shooting the calf, but his point had been made.

She jumped in front of his gun as he pulled back the hammer.

He swung the gun aside. "You trying to get yourself killed?"

"No, I'm making sure that calf doesn't." She stepped closer. "Please, mister. There's a woman I'm taking care of. She's about to have a baby, but is ailing. She needs the milk and butter this cow can provide. If you won't trade me for them, loan them to me. Just for a few weeks. You can come back and get them when the calf is big enough to travel. Take them to the sale barn then."

Her pleading was far more difficult to deal with than her demands. He wasn't wavering though. "I sell cows by the lot, not singularly."

"Garth," JoJo said. "What's one cow? You got over two thousand others."

Though the cook had spoken to him, JoJo's words had caught the woman's attention. Her head had snapped up and her stare grew intense. Like she was trying to see something inside him. Or maybe she was just staring at his swollen face. Either way, her eye-to-eye stare made Garth's stomach quiver. Very few things made his insides quiver. "Stay out of this, JoJo," he said without breaking eye contact with her.

"Garth?" she asked almost as if testing if she could say it or not.

"That's my name," he said. "It's not a long or complicated one."

"Garth what?"

"McCain. And those twenty-five hundred cows JoJo just mentioned are all mine."

"Garth McCain." She repeated it as if it was a curse like no other.

Then along with a hiss, she hauled off and smacked his cheek so fast and hard he had to blink at the shock. And hold his breath at the renewed throbbing of his eye.

He grabbed her wrist before she could strike a second time. "What's wrong with you?"

Bridgette wondered the exact same thing. If this was Garth. The Garth McCain she'd been waiting to see for the past nine years, why wasn't she happy? Ecstatic? And good heavens, why had she slapped him? His face was already swollen and red, and looked extremely painful. The mud had dried and cracked making his eye and cheek look horrific.

The whiskers didn't help either. He looked nothing like the boy she remembered, or the man she'd imagined he'd become. He didn't act like him either. Her Garth wouldn't have ordered a calf killed, or threatened to kill one. Yet, there couldn't be two Garth McCains. Could there?

"Where are you from?" she asked while continuing to search for familiarity somewhere in his features. His eye that wasn't swollen shut, was so narrow she couldn't see if his eyes were brown or not and the dark hair that hung past his shirt collar was as coated with dust as his clothes.

The last time she'd seen him, his hair had been short. Shaved clear to his scalp. That had happened to all the boys before they'd left New York. She and the other girls had received a good dip in a kerosene bath. Both measures had been to prevent any of them from carrying the head lice that lived at the orphanage along with them.

"Texas," he said.

"Before then?"

"Why?"

Bridgette didn't realize she was nibbling on a thumb nail until his eye widened a touch, as if noticing that was exactly what she was doing. She pulled her hand away from her face. Mrs. Killgrove had used whacks from a wooden ruler to break her of her nail biting habit back in the orphanage, and she hadn't bitten them for years.

Suddenly she didn't want to know if this was Garth—her Garth—or not. Didn't want to believe he could have changed that much. Or maybe she didn't want to believe he had deserted her. Forgotten she existed.

Walking around him, she said, "Keep your cow and your calf."

The cook, who had introduced himself as JoJo—no last name, just JoJo—fell in step beside her. "Listen up here, missy. That's a fine cow and Garth there—"

"I no longer want the cow and her calf, but you can keep the eggs and green beans for the trouble."

"That wouldn't be right. Garth is a fair man and he won't—"

"Good day, sir." She'd arrived at Cecil's plow horse, and gathered a handful of her skirt to climb into the saddle.

"What's your name?"

The question didn't surprise her. Footsteps had followed her to the horse. The fluttering inside her wasn't surprising either, nor was it welcomed. Whether this was her Garth or not, she had nothing more to say to him. Without answering, she stuck a foot in the stirrup and using the horn, hoisted herself into the saddle. Before he could stop her, she slapped the reins over the horse's rump.

The animal wasn't overly fast, but she urged it into a gallop that was surprisingly smooth for an animal of its size. It felt as if she was running away, and that wasn't something she did. Despite how often she'd dreamed of it. Furthermore, if she was hoping for freedom, there wasn't any. Not from inside her that is.

The heat of the sun was sweltering, yet, she was cold. Shivering. The hope, the dream of Garth finding her and finally living a life full of brightly colored rainbows, seeped out of her like a bucket with a hole in the bottom. She wasn't exactly sure what she'd expected him to be like when they met again, but this man—the one who'd order a young man to kill an innocent calf—wasn't it. Nor was one who would shoot the calf himself, just in order to prove a point. That's what he'd been doing. Proving a point.

A heavy sigh left her chest and she let the plow horse slow to its regular sluggish pace. Proving a point was something Garth would do. Always had. From the time he'd arrived at the orphanage, he'd taken it upon himself to be a leader. A guardian to those who needed one. He'd also been a teacher. Making sure if there was a lesson to be learned, it was learned.

That was where the problem lay. She could believe the man she'd just encountered was her Garth. The Garth McCain she'd wasted nine years waiting for. What angered her, what hurt, was what JoJo had told her before he'd arrived.

JoJo had only called him the boss man, and had said he was fair and honest, and would be the one to decide upon her trade. He'd also said the boss man had been bringing cattle from Texas to Kansas for years and had often made trades such as the one she'd offered.

Years. He'd been traveling past her home for years and never once bothered to look for her. Not once, and that hurt. Hurt her more than she'd ever been hurt before.

She understood on the way north he might have been too busy. Driving thousands of cattle wasn't an easy job. But, once the cattle were delivered, men often hung around, spending a large portion of the money they'd earned in Dodge before slowly making their way back down to Texas.

The idea of Garth chasing naked women down the street and hooting and hollering when he caught one turned her stomach rock hard. Of all the people who'd deserted her, disappointed her, this betrayal hurt the worst.

Straightening her spine, she drew in a deep breath. That she wouldn't stand for. She'd forget all about him, just as he had her. That would be easy.

A low moo had her looking over her shoulder. Sure enough, a horse and rider followed her, leading the cow and calf. She wasn't sure if she was more disappointed, or simply beyond caring when she recognized the young cowboy as the rider.

Garth hadn't bothered to look for her in over nine years so there was no reason he'd come after her today. Which was fine, because after today, she was going to forget Garth McCain ever existed.

The bawl of a calf had her stopping the plow horse. She'd learned the freckle-faced cowboy's name was Brad Martie when JoJo had sent his young helper, Bat, out to find Brad when she'd arrived at their camp with the calf.

Brad had the calf laid over his lap, and her heart took a tumble for the little animal. Unlike when she'd ridden with the calf, it was struggling, wanting down now that it had been reunited with its mother. The mooing said the cow wanted her baby near her, too.

The leaner cattle horse walked much faster than the plow horse, and in no time, Brad arrived at her side. "The boss wants you to have the cow and the calf. Told me to follow you home, make sure you got them both there."

Holding no animosity toward the cowboy, she replied. "Thank you." Despite the encounter, she truly hadn't wanted to arrive back at the Chaney residence without either the calf and the cow, or the eggs and beans. Cecil would have been furious. That wouldn't have bothered her as much as failing Emma Sue. "It's not too far," Bridgette said, setting the plow horse in motion again. "Only a few miles."

"Don't rightly matter to me how far it is," Brad said. "I'm glad to get away from those cows even for a bit. Reckon I didn't realize what I was getting into when I signed up."

"This is your first cattle drive?"

He nodded. "Yes, ma'am. Ain't never been outta Texas afore."

"How old are you?"

"Sixteen."

Over the years, she'd encountered people of all ages, and had figured out that age didn't mature a person as much as the life they'd lived, despite the number of years. She stopped the plow horse when the calf bellowed again. "Go ahead and put him on the ground. He'll be happier walking next to his mother."

"Reckon he will."

She waited as he dismounted and then lifted the calf down. The baby latched on to nurse almost instantly. "Let's wait a bit," she said as Brad climbed back into his saddle. When he glanced around nervously and twisted the reins in his hands, she asked, "Why'd you decide to join a cattle drive?"

He bowed his head and shrugged. "Mr. McCain is somewhat of a legend down by San Antone, and I wanted to be like him."

"Do you mean San Antonio, Texas?"

"Yes."

"What sort of legend? Why would you want to be like him?"

"He's the youngest trail boss ever. Been leading drives north for over six years. He started out as a cowboy, but within two years, was leading drives. Has been ever since." With another shrug and while twisting the reins in his hands, he said, "Guessing I got more to learn than he did."

"Some people take more readily to things than others." Forgetting Garth might be easier if she knew a bit more about him. "How old was Garth—Mr. McCain when he became a trail boss?"

"Seventeen. Some folks didn't believe it, but Mr. Johansson, that's the rancher he worked for, said it sure enough was true. That Garth McCain was only seventeen when he became a trail boss. One of the best, too. If not the best."

Seventeen. Garth had been fourteen when they'd traveled on the Orphan Train West together. The last time she'd seen him, when he'd been called out to the platform at the rail station, he'd told her he'd see her again. That she just had to follow the rules, be good, and that he'd find where she ended up as soon as he could.

That was a broken promise if there ever had been one. Had she known that he'd forgotten all about her, she wouldn't have stayed here all these years. Waiting for him.

"That calf could nurse all day if we let him," Brad said. "We best get moving again. I don't want to be too late getting back. Gotta take my turn at night watch."

"Of course," Bridgette agreed. After the cow and calf were tranquilly following along, she asked, "How much is that cow worth?"

"Can't say until we get to Dodge," Brad answered. "On average the yards pay nine bucks for a young steer and eight for a heifer. But that's an average. Some go lots higher and those were last year's prices. Mr. McCain wants his cattle to be the first to arrive. That's when the prices are the highest. Top dollar can go upwards of fifteen a head. By the end of the season, the prices drop. Course it also depends on the cows. McCain has good cows and doesn't push them too hard. We came across some good grass and water near the state line and he let them eat and rest up for two days. We had time to do that because we left McCain's place two weeks ahead of everyone else."

"McCain's place?" The bitterness that had set roots inside her turned to fury. "He has a ranch in Texas?"

Brad nodded. "Must be next to Mr. Johansson's place. That's where we headed out from. Maybe they'd partnered up or something. That's how I figure it since these cows are McCain's. Years past he's driven cows north for Johansson. But not this year. This year he's driving his own cows north."

"Is that so?" Bridgette muttered, mainly to herself. Boy, was she mad now. Increasingly so. If Garth thought he could break his promise without retribution, he'd soon discover how wrong he was. After all, he'd been the one to teach her an eye for an eye.

Chapter Five

"Ain't those about the best green beans you ever ate?" JoJo asked, dumping another spoonful onto Garth's plate. "That little gal told me how to make them. Said to boil them until tender and then give them a toss in the frying pan with bacon grease. Cain't believe I never thought of that before."

Garth didn't comment. He'd eaten the beans because whether he was hungry or not, he needed to eat, but couldn't say he'd actually tasted a bite. The rest of his men had. The beans and the eggs had the entire outfit grinning and asking for third helpings.

His attention wasn't on the men any more than it was on the food. It was on the horizon to the northwest, watching for Brad's return. He still couldn't see out of one eye, but the other one was doing better. His face wasn't. JoJo had scraped off a generous amount of skin trying to get out the stinger. Garth had put a stop to the scraping, but not soon enough. Rather than burning from the hornet's sting, the entire side of his face stung as if he'd shaved with a dull razor and no soap.

The pain though wasn't what he was thinking about. It was her. That woman. She'd been snippy and uppity, and he just couldn't get her out of his head. He hadn't thought this long and hard about someone in a long time.

Actually, he'd only ever thought this much about one person.

Bridgette.

"You ain't heard a word I said, have ya?"

Garth focused his good eye on JoJo.

"I didn't think so," JoJo said.

Handing his plate to the cook, Garth stood. "When you say something worth hearing, I'll listen. Until then, I'll just let it go in one ear and out the other."

"You got that right," JoJo said. "There ain't nothin' betwixt those ears in your noggin 'cept air. You oughta have a constant earache from the wind blowing through your head."

Normally he gave JoJo back as much as the man gave out, but he wasn't in the mood, and turned about.

"Where you goin'?" JoJo asked. "I was only telling you we got enough eggs for breakfast, too."

"Good," Garth replied. "I'll go relieve the last two cowboys."

JoJo mumbled something about being ornery as a snake before saying, "You cain't even see yet, and no one's expecting you to take over for them."

Garth walked toward his tack. He was ornery some days. It was his nature. He doubted he'd been born that way, but for as long as he could remember, he'd been mad, and that alone was enough to leave a person ornery.

That didn't mean he never laughed or had fun. Some of his earliest memories were of the big ships that docked in New York. The sailors were often willing to pay a penny for directions or to have a message delivered, and he and other boys spent a lot of time in that area, earning enough to buy a warm meal now and again. They'd had a lot of fun at the docks, especially teasing the laundrymen who washed the sailors' clothes. Those men could run, and often chased him and the other boys with hot irons, threatening to turn them in to the officials.

They had never caught him, or turned him in—that had all been his own doing. His lesson in not thinking things through.

Garth swung the saddle over one shoulder and grabbed the bridle and blanket with his other hand. Spinning about, he all but ran over Bat. He hated only having one good eye.

"You want me to fetch you a horse, Boss?" the boy asked.

"I can do it," Garth answered.

"No, he can't," JoJo said. "Go get him a mount, Bat."

The horses were kept a distance away, between the cattle and the camp. His sight was good enough to walk that far, and good enough to keep an eye on the cows while the others came in to eat. He didn't tell JoJo that. It would be a waste of breath, as had telling the truth all those years ago.

His capture, as he'd labeled it, had come about when he'd witnessed a man bludgeon one of those little laundrymen. He'd gone to the authorities and the man was captured, but had claimed the opposite. That Garth had done the bludgeoning. Because he'd been the one with blood on his clothes from dragging the laundryman into the back door of the laundry shop, he was the one arrested. The authorities hadn't put him in jail, instead he'd been sent off to the Children's Home at age eleven. The horror stories he'd heard had been true, at

least in part. It was a prison for children if there ever
had been one.

His second lesson in not thinking things through
came about when he ran away from the orphanage. He
hadn't been an orphan, not then. His mother had worked
in a crib close to the docks, but when he got there, she
was gone. Turned out, she'd run off with a sailor as
soon as she'd heard he'd been taken to the orphanage.
As far as he knew, his mother could still be alive, living on some other continent. Gertrude, the woman his
mother had shared a crib with had told him to go back
to the orphanage, that it was where he belonged, and
didn't waste any time in alerting the authorities. It was
only a matter of days before he was hauled back to the
Children's Home.

He was kept under lock and key, as were most of
the others. When given the opportunity to go West on
one of the trains, he'd jumped at the chance. And told
Bridgette she should, too.

Unlike him, she'd lived most of her life at the orphanage, and believed her parents were coming back
for her, some day. He knew that wouldn't happen, and
had told her so. She didn't believe him and attempted
to run away. Thought she could climb the big oak tree
that had branches hanging over the back fence. She'd
fallen instead and broken her arm.

In an attempt to keep her from doing that again, he'd
snuck into the office and looked up the information
they had on her. He'd found a baptismal record from
a church on Staten Island and a note from her mother
saying her husband had died and that she was too ill to
take care of Bridgette. Another note stated her mother
had died a few days later.

Looking back, Garth figured Bridgette had always

known her parents had died, but hadn't wanted it to be true. Hadn't wanted to be an orphan. He could relate, and grinned at the memory of sitting beside her beneath the same big oak she'd fallen out of. It had been a cold fall day and the two of them had been assigned to gathering the dead leaves. She'd been mad about him sneaking into the office. Told him he could have gotten caught and then they'd never be able to go West.

That's when the waiting had started. For both of them. Over a year of wondering if there would be room on the next train or not. Bridgette had come up with all sorts of wild plans of how they could sneak onto one of the trains, and he'd had to stop each one of them, telling her she had to think things through before jumping into action or she'd break another arm. She'd been frustrated, but conceded—until she'd come up with another harebrained idea that would threaten to get them both in trouble.

He'd been almost fourteen and she had just turned nine by the time they'd finally boarded a westbound train.

"Here you go, Boss."

Bat's voice brought Garth's mind back to the present and his feet to a stop.

"I know you like this one, Boss," Bat said. "She's a good horse, no?"

"Yes," Garth answered. The big brown horse had three white socks and was one of the best cattle horses he'd ever ridden. "You know a good horse when you see one, Bat. And you are good with them." The boy deserved the compliment. After helping JoJo all day including gathering an ongoing supply of firewood, the boy visited the remuda each evening, making sure the mounts had all been taken care of. The job hadn't been assigned to Bat, he'd just taken it upon himself, and Garth had taken notice of that.

"I like horses," Bat said. "Afore my ma died, I had a black-and-white horse all of my own."

That was the most the boy had ever said about his past. At least the most Garth had heard. Then again, he'd never asked. He hadn't this time, either. Bat must have just figured it was time. That's how it was with orphans. When the time was right, they'd share their past. Usually in bits and pieces.

"It shows you like them," Garth said. "I appreciate how well you take care of them."

Bat handed over the rope. "I'll put on his bridle while you saddle him."

Garth nodded. Just as he suspected, Bat was done talking about himself. JoJo had never mentioned where he'd found Bat, or how, and Garth hadn't asked. It hadn't mattered. Today, with all his own ghosts roaming about in his head, he found himself thankful JoJo had taken Bat in.

"Unless you cain't see well enough to put on the saddle," Bat said. "I can do it if you need."

Garth stepped forward and threw the blanket over the horse's back. "Can't see well enough."

"You cain't?" Bat asked.

"I can see well enough," Garth answered, settling the saddle on the horse. "The word is can't not cain't. Cain't isn't a word."

"It ain't?"

Garth grinned and the tightening of the muscles said his face still hurt too bad to go into a lesson right now. The salve JoJo had put on it after scraping off his hide stunk as strongly as it burned. "Run back to camp now," he said. "I'm sure JoJo has something for you to do. Thanks for gathering my mount."

"You betcha, Boss," Bat answered, already hightailing it toward camp.

Once he'd tightened the cinch, Garth couldn't help but press a hand to the side of his face. The swelling didn't feel like it had increased, but the hurting sure hadn't eased. Ignoring it seemed his best, and only, choice, so he mounted and headed toward the herd.

Not in the mood for conversation, he merely gestured for both of the two cowboys riding watch to go to the camp. There were always to be no less than two men with the cattle, but that was his rule, so only he could break it. Another man would ride out before long. As soon as he'd had his fill of eggs and green beans.

As Garth slowly made his way around the circumference of the cattle, he found himself thinking about Bridgette again. Over the years, that had happened more than he'd wanted. Usually when things were slow or he'd find himself alone, often in his bedroll staring at the night sky. He'd wonder if the people who had adopted her were good to her and if she ever thought about him. When he first left Orson's place he'd contemplated finding out what had happened to her, where she'd been dropped off, but concluded there wasn't anything he could do if he did know. What Orson had shouted while whipping him had been true. Bridgette was better off without him. He never discovered how Orson knew about her. It could have been Fredrick Fry, considering Fry had said the same thing, but in truth it didn't matter. As the years went on, he told himself to forget about her, forget about everything that connected him to his past. He had nothing to gain from it.

Malcolm Johansson had told him that a man couldn't create a future while living in the past, and that's what Garth wanted. A future. One that held no connection to his past.

It had been over nine years since he'd seen Bridgette. She'd be eighteen now. Could be married. Have children of her own. The idea of that, of her being married, made him crack another grin. She'd been so sad about admitting she was an orphan that day under the oak tree, he'd pretended to perform a ceremony, marrying the two of them so neither of them would be alone. Kids. Life seemed so simple to them.

Not one but two men arrived to take over watching the herd. Garth waved at them as he finished his slow trek around the cattle and then headed back toward camp. His head still hurt. Not just from his injury. It ached from thinking too much.

As he rode into camp, he noticed Bat leading Brad's horse and scanned the area for the young man. At least his good eye was no longer watering, leaving his limited sight a bit clearer. Sitting cross-legged on the ground, Brad spooned beans and eggs into his mouth as fast as the others had.

"Want me to take your horse back to the others, Boss?" Bat asked.

"No, I'll ride back out to the herd once more yet this evening." Garth dismounted and dropped the reins of his horse. Every animal in his remuda was trained to stay where it was left and didn't spook easy. He put as much effort into training his horses as he did his men.

On his way across the camp, Garth paused long

enough to fetch a cup of coffee from JoJo before walking over to sit down next to Brad.

"How'd that go?" he asked, taking a sip of coffee.

"Fine." Brad swallowed the food in his mouth. "She was real nice, and thankful."

Although it didn't matter, Garth couldn't stop from asking, "What's her name?"

"I dunno," Brad said.

"You didn't ask? She didn't tell you?"

"Nope. I might've but as soon as we got the cow in the barn, the man came out of the house yelling that she was needed. That something was wrong. She took off for the house and I got my rope and skedaddled. That fella's an ornery one."

Garth pitched the contents of his coffee cup onto the ground. "You left her there? With the man yelling that something was wrong?"

"She told me to go."

"Where's the house?" Garth couldn't say why that bothered him. He wasn't one to put his nose in someone else's business, but his gut was churning and he couldn't ignore it.

"About five miles northwest," Brad said. "You want me to go back? See if she's all right?"

"No," Garth answered as he stood. "I'll go."

"Want me to go with you?" Brad set his plate down.

"No. You're on duty soon."

"Just follow the creek," Brad said. "When it veers east, go west about half a mile. It's a sod house and a barn that's about to fall down."

"I'll find it," Garth answered.

JoJo's frown couldn't go unnoticed, nor could how the man fell in step beside him. "You think she's in trouble for giving us the eggs and green beans?"

Garth shrugged as he gathered the reins of his horse.

"I didn't see that fella earlier," JoJo said, "only Brad did."

"I'll be back." Garth swung up into the saddle.

"Maybe you oughta take someone with you, with your eyes hurting and all."

"My eyes are fine."

"One ain't," JoJo supplied.

Garth steered the horse around and headed northwest. He knew damn well one eye wasn't fine. He couldn't see it, or see with it. Didn't need to. The pain told him all he needed to know. Next time he got hurt, he'd stay far away from JoJo. Doctoring was not JoJo's strong suit, but cooking was, and although Garth hadn't admitted it, those green beans and eggs had been a much needed change to their diet of late.

As he rode, he wondered about the woman who'd traded the eggs and beans for the cow. And he wondered about Bridgette. Normally, he planned rather than wondered. Bridgette hadn't. She'd wondered about everything, especially rainbows. How they formed. Why they formed. Where they started and ended. Every time she saw one she was ready to take off in search of discovering the mythical pot of gold. He'd tried to tell her that riches aren't found, they have to be made, just like the sun makes rainbows. She'd scoffed at that, told him he needed to have more imagination and belief.

He had belief all right. That life wasn't full of rainbows.

In some ways, he hoped that she'd finally learned that; in other ways, he hoped she never would.

Just as Brad had instructed, Garth shifted direction when the creek veered, and sure enough, a sod shanty and run-down barn appeared a short distance later. A bit of injustice flared inside him. The place needed work. He could understand money being tight, even nonexistent, but ambition was free. A man not using that irritated him more than fidgeting.

He found a place where the barbed wire fence had been cut and followed the trail through the tall grass to the barn. His horse hadn't stopped yet when a man exited the doorway of the ramshackle building. One of the double doors that would be needed to keep animals inside was missing and the other door, gray and rotting away, hung crooked on its one hinge.

"What you want?"

Using only one eye, Garth didn't have time to completely size the man up before he spoke again.

"If it's doctoring you need, head out," the man said. "She's busy."

"I don't need a doctor," Garth said.

"Looks like you do to me."

The man was of fair size, but it came from laziness rather than hard work, and the bottle he'd slid in his back pocket could be part of the cause. Garth dismounted. "I'm with the cattle drive."

Taking a step back, the man folded his arms over his portly stomach. "I told her you'd be back to get your cow. No man, not one with a brain that is, trades a cow for eggs and beans. I sure enough told her that. And I told her I wouldn't be taking the blame for her foolishness." Waving a hand toward the barn doorway, he continued, "The cow and calf are in the barn. I can't help you take them back. I'm busy."

Even with just one eye, Garth saw plenty that had been ignored for a long time and wasn't receiving any attention right now, either. "Doing what?"

The man rubbed his nose with the back of one hand. "Waiting. The wife's pushing out a baby."

Garth's glance toward the house didn't tell him anything other than it was in better shape than the barn. At least the door had both hinges and was tightly closed. "Your first?" he asked, turning his attention back to the man.

"Yes. If it lives that is." Worry filled the man's eyes as he glanced toward the house. "A couple ones before this didn't."

Compassion didn't come easily, but in this instant, it seemed to. "Name's Garth McCain," he said, holding out a hand.

"Cecil Chaney."

"I hope congratulations are soon in order, Mr. Chaney," he said while shaking the man's hand. Every child's life was important, even this man's. As Cecil's eyes lightened up, Garth continued, "I'm not here to collect the cow or the calf. I wanted to say thank you for the trade. My cowboys were greatly pleased with the eggs and beans. We don't get foodstuff along those lines too often while on the trail."

Cecil's face had completely brightened and his chest puffed. "I told her that."

Satisfied there wasn't trouble here, Garth reckoned he could head back to the herd, yet couldn't stop from saying, "You seem to have told her a lot of things."

"Have to. A girl that uppity needs some direction or she'll go flying around like a moth, flapping her wings and getting nowhere."

"Are you referring to your wife?"

"No, no, no. My wife, Emma Sue, she's the one having the baby. I'm talking about Bridgette. That girl…"

Garth had started for his horse, but stopped as his

stomach shot past his heart to land some place near his throat, where it dang near strangled him. After telling himself Chaney couldn't be talking about his Bridgette several times, that his ears must be as swollen as his eye, he managed to catch enough breath to ask, "Bridgette who?"

"Don't rightly know her last name. Rodgers I guess. She's the doc's adopted daughter. He farms her out to folks needing doctoring. Costs plenty for what ya get, but—"

"And she's the one who traded for the cow and calf?" Garth asked, staring at the house. That couldn't have been Bridgette; she'd have said something. Especially when he told her his name. Suddenly, the side of his face, where she'd slapped him, stung again, and irritation flared. Why the hell had she slapped him?

"Where you going?"

Garth had started for the house, and didn't slow at the man's question.

"You can't go in there! My wife's having a baby."

That shout stopped him. At least it stopped his feet. With his insides gushing about like flood waters, Garth spun enough to see Cecil with his good eye. "Go get her."

"My wife?"

"No," he growled. "Bridgette."

Cecil shook his head. "I can't. She told me not to open that door." Wiping his lips with one hand, he added, "I thought the baby would come before she got back. I don't know nothing about birthing babies and I don't want to learn."

Garth spewed a mouthful of curse words as he swung back around to glare at the house. He didn't want to learn about birthing babies either, but he did want to see Bridgette. Wanted to know why she'd smacked him and why she hadn't told him who she was.

"She swindle you out of that calf and cow?" Cecil asked. "She's like that. Has you doing things you don't know you're doing 'til it's done. She's had me doing more work around here since—"

With his head hurting and his guts twisting, Garth spun back to Cecil. "Give me that bottle."

Clamping his mouth shut midsentence, Cecil glanced around before asking, "What bottle?"

"The one in your back pocket." Garth took a step forward. "Now."

Cecil shuffled his feet while dipping his head. "Oh, that one." He pulled a bottle out. "I was just calming my nerves. You know how it is. Had to get me a couple extra bottles lately, with Bridgette living here and all. That woman could drive a man batty."

Garth took the bottle and a long swig. It burned his throat, proving the whiskey—if that's what it was supposed to be—was far from good, but that didn't stop him from taking a second swallow. There was no reason, not a single one, for Bridgette not to have told him who she was.

"I told her there ain't nothing wrong with being an orphan, ain't no one to blame, but she didn't take to my…"

Cecil kept talking. Garth wasn't listening. There had been times in his life when he'd said those exact words. Events happened. Children were left without parents. Some, like him, were simply not wanted; others, like Bridgette knew of their beginning but no more; and others still, knew the exact moment they'd become an orphan. He'd spent a good amount of time being angry that he'd been an unwanted one and had spent a fair amount of time searching for a way to get back at life for that. At getting even. Until he'd decided to forget his past.

The injustice of life, the unfairness, the inequality still got to him at times. Being older helped. Knowing life was life, that you got out of it what you put into it. But this, Bridgette treating him like a stranger, hit him almost as hard as learning his mother had run off all those years ago.

Bridgette had been in the hallway when he'd arrived at the Children's Home, on her hands and knees scrubbing the floors, and so skinny and scrawny the bucket of water had been bigger than her. He'd been mad, upset about being taken to the orphanage, and had been trying to get out of the constable's hold. When the man had raised a hand to whack him, Bridgette had thrown her scrub brush toward them. It had missed the constable, and bounced off the wall. She'd run to retrieve it and prepared to throw the brush again.

He'd known plenty of girls on the streets, but he'd never seen or heard of a girl who'd laid into a constable the way Bridgette had. Even while being carried down the hall by one of the nursemaids, she'd continued to rant about the wrongness of hitting a child.

Later, when he'd seen her again, he'd pointed out that she was a child. She'd said exactly, who was better to know the wrongness of hitting a child than a child.

He hadn't been able to argue that point, but they hadn't formed a friendship until after he'd been brought to the Children's Home the second time, when she'd snuck food to him when he'd been forced to complete chores during mealtimes as punishment for running away. After that, they'd spent plenty of time in each other's company.

Until Kansas City, where he'd been *distributed*.

"You, uh, gonna give that back?"

Garth looked at the bottle and then Cecil before answering, "No." He walked toward his horse.

"You heading back to your herd?"

Cecil was on his heels, and Garth barely paused to grab the reins of his mount. "No." He led the horse to the side of the barn, into the shade, and loosened its girth.

Chapter Six

Bridgette tucked the swaddled baby, a girl, beet red and with a healthy set of lungs, into the crook of Emma Sue's arm. "She's perfect, just like her momma."

Emma Sue smiled as she kissed the top of the baby's head. "She is perfect." Lifting tear-filled eyes, Emma Sue shook her head. "Thank you, Bridgette. Thank you. Oh, I truly don't know what else to say. I was so scared when the pains started right after you left. Cecil told me not to be, but I was."

Grateful all had turned out well, Bridgette refused to focus on what could have been. What might have happened if she hadn't returned when she had. Dr. Rodgers still hadn't arrived, so Emma Sue would have been on her own. "Everything would have been fine," she said, for Emma Sue's sake. "You did wonderfully, and your daughter is beautiful. What will you name her?"

"I don't know yet." Emma Sue kissed the dark curls covering the baby's head again. "I'll have to ask Cecil. Can he come in now?"

"In a few minutes," Bridgette answered. "Let me get everything in order first."

"Of course. I'm just so excited for him to see her."

"I'm sure you are." Whether she liked him or not, Emma Sue loved Cecil, and for that reason alone Bridgette hurried about. Without any windows, the room was dark even with both lamps lit, but having cleaned up after a birth many times, she could complete the tasks with her eyes closed. The adverse effect of that meant she didn't need to concentrate on what she was doing, which left her mind wide open to wander. And wander it did. Straight back to Garth McCain.

The audacity of that man! Traveling right past her for all these years and never once even attempting to see her. She had half a mind to ride back out to that herd and tell him exactly what she thought of him. That wasn't possible, at least not until after Dr. Rodgers arrived and confirmed both Emma Sue and the baby were indeed fine. Considering he hadn't arrived yet, she guessed he was seeing to another patient, therefore, it could be some time before he received the message and made his way out here.

Withholding a sigh, she neared the bed again. "Still doing fine?"

"Yes," Emma Sue answered. "She's sleeping."

"She's had an eventful day," Bridgette replied, stroking the soft skin along the side of the baby's cheek with a knuckle. "She really is beautiful." This baby was. Though all were cute in their own right, some she'd seen could never have been called beautiful. "She looks just like you."

"I see Cecil in her," Emma Sue answered. "She has his eyes and nose."

Not wanting to subject her mind to that consideration, Bridgette gathered one lamp. "I'll carry everything out of the room and then go get him."

"Thank you."

After setting the lamp on the kitchen table, Bridgette went back into the bedroom and collected the basket containing the used linens and the bag of supplies Dr. Rodgers provided for her use each time she went to live with a family. She'd wash the instruments after Cecil visited with Emma Sue, and take care of the linens in the morning. The thought of Cecil had her taking a moment to return the pot of rabbit stew onto the stove. The egg noodles were good and dry, but that didn't hurt them. She'd add them once the pot started to boil again.

Bridgette opened the door and was a bit surprised to find the cloaking dusk of evening. Husbands were usually sitting right outside the door, but that wasn't the case with Cecil. She should have known. Pulling the door shut so as not to disturb Emma Sue, Bridgette shouted, "Cecil?"

A clatter had her turning toward the barn. Her insides hardened, and though she thought it impossible, her dislike of him increased. Weaving, and acting as if it took all his concentration to make his feet move, Cecil walked toward her.

Furious, she stomped forward. "Are you drunk?"

"I—I—I's set—settling my n-nerves," he said between hiccups.

If she had a frying pan handy, she would have smacked him with it.

"A boy?"

Bridgette took a deep breath and held it until calm enough to say, "You have a beautiful, healthy baby girl."

"A girl?" Grinning, he turned toward the barn and waved an arm, but then frowned for a moment before turning back to her. Wobbling, he asked, "Can I go in?"

As much as she'd like to say no, she nodded. "But only for a little while. Emma Sue and the baby are tired."

Arms out for balance, he started for the house. She'd been here six weeks, and hadn't seen him in that condition, yet knew he sipped off his bottles of hooch every night. Taking that into consideration, she asked, "You did go summons Dr. Rodgers when I told you, didn't you?"

He nodded, but then shook his head. "I went to the Jamison place and sent one of their boys to town, 'case you needed me here."

"When?"

"Right away."

The Jamison place was only a mile away, so he could have made that trip relatively quickly, giving him plenty of time to get sloshed. Mrs. Jamison would have made sure one of her sons went for the doctor, therefore Bridgette dropped the subject, and turned away from watching Cecil wobble his way to the house.

As she scanned the yard, looking for a place to wait, the flicker of a light had her walking toward the barn. "Leave it to Cecil to leave a lit lantern in the barn," she muttered. As she approached the one door that creaked against the evening breeze, she added, "At least I don't need to light one to see to the cow and calf. Heaven knows he wouldn't have thought of feeding them."

"You're right, he didn't, but I did."

With one foot lifted midstep, Bridgette found herself wobbling as Garth appeared in the doorway. Drawing a breath, she lowered her foot slowly. Even once it settled upon the dirt, she was still off-kilter. Especially her insides.

"Hello, Bridgette."

The disdain in his voice made her name sound like a curse. Contempt filled her. "Garth," she answered, just as dark and snarly. "What are you doing here? Come to shoot the calf." Sneering, she added, "And the cow?"

He had one arm braced on the frame of the narrow and short doorway, which made him look taller, wider. "No." He let go of the frame, but planted his hand back against it just as quickly. "Why the hell aren't you in Wyoming?"

The question or curse didn't catch her attention as much as the other sound he'd made. It sounded like a muffled hiccup. She stepped close enough to sniff the air. Fury overshadowed everything else. "Are you drunk?"

He straightened his stance, but never let go of the wall. "No."

"You smell like you are."

Leaning a bit more toward the wall, he touched the side of his face with his other hand. A hint of compassion rose inside her. There was just enough light to show how swollen his face still was, and how red. In fact, it looked worse now than it had earlier.

"What are you doing here, Bridgette?"

"What are *you* doing here?" she asked, rather than answer. Injured or not, she couldn't afford to feel sympathy for him. He'd deserted her. Left her waiting and waiting.

"Driving cows to Dodge," he said.

"Like you have every year for the past nine," she snapped.

"Eight."

Flustered, she brushed past him and walked the length of the small barn. The cow and the calf were in the back pasture. Both seemed content, the cow chewing

and the calf nursing. She checked that the gate blocking the doorway was secure, and then finding nothing
else to do, spun around.

Garth had turned about, but still leaned against the
doorframe. "Why didn't you tell me who you were?"

"Why should I have?" She lifted her chin in order
to meet his stare. "It was fine for you to have forgotten
me, but not for me to have forgotten you?"

He frowned slightly and shook his head. "I hadn't
forgotten you. Why aren't you in Wyoming?"

"Why do you keep asking that? I've never been to
Wyoming. Never planned on going to Wyoming."

Shifting his feet until he leaned against the wall, he
folded his arms across his chest. "That's what Fredrick
Fry told me. That you'd been adopted by a doctor near
Topeka, and from there you'd moved to Wyoming."

Shaking her head, mainly to toss aside the thought
he might actually have tried to find her, she said, "Fredrick Fry didn't tell you that. You were already gone by
the time I got off the train."

"I—"

"Stop." Unnerved by the hope that was trying to
work its way into her heart, she held up a hand. "Just
stop. There's no need to lie. No need to pretend."

"I'm not lying," he said, "And I've never pretended
anything in my life."

"You are right now." Rather than say he was pretending to care, she said, "You're pretending to be something
you aren't." A caring, honest man. A man who cared
enough that he had looked for her. She had to blink at
the sting in her eyes. That's who she wanted him to be,
not who he was. Who he'd become.

"I've never pretended to be something I'm not."

"Really?"

He pressed a hand to his forehead, and sighed. "Other than sober. I've pretended to be sober a couple of times in my life."

His grin stole her breath. Even with the bottom half of his face covered in whiskers and the other half swollen, she recognized that grin, the twinkle in those dark eyes—one eye anyway. The old Garth, the one she'd been waiting on, was in there, and that made her knees wobble. However, it also reminded her of how long she'd been waiting for him. "How's that working for you?" she asked. "Pretending to be sober?"

His body gave a little jerk as he muffled a hiccup. "Not so well." Shaking his head and rubbing his forehead, he said, "My head hurts. What the hell is in those bottles?"

She glanced in the direction he pointed, to where two bales of hay had been situated on each side of a barrel, upon which sat a checkerboard. Empty bottles littered the floor around the barrel.

"I was keeping Cecil company. Keeping his mind off his wife."

"Getting him drunk you mean."

"No, I think it was the other way around. He kept pulling out bottles two at a time."

Bridgette walked closer to the bales and counted six empty bottles. "Graham Linkletter brews it. I've heard it's awful."

"It is." Garth groaned and rubbed his forehead again. "I thought it would take away the pain, but it's made it worse."

She lifted the lamp from where it hung, off a hook on the center beam and walked a bit closer in order to shine the light on his face. Her heart took a tumble. "What did you do?"

"I got stung by a hornet."

"After that. It didn't look this bad at your camp."

"JoJo scraped out the stinger."

As well as a layer of skin. She didn't tell him that. The misery in his eyes said he was in enough pain. "Sit down," she said. "I have some cottonwood ointment in the house. I'll go get it."

His hand wrapped around her wrist and though it was much larger and more calloused than the one she remembered, the warmth was familiar.

"You'll come back."

She had to swallow at how the warmth raced up her arms and into her chest. "Yes."

"You promise."

A part of her wanted to say that unlike him, her promises meant something. Biting her tongue, she nodded. "I'll be back."

"I'll be waiting."

She ought to be questioning her wisdom, but doctoring injuries had been her focus for the past nine years. It some ways, it had taken the place that Garth's absence had left empty. She pulled her arm from his hold and hurried for the door. Over the years, when she'd found herself missing him intensely, she'd told herself that a nine-year-old child couldn't fall in love. During those same times of intense longing, she'd concluded that children could love, and that's what she had done. She'd loved Garth. That's why she'd married him. The problem was, she'd thought he'd loved her, too.

Arriving at the house, she paused before opening the door and took a moment to clear her mind. She'd doctor his face and send him on his way. And then forget he ever existed.

The quilt separating the bedroom from the rest of

the house blocked her from seeing in there. She could hear muffled voices, and hoped that meant Cecil was behaving. From her pile of belongings, she gathered what she needed and then the dishpan. She left the house as quietly as she'd entered, and stopped near the well to pour water into the dishpan before continuing to the barn.

Garth was sitting on one of the bales and holding his head with both hands. Despite everything, deep inside, a place she'd kept hidden, responded to the reality that this was Garth. Warmth spilled out, encircling her heart. She tried to ignore it, but he'd lifted his head and the pain reflecting in his eyes was enough to make her gasp. Setting the dishpan atop the checkerboard, she knelt down. "Let me clean this up. Then I'll make you some tea for the pain." She bit her lips for a moment before adding, "This might sting. I have to clean it."

He removed his hat and set it on the hay beside him. "Go ahead. It can't hurt any worse than it does."

She didn't doubt it hurt, but knew, no matter how gentle she was, her actions would irritate the injury, make it hurt worse. Wringing the water out of the cloth she'd dropped in the basin, she asked, "What did JoJo put on this after he scraped it?" His answer wouldn't make a difference, but she wanted him to think of something besides what she was doing. That wasn't completely true. She needed something to think about other than touching him.

He was far broader and more solid than the Garth she remembered, and his features sterner, more set and seasoned. The sun had left permanent tiny crinkles near his eyes, which gave him an aged appearance that was far more of an enhancement than a determent to his good looks.

He sucked in air as she pressed the cloth to his face. "I don't know. Something that smells as rank as he does."

"You mean as rank as you smell."

"It's the ointment."

"No, it's not," she argued. They'd always bantered back and forth. She hoped recalling that would anchor her, ground her, because being this near to him had unlocked an unusual sense of chaos inside her.

"Still smelling that hooch, are you?"

"That, too." With her heart racing, she continued to dip the cloth in the water, wring it out, and softly wipe the side of his face. She'd doctored men and woman alike, and had never been this nervous.

He let out a small groan. "You're enjoying this, aren't you?"

"I should be," she said truthfully.

"Fredrick Fry told me you went to Wyoming."

Finally something to focus on. "When did you talk to him?" Fredrick Fry had been the agent who'd overseen the boys on the train while Agatha Killgrove had overseen the girls. Of the two, Mr. Fry had been far more pleasant.

"I didn't talk to him." Garth groaned again as she continued wiping. "I wrote to him my first winter down in Texas. He wrote back that you'd been adopted out in a town named Oskaloosa, near Topeka, and that the doctor who adopted you had said he was on his way to Wyoming."

Bridgette twisted the water out of the cloth again while what he claimed settled in her mind. She couldn't recall any talk of Wyoming. "They collected me in Oskaloosa, but we came directly to Hosford, and have lived here ever since. In the exact same house. It's a big house on the edge of town. You can't miss it." She wasn't exactly sure why she said all that, other than she'd always wanted him to find her.

"Fry said he'd forward me any additional information, but never did."

"Because he lied to you."

"There was no reason for him to do that."

"There wasn't?" Having cleaned off JoJo's greasy salve and the lingering film of mud, she collected her tin of cottonwood ointment. "Both Mr. Fry and Mrs. Killgrove tried to keep us separated as much as possible."

"That's true." He turned enough to look at her. "They thought I'd corrupt you."

Unable not to, she grinned, thinking about some of their escapades. "It was a little late for that."

He turned and grasped her wrist, stilling her fingers. The way he was looking at her made her quiver on the inside. A warm and wonderful quiver. She couldn't pull her eyes away, nor could she stop her hand from cupping the side of his face. She'd missed him so much. It had been as if she'd lost a part of herself when he'd gotten off the train in Kansas City. A part she'd never found again.

"I worried about you."

His whisper was gruff, as if he rarely spoke that softly.

She swallowed against the quickening of her heart and breath. "There was no need to worry," she answered softly. "The Rodgerses have provided well for me."

"That's good. I hoped whoever had taken you in was good to you. Hoped you were happy. Had food, clothes, a house." A twinkle flashed in his eyes as he whispered, "Rainbows."

If a heart could melt, hers did, clear to her toes. Only

Garth knew how much she loved rainbows, and suddenly, it didn't matter how long they'd been apart, he was here now. She took a breath, preparing to tell him she'd been fine but that there hadn't been any rainbows, when her name echoed inside the barn.

"Who's that?"

It was a moment before she recognized the voice. "Dr. Rodgers." The doctor would expect her to be at Emma Sue's side. Bridgette scrambled to her feet. "He's here to check on Emma Sue and the baby. I'll have him look at your face, too."

He didn't want to, but Garth let go of her wrist, and watched her hurry to the door. His mind was still trying to figure out something to say when she spun around.

"Stay here." Briefly glancing out the doorway, she brushed aside a strand of hair that blew across her cheek while saying, "But stuff those bottles under the hay."

Garth let the heavy air out of his lungs as she disappeared into the night. His face might still hurt, and his head from Cecil's hooch, but neither bothered him as much as the pain centered in his chest. He should be elated. Happy to see her after all these years. The problem was, he didn't know what to do about that.

She wasn't the same. The softness of her features had changed. The round, youthful plumpness of her cheeks was gone, giving her a more angled, womanly look. She'd always been cute, now she was pretty, beautiful. Her hair was darker, honey colored rather than yellow, and the curves of her body—something he couldn't help but admire and sincerely had wished both eyes were working to do so properly—said she'd matured in all ways.

That had another sigh building tight in his lungs. She'd grown into a woman, and he'd be the first to say women couldn't be trusted. They were always looking for greener pastures.

Before standing, he stuffed the bottles under the hay and blew out the lantern. At the doorway, Garth paused long enough to watch Bridgette follow a tall man into the house. He took his time saddling the horse he'd tied beside the barn, and kept glancing toward the house. Leaving was the smart thing to do, but he'd yet to find the wherewithal to actually mount up.

Maybe because he was still feeling the effects of Cecil's home brew. That could be why he hadn't told her everything Fredrick Fry had said in his letter. Fry had said that if Garth really cared about Bridgette, he'd forget about her. She was with good people and would have a good life. The kind of life he could never give her.

Fry had been right. Even Malcolm, a man Garth had already learned to trust back then, had agreed.

With a final glance over his shoulder, Garth stuck a foot in the stirrup.

Chapter Seven

Garth didn't welcome the daylight as fondly as he usually did. His head felt like he had a bull rummaging around inside it, and he couldn't blame that pain on anyone other than himself.

"On your left!" he shouted. "Heading west!"

A cowboy named Randy took off toward the brush where Garth had seen a steer running. The cattle seemed as ornery as he felt this morning. Almost as if they didn't want to leave this place any more than he did.

Leave Bridgette.

Garth shook his head at his own thought. Now that he knew where she was, he could come back if he wanted. But that was exactly what he should not want.

Tarnation but that woman had left his mind a mess, which was exactly why he shouldn't want to come back. In the years since he'd moved to Texas, he'd kept himself clear of women. All women. And more than once had felt a sense of empathy for those men who found themselves shackled by one.

A flash at the corner of his eye had him spinning his horse around. Squinting to see through the dust, he hollered at the cowboy entering the center of the herd, "Willis! Get that white-faced one out front!"

"Got it, Boss!"

The cattle, stubborn and irritable, were bunching up, blocking the leaders from doing what they did best— leading. Willis was an experienced point rider, and convinced he'd get the herd straightened out, Garth steered his horse around to help the wing riders set the perimeters of the herd.

It took longer than normal, and he'd eaten a good couple of pounds of dust and dirt by the time the front section had calmed down enough to start moving forward in unison, which set the others to follow. Dusty and sweaty, Garth once again swung his horse about to ride farther back along the herd, to the flank riders.

"Got any strays still out there?" he asked Lowell Krebs.

Krebs shook his head. "Got 'em all rounded up. They're feisty this morning."

"More so than usual," Garth replied.

"Think that means there's a storm brewing?"

The sky was as blue as the gulf waters and the sun was shining, but in these parts, that didn't mean much. A storm could come out of nowhere. "I hope not," he answered. "JoJo complaining about his knees?" The cook swore the bones in his legs could predict a thunderstorm, and along this trip, his predictions had been right more often than not.

"Not that I heard," Krebs answered.

"Then let's just hope the cows liked the grass they've been feeding on all night too much to move out." Garth waved a hand before he took off again to meet up with the drag riders.

The cowboys were busy pushing the cows trying to

lag behind, and Garth took note of each man and the due diligence they used. He also helped. When caught between two cowboys, a cow would easily give up and hurry forward to join the others of like kind.

Here, too, once all was settled, he steered his horse back up the other side of the herd. The cows were calm now, and moving at a steady pace that didn't take too much energy but would get them several miles closer to Dodge by the time the sun set. It was a sight to see, one that even after eight years, he wasn't tired of seeing. This sea of pointy-hipped critters, some red, some black, some brown, some white and most a combination of colors, filled him with a satisfaction he couldn't have explained if he'd had to. Which was close to how he felt about Bridgette—couldn't explain what he felt toward her if he had to.

He spoke to the flank and wing riders before making his way to the point riders at the front of the herd. Riding up next to Willis, he had to shout above the noise of the herd, "Good job!"

"That was a rough morning," Willis shouted in return. "Stubborn critters."

"They may get more stubborn," Garth warned. "We'll be crossing a river midday tomorrow. I'm riding up to check on the crossing now. We may have to steer east."

"How far?"

"I'll know by evening." Garth gestured toward the herd. "Keep them heading straight north. The route won't change much. It'll depend on the condition of the banks. Don't need any broken legs."

"Good enough. We'll put some miles behind us today," Willis answered.

Garth nodded and rode forward to catch up with JoJo

and Bat who had set out right after feeding everyone the last of Bridgette's eggs.

Without the cattle holding his attention, his mind drifted and settled on her again. A man couldn't have a future while living in the past. He'd been successful since figuring that out. Since leaving his childhood behind him. Bridgette certainly had been a part of his childhood. Now that he knew she was safe, taken care of, he should be able to completely forget about her. Shouldn't he?

Garth rubbed his beard and twisted the longer stands, pulling at them as if the sting it caused might, in some warped and perverse way, help his thinking. It didn't of course.

The clanging and banging of the chuck wagon had him focusing his gaze on the trail ahead of him, and what he saw had him accidently plucking a handful of whiskers from his chin.

"Damn it," he muttered at the sting…and the sight of the plow horse. The next moment, he found himself trying not to smile. Deep down, he'd known she would come after him. She hadn't changed that much. She'd always thought she had to take care of everyone. Especially him at times.

He spurred his horse to catch up with the wagon and her. The last thing he needed was JoJo chewing her ear off.

"What are you doing here?" he asked as his horse sided up next to hers.

Swifter than the plow horse, he had to bring his mount to a stop and wait a moment for her to catch up.

"I wanted to make sure you made it back to camp last night," she said. "I told you to wait in the barn. Why didn't you?"

He shrugged. "No reason to."

Her smile was a disguise. The anger that flashed in her blue eyes told him that, and the lump that formed in his stomach told him he should be wary. Bridgette's wrath had been something to contend with years ago, and most likely had grown as much as the rest of her had.

"I see your eye is no longer swollen."

He grinned. "I can actually see you today."

"You could see me yesterday," she said.

She was making a point, he just wasn't sure what it might be. Changing the subject, he asked, "How's Cecil's baby this morning?"

"The baby and Emma Sue are doing fine." A hint of disgust was included in her glare. "Cecil, however, is moving a bit slow. As I suspect you should be."

"Slow?" He chuckled. "I never move slow."

"Perhaps you should. It might make you think before you act."

She'd always been the impulsive one, not him. "You ride out here just to argue with me this morning?"

"No, I came to make sure you'd made it. You were in no condition to go anywhere last night. I figured maybe I'd find you lying on the ground with buzzards circling above your carcass."

"Figured or hoped?"

She shrugged.

Despite knowing better, he was enjoying this. So was she. They always had enjoyed shooting gibes at each other. "Buzzards don't show up that fast."

"They do when they smell something rotten."

A snicker reminded Garth they weren't alone. JoJo had slowed the chuck wagon to the pace of the plow horse, and there was no doubt his ears were as fine-tuned as a church organ.

With a nod, Garth told Bridgette, "Follow me."

Being politer than him, she bid farewell to JoJo and Bat before encouraging the plow horse to veer westward. The Chaney place couldn't be more than a couple of miles away and that's where he'd lead her to. Back where she belonged. He'd asked Cecil every question he could think of last night, but the man hadn't had many answers. He'd been too focused on the baby being born inside the sod shanty.

"You've done a lot of doctoring, I hear."

"That's why Dr. Rodgers traveled to Oskaloosa," she said.

He glanced her way, mainly to read her face and learn more.

She shrugged. "That's the reason most folks took us older kids off the trains. They needed the help."

Garth knew that, but had hoped differently for her. Had hoped someone had taken her in because they wanted her. Years ago, back at the orphanage, he'd asked Fredrick Fry why no one had ever adopted Bridgette. Fry had said because she'd been a sickly child, and no one wanted that. "You've been working for the doctor the entire time?"

"I didn't start seeing to patients until I was twelve, but yes, I've worked for Dr. Rodgers and his wife the entire time." She was staring straight ahead, as if the vast and somewhat barren landscape held her attention. "I can't complain, though. They've treated me well." Turning, she made her point with a solid stare as she said, "Seems like you can't either."

He could complain, but wouldn't. He'd given that up along with his past, shortly after Malcolm had pointed out that doing something about tomorrow got a man a lot further than complaining about yesterday.

The Chaney place was still a good ride ahead, but in sight. No more than dark lumps on the horizon, but he'd gone far enough. Garth pulled his horse to a stop and while it tossed its head and snorted, he glanced her way. They were no longer best friends, that was clear; they were strangers who had lived apart for more years than they'd lived together. "I have to get my cows to Dodge now. It was good seeing you."

Bridgette bit the tip of her tongue. She wasn't exactly certain what she'd expected to happen this morning, but knew this wasn't it. A part of her had imagined him asking her to join him, which of course she would refuse. She would tell him that she had a life here. But she didn't have a life here, not the life she wanted. The one she'd dreamed of, complete with a house and rainbows. Then again, he'd been the one to put those dreams in her head in the first place, so maybe it wasn't the life *she* wanted, not anymore. Following a herd of cows and sleeping on the dirt with more than a dozen cowboys wasn't either.

She nudged the plow horse forward. "It was good seeing you, too. At least now I don't have to wonder if you're dead or alive."

"Take care of yourself."

"You, too," she said without glancing over her shoulder. He wasn't following her; she hadn't thought he would. Garth wasn't a follower, he was a leader. Always had been. From the day he'd entered the orphanage, he'd expected others to follow him. Expected her to follow him. And she had. That had been one of the things that had made being separated from him so very hard. She'd had to learn to think for herself. Learn to make her own decisions.

That hadn't been easy at first. Garth had always been her point of reason. He'd always pointed out why her ideas wouldn't work, told her she had to think things through. That took patience. Something she'd been short of back then. She still didn't like waiting for anything. When she wanted something, she wanted it now, not years from now.

Letting out the air burning her lungs, she admitted she had learned far more than she'd expected to in the past nine years. Yet the fading thud of his horse galloping away tore at her insides. Part of her wanted to turn around, but the other part of her didn't want to see him leaving. Not again. The image of him walking away from the train had stayed with her for years.

The words he'd said to her long ago, when he'd been called off the train, echoed inside her head. *Don't watch me leave, Bridgette. It'll just make it harder.*

She'd watched him then, but didn't now.

By the time she arrived at the Chaney residence, tears no longer threatened to spill forward. The sting in her heart would take longer to heal, as would the dull emptiness. She knew that from experience.

Her feet had barely touched the ground when Cecil appeared at her side.

"I'll unsaddle the horse," he said.

"Is something wrong with—"

"No, no," he said quickly. "Emma Sue and baby Charlotte are resting, so I came out here. Thought I'd get a few chores done."

His friendly tone made her spine shiver slightly, but when she turned in the direction he'd gestured, she was stunned. "You fixed the barn door?" He'd not only attached the one to its second hinge, he'd found and hung up the other door that had been absent since her arrival six weeks ago.

"Yep, that calf and cow are gonna need to get out of the rain, if it rains that is. Figured they'll need to get out of the sun on hot days, too."

She would swear he was blushing; then again, maybe his face was just red from lifting down the saddle, or from the work of hanging the door. "They will," she said, with a sense of unease.

"It was right smart of you to trade for them. Charlotte will need the milk soon."

Feeling as if she'd arrived at the wrong homestead, or at least encountered the wrong Cecil Chaney, she advised, "It'll be some time before Charlotte's drinking cow's milk."

"Oh, I know, I know, but the time will come." He hefted the saddle over one shoulder and grasped the horse's reins with his other hand. "I got plenty of other chores to see to. Gonna dig a ditch from the creek over yonder to water the wheat. I'll make my way into the house around lunchtime. Emma Sue and the baby should be awake by then."

Bridgette was too stunned to reply, so simply turned about and made her way to the house, where she was equally surprised.

"Emma Sue, what are you doing up?" Bridgette hurried across the room to take the kettle from the woman's hand.

"I have it," Emma Sue said, not relinquishing the pot. "I'm putting some eggs on to boil for the noon meal. We can have them with the rabbit and noodles you made yesterday." Smiling she added, "Charlotte's arrival meant there were plenty of leftovers."

"That it did," Bridgette answered. "But you should be resting while she's sleeping."

"I feel too good to rest," Emma Sue said. "I can't begin to tell you how wonderful I feel. I don't think I've ever felt this good."

Emma Sue was beaming. Her cheeks were flushed, and she looked twice as healthy as she had yesterday.

"I'm glad," Bridgette said, "but you don't want to overdo it."

"I won't." Emma Sue pressed four fingers to her lips as she giggled. "Cecil will see that I don't. He hauled in water this morning and gathered eggs."

"When?" Bridgette asked. Cecil had all but crawled to the breakfast table and after a single bite had stumbled out the door. He'd been nowhere in sight when she'd left a short time later to ride out to Garth's camp.

"After you left." Emma Sue giggled again. "And after he took a bath."

"A bath? Cecil?"

"Yes. He used the rain barrel behind the house. Didn't you notice he'd shaved?" Emma Sue sighed. "He certainly is a handsome one all shaven and sparkling clean."

Bridgette didn't know what to say. At least not aloud. Would wonders never cease? That's why he'd looked like he was blushing. His face was red from shaving. She hadn't even noticed his whiskers were gone. Her mind began to wonder what Garth would look like all shaven and sparkling clean, but only for a moment. She had the wherewithal to stop those thoughts dead in their tracks. He'd left her again, just like he had years ago, and this time, she wasn't going to sit around pining for him. She would make her own plan, one that would lead her to the life she'd always wanted. Despite him. Without him.

"Well, I have laundry to do." Last night she'd set the sheets and towels used during Charlotte's birth to soak and had felt a tinge of guilt riding out this morning without seeing to their washing.

"You go ahead," Emma Sue said. "I'll see to the noon meal, and of course to Charlotte when she wakes."

Bridgette washed the laundry, but regardless of just having given birth and Bridgette's constant pleading to take it easy, Emma Sue saw to most everything else. Cecil took care of the chores, most of which Bridgette had been used to doing.

By the time Dr. Rodgers arrived the following evening, Bridgette was doing little more than twiddling her thumbs. With her hands and body that is, her mind was constantly on the move, going places and thinking about things she hadn't wanted to contemplate. It didn't help that Emma Sue and Cecil had turned into a couple of lovebirds, cooing over their baby and each other nonstop.

In a matter of minutes, Dr. Rodgers proclaimed Emma Sue and Charlotte fit as fiddles and told Bridgette to pack up her belongings.

While doing so, she discovered, as unbelievable as it was, she was sad to leave the Chaney place. That wasn't unusual for most places she'd stayed—overall the families had been good to her—but she hadn't expected to be sad to leave here.

"I'm sorry I never had the chance to teach you any embroidery stitches," Emma Sue said as they hugged goodbye beside Dr. Rodgers's buggy.

"That's all right," Bridgette said. Her gaze went to

Cecil, who stood in the open doorway of the house. "You taught me something far more important."

"Oh? What's that?" Emma Sue asked.

Bridgette had to swallow around the lump that formed in her throat. "That love is blind," she whispered. If there was anyone who couldn't see faults in the person they loved, it was Emma Sue, and that had given Bridgette plenty to think about.

Emma Sue frowned.

Bridgette kissed her cheek. "And that's a good thing."

"You'll come visit?" Emma Sue asked.

Climbing into the buggy, Bridgette answered, "Every chance I get. I'll want to see that rabbit fur hat you're going to make for Charlotte."

Dr. Rodgers flayed the reins over the back of the horse. The buggy creaked as the wheels started turning, and Bridgette couldn't help but accept her life would never be the same. Emma Sue and Cecil had changed it. So had seeing Garth, but more so, it was going to change because she was going to make it change. There'd be no more waiting around for rainbows.

"Rose Canton's time is nearing," Dr. Rodgers said before they'd rolled out of the Chaney yard. "I'll ride out there today and let them know you'll be ready to move in by tomorrow afternoon. That should give you enough time to replenish your supplies."

Bridgette didn't comment, even while wondering why the Cantons would want her assistance. Rose had several children already, and had never needed help before because her mother-in-law lived with Rose and Al, her husband.

With very little conversation during their trek to town, Bridgette had time to formalize the idea that had appeared in her thoughts yesterday and floundered there all day today. Though most of the people she'd stayed with handled the payment like the Chaneys had—given all of it to Dr. Rodgers, where it stayed—it was *her* contribution to the family budget. Mrs. Rodgers had explained it like that when Bridgette had questioned it once long ago. However, a few people had slipped her some coins, stating they wanted her to have it and that they wouldn't tell the doctor. It had never been much, but over the years, had added up to a small sum. Enough to get her to Dodge and provide for accommodations until she decided what to do next.

If Garth could get on with his life without her, she could get on with her life without him.

Chapter Eight

The expanse of the night sky full of twinkling stars that went on for as far as he could see matched the emptiness that had settled deep and dark inside him as soon as he'd ridden away from Bridgette three days ago. Garth rolled far enough onto one side to pick up his hat, and when once again lying on his back, he set the hat over his face, blocking the stars, the sky, his thoughts.

It didn't help. Blocking his view wouldn't make him stop thinking about Bridgette. He should be happy. Happy to know she was healthy, doing fine. Happy the drive was almost over. They'd arrive in Dodge tomorrow. The first herd of the year, just as he'd planned. Dodge would become his town, just as Wichita was Malcolm's. That's why he'd chosen not to take his herd there. He wanted to be known as his own man, not Malcolm's trail boss. He'd imagined what it would feel like bringing in this first herd, and those that would follow. How buyers would eagerly await McCain cattle, knowing they'd be getting prime beef.

His cattle were prime. Not a one ailing or limping or exhausted from the long trip. He'd taken measures, found plentiful grass and water along the way, yet none of that seemed to matter right now. None of those heightened emotions he'd imagined were swirling about inside him.

That goaded him. The drive had gone exactly as he'd planned. The only accident had been him getting stung by that hornet. The only unexpected loss of cattle had been the two traded to Bridgette for her eggs and beans. He hadn't even had a man quit on him, and that was a first.

He pulled the hat off his head and slapped it on the ground.

"Hot night," JoJo said from his bedroll a short distance away. "You'd think this crazy wind would cool things off."

"All it does is stir up dirt," Willis said, his voice farther away.

"At least it keeps the bugs from biting," Bat said with his child's optimism that never failed.

Despite all the darkness inside him, Garth had to smile. He liked that kid. Even when he'd looked rather comical after JoJo had taken a bowl and a pair of scissors to Bat's straight black hair that had been covering his eyes. JoJo had been threatening to do it again a couple of weeks ago and Garth had told him not to. He'd decided to buy Bat a hat in the next town instead, and he had. The boy sported it daily, and proudly.

Bat had made a good cook's helper, and Garth had already said he'd hire the boy on again for the drive next year, but he shouldn't have. The boy needed a better life. He needed a home, a real bed and an education. All kids needed those things. He wouldn't have thought that at one time, but he did now.

A pang shot across his stomach, and no longer listening to the quiet conversation that continued from bedroll to bedroll around the camp, Garth once again stared at the sky. Was this why finding Bridgette weighed so heavy inside him? Because deep inside where all his secrets were hidden, she made him remember things. Such as what kids needed. She'd always talked of having a house, a place that was her own and one she never had to worry about leaving. He'd never had those things, and didn't need or want them. He liked what he had right now. Where nothing held him in one place. He had the freedom of seeing different places every day. Not only on the trail, but down in Texas. He enjoyed the months of roaming the range, rounding up cattle. Last winter he'd gone deep into Mexico for some of the cows he'd deliver to Dodge tomorrow. Renting a chunk of land for his cows from Malcolm had worked perfectly, and would for years to come. He didn't need a place to call home. Not even for his cattle.

But others did. Bridgette. Bat. Hell, even JoJo was getting too old to keep up this way of life for much longer.

That wasn't his fault, or his problem, so why was he contemplating it all now? Why was it keeping him awake?

It wasn't. The thing that was keeping him awake was Bridgette.

She was no longer a scared little girl he felt compelled to protect—mainly because her smart mouth and impulsiveness was forever getting her in trouble. He'd been afraid leaving the train before her and had made Fredrick Fry vow on his mother's grave he'd find a good, solid family to take her in. Had gone so far as to warn Fry he'd find him and take it out of his hide if anything happened to her.

Garth cracked a smile at that. He'd been a kid then. A smart-mouthed orphan with a chip on his shoulder and a soft spot in his heart. Bridgette had put that spot there, and he'd tried hard to get rid of it the past few years. Hell. A little girl was one thing, a grown woman was an entirely different thing—one he didn't want or need. Not now. Not ever.

His thoughts detangled themselves and he sat up, listening for what had triggered his alertness. Faint, but chaotic enough to raise the hair on his arms, he heard men shouting and cattle bawling. "Stampede!" he yelled, jumping to his feet.

With their saddles over their shoulders, every man in the camp ran to the remuda. Throwing their gear onto whatever horse they came to, they were mounted and heading for the herd within a matter of minutes. The shouts and bawling were closer and the dust already filling the air made seeing through the darkness almost impossible. It made the horses nervous, too. They stomped and bounced, fighting against the riders forcing them to move toward the noise.

Garth shouted for Willis to find the lead cows and turn them about, for Krebs and Thomas to head to where the front of the herd should be and for Brad and Akin to head to the back end. They'd had a few minor stampedes along the way, every drive did, but one at night was a trail boss's worst nightmare. One slip, one turn taken too sharply, and a man could fall off his horse. Be trampled to death before anyone knew it.

He continued shouting orders at others that included telling each man to hold his seat. Garth also shouted at himself, silently, but with solid anger. He'd let his guard down. Some thought the most precarious part of the trail was the barren miles of northern Texas or the highly talked about Indian Territory between the borders of Texas and Kansas, but he knew the greatest danger lay right before arriving. That's where rustlers preyed, and those men were far more menacing than all else on earth.

Rustlers would start a stampede and during the chaos make off with a few head. Then, after the drives were done for the year, they'd take them to the stockyards, claiming the cattle as stragglers they'd found. Everyone knew about it, but most trail bosses didn't hang around to claim those cows. A dozen or so cows weren't worth the time and hassle.

They were to him.

Disarray surrounded him. Cattle running in all directions, shouts, bawls and gunshots as his men fired bullets into the ground near the cattle's hooves in order to turn them back into the herd. If they could get the cows gathered close, they'd lose their momentum and the stampede would cease. Garth fired his pistol into the ground too, turning cattle about while making sure he wasn't caught between any. Ending up in the middle of the stampede was a death wish for any cowboy.

Dust stung his eyes and the smell of dung burned his nose. When riled cattle squirted themselves, each other, horses and cowboys. Slimy muck covered his britches and his muscles burned from holding his seat as he steered his horse left and right.

The battle was fierce, that of man against cow, and black emotions filled him as he couldn't make out more than a couple of his men. His mind flashed scenes of him returning to Texas without one or more of them, how it would be up to him to tell their families what had happened. He'd had to do that once before. It had been unpleasant, and had filled him with a sense of shame and failure.

He'd vowed that would never happen again. "They're turning in!" he shouted to no one in particular, hoping whoever heard would be renewed at the idea the stampede would soon end. "They're turning in!"

As if saying it aloud made it true, the mayhem slowed. The bawling dulled into snorts and moos. "Keep 'em moving, boys!" Garth shouted. Letting up now could reignite the stampede. "Keep 'em moving!"

Garth waited until the cattle were unified, moving as one massive dark cloud across the land, and until the air had lost the tense heaviness it had held earlier before he shouted again, "Tell someone you're alive, boys! Your momma wants to know!"

He listened as faint shouts grew louder. Each man not only shouted their name, but the names of the others near them in order for all names to make the full circle of the herd. It wasn't until he'd heard the name of every man, all fifteen of them, that Garth let out a sigh of relief, but there was no time for rejoicing.

Taking it slow so as not to disturb the calm, Garth started searching for one of the two men who'd been on night watch. Upon encountering Gil, he asked, "What happened? You see anything?"

"No, sir," Gil answered. "Even ole' Hickory was settled in for the night when all hell broke loose. Trace was on the other end, but I ain't seen him since it started."

Garth nodded and continued on his route. Hickory had been a cow too stubborn for his own good when they'd started out and Gil had taken extra caution with the steer by sewing its eyes closed so it had no choice but to follow along. By the time the thread had rotted away, Hickory had practically become Gil's pet.

The sky was turning pink, and as Garth rode past the others, he told them to get comfortable because it was going to be a long day. There wasn't a grumble among them. They already knew the opportunity for sleep had long passed.

Trace, a well-seasoned cowboy who'd been on several drives, was bringing up the rear, shooing in a stray by slapping his hat against one knee.

"Any idea what happened?" Garth asked.

"No," Trace answered. "I was halfway through a rotation when I heard some commotion behind me. Next thing I knew, cows were going in every direction."

"You think we lost any?"

"Won't know until we get a bit more daylight, but I've seen most of mine."

Garth nodded. The men had been with these cattle for the past three months and knew them by sight and sound. Just as Gil had Hickory, the others had singled out specific cows. Some because the cow had needed a strong hand or a gentle shove, others because they just liked specific critters for one reason or another. "Have you seen Drake? I'll take him with me to have a look around."

Trace gestured behind him. "His name came from back there."

"Keep 'em moving," Garth said. "We'll be in Dodge before dark."

"I'll be glad about that," Trace answered. "Damn glad."

"Start a head count as soon as the sun comes up," Garth said as he sent his horse onward to find Drake. Not only a good cowboy, Drake could tell which type of critter—four-legged or two—had stepped on a blade of grass and how long ago. He'd also been the first man

Garth had hired years ago for Malcolm and then last year for himself.

Garth and Drake didn't say a word when they met up a short time later, they just started riding south, back to where the stampede had started.

Chapter Nine

Her plan had flaws. Several of them. Which was what usually happened when one didn't think things through—that's what Garth used to tell her. Bridgette had sure done a lot of thinking, but just now she concluded that perhaps she hadn't thought hard enough about the *right* things. Her thoughts had included Dodge and Garth. Mainly Garth. Rather than thinking about how wonderful it would be to show him she could get along without him as well as he could without her, she should have thought about how she was going to do that once she got there.

Revenge certainly was a double-edged sword. But the more she'd thought about all those years of waiting for him, the angrier she'd become. She wanted a life of her own, and she was going to get it.

Except that hadn't worked out very well so far either. This was not what she'd expected.

There weren't any women running naked down the streets, though you couldn't walk down Front Street without coming across what Bridgette thought of as the type of woman who might. More important, not a single thing cost less than two bits in Dodge. Not a spool of thread or a needle, and certainly not a meal or lodging. All that meant the meager amount of coins she'd had left after paying for the stage that had deposited her in the middle of town three days ago were not going to last long. Already hadn't.

The fact she needed to keep her precise location as secret as possible added to her dilemma. By now Dr. Rodgers would know she hadn't gone to Rose Canton's place as she'd told Mrs. Rodgers she would when carrying her bag out the front door. Bridgette held no misconceptions that Dr. and Mrs. Rodgers would come looking for her because they were worried about her. They'd taken her in nine years ago because Shelia had been born only a few months before and taking care of the baby had been too strenuous for Mrs. Rodgers. Upon her entrance into the big house, though it had been quite late, Mrs. Rodgers had told her the baby was now Bridgette's responsibility. *I haven't had a full night's sleep since she was born,* Mrs. Rodgers had said. *See that I do tonight.*

Bridgette had seen to Shelia that night, and for the next three years. She hadn't minded. Though she'd always wanted her own family, she hadn't planned on being adopted in order to get it. Garth had been her family. Their pretend marriage had made it so. Even back then her plan had simply been to wait for his arrival and then, together, they'd start living their lives. The life she always wanted. Her role as nursemaid had seemed a fine way to fill the time, and she'd taken care to do an excellent job.

That was no longer her plan. To wait on him. That plan had been as flawed as this one.

She glanced around the windowless room and

couldn't help but sigh and wonder how she'd ever manage to get out of this pickle.

Her first day in Dodge, while contemplating the prices for food and lodging as well as the idea of Dr. Rodgers sending someone to find her, she'd quite accidently acquired accommodations here. It certainly was a place no one would look for her, and a place where she could barter for room and board.

Staring at the small cot, she sighed again.

It had all come about respectfully enough. She'd merely been walking along the boardwalk when a young girl looking for a doctor had bumped into her. Upon the girl's pleading, Bridgette had followed her to the Crystal Palace. The house was far from being a palace and there wasn't a piece of crystal to be found, but the young woman whose blood had been soaking through into the straw mattress had indeed been in need of medical help.

The infant had already been miscarried, but Michelle, the ill woman, had been close to losing too much blood to survive by the time Bridgette had arrived. After packing Michelle with gauze, Bridgette had propped the foot of the bed up on blocks to stop the blood from draining out of Michelle, and hoped it would work. Several frightening hours had passed before the bleeding had become manageable, and now, two days later, Michelle was no longer in danger of dying. Not from the miscarriage, but her profession could very well serve that ultimate consequence. The life of a soiled dove was not one to be envious of.

Stifling a yawn, Bridgette was too tired to care who was or wasn't happy. She pulled the sheet off the cot, wadded it into a bundle and tossed it in the basket. The small room she'd been assigned was off the kitchen, and a bit crowded considering it housed the large brass tub the doves used for bathing. A cot had been situated in the corner, both for her to sleep on and to perform examinations on each and every girl working at the Crystal Palace.

Bridgette washed her hands with the strong-smelling lye soap before taking down a clean sheet from the shelf and laying it over the mattress. Though lumpy and well-worn, the cot, now covered in a clean sheet, was inviting. The days here were long, but the nights were longer, and she needed to catch a few hours of sleep while she could.

Willow, no last name, just Willow, prided herself upon being the owner of the Crystal Palace, and had hired Bridgette even before she'd declared Michelle would survive. Dodge had several doctors, Willow had explained, and they were willing to come to the palace when called, however, the prices they charged were far beyond what the girls could afford.

Letting out a long sigh as she lay down, Bridgette closed her eyes. The music from the parlor made the wall behind her rumble, but it wouldn't bother her for long. She'd quickly learned which noises to sleep through and which ones meant trouble.

Besides taking care of Michelle, she'd spent the last two days examining every one of Willow's girls. Earning her keep had taken on a new meaning in a very short time. She'd mixed up douches, applied cotton-wood ointment to all sorts of rashes and ailments and even stitched up Ellen's finger when the girl had sliced it open. All for the price of this tiny room and three meals a day.

Willow had said Bridgette could work on the side, to earn actual cash money, if she wanted. Appalled, for she knew exactly the type of work Willow had referred to, yet, not having any other options, Bridgette had said she wouldn't be working on the side, or staying long, that she was only in Dodge to meet her husband.

On impulse, that's when she'd done it. Called herself Mrs. McCain.

There had been several reasons for saying what she had, and at the time, they'd seemed perfectly sensible.

Yawning, she rubbed the back of her neck. It wasn't until times like now, when she lay down and her mind slowed that she thought about what she'd done and the repercussions she'd face eventually.

Right now, she didn't even care about them. She had to catch a bit of sleep while the girls were all busy. Dressed in their finery that left plenty of skin showing, the girls were all outside, waving and coaxing any man walking or riding by to enter the parlor where the music played and the drinks flowed. A trainload of stock buyers had arrived yesterday, and every business providing the same services as the Crystal Palace vied to keep those men happy until the cowboys started to arrive—which would be any day.

Dirty, tired and hungry, Garth was in no mood to stand around any longer. He'd been here almost an hour and the yard agent had yet to arrive. His men hadn't slept in almost forty-eight hours, and as it stood, it would be good and dark by the time they closed the gate on his last cow. He stormed back into the stockyard office, not caring how the glass rattled when the door banged against the wall. "My boys are going to be driving twenty-five hundred head of cattle into these pens within the next hour," he shouted at the pipsqueak standing behind the counter.

The balding little man wiped at the sweat that beaded

his upper lip. "I know, sir, and I expected Mr. Williams back by now." He pointed at the stack of papers on the counter. "I have the paperwork ready and can assign counters to every pen, but—"

"Until Williams is here to visually verify they're mine, anyone can claim those cattle," Garth finished. "I know the routine. That's why I'm here a good two hours ahead of my herd to make sure there's not a single mistake." It wasn't likely another herd would hit the stockyards at the exact same time as his, but by this time tomorrow, every pen could be full and he'd seen plenty of mix-ups when it came to verifying which pen belonged to whom. During drives, yard agents were to be on-site at all times.

"As I explained, Mr. Williams escorted several buyers into town," the man said. "I'm sure he'll be back shortly. He knows a herd was scheduled to arrive today. Once the drives start rolling in, more agents will be assigned twenty-four hours a day, seven days a week."

Garth banged a fist on the counter. "The drives have started rolling in. Mine!"

The pipsqueak nearly jumped out of his boots. "I know, sir."

"Then get another agent in here!" Garth shouted.

Jumping back, the man shook his head. "I can't. They haven't been assigned yet. Mr. Williams has to do that. He's scheduled it for tomorrow morning."

Scaring the little clerk wasn't helping; Garth knew that. "Where'd Williams take the buyers?"

"I'm sure he escorted them to their hotels."

"And?"

The man once again wiped the sweat off his lip while his face turned red.

Garth's last nerve snapped in two. "Which whore-house?"

"Sir, I didn't say—"

"I did!" Garth shouted. "Which one?"

"Mr. Williams has a special liking for the Crystal Palace." Darting his eyes toward the window, the man added, "It's just a block up the road. Has a sign in the front yard."

Garth grabbed the stack of papers and scribbled his name to the bottom of the first page as well as drew a quick picture of the McCain brand. A large M with a slash through the center. "What's Williams's first name?"

"Elroy."

"And yours?"

Blinking and swallowing, the man said, "Ludwig. Ludwig Smith."

"Well, Ludwig, here's my name and brand. Get your boys ready to count. I'll have Elroy back here in ten minutes to approve it."

Garth didn't bother riding his horse. It would be just as fast to walk and he wouldn't need to worry about the mount while dragging Williams out of the whore-house. The stock association would hear about this. If they wanted Dodge to reach the potential it had of be-coming the greatest cattle town in Kansas, they'd bet-ter get the right men at the helm.

The Crystal Palace was easy to find. Besides the large sign in the front yard, girls with their faces painted and the upper halves of their bosoms popping out of their low-cut dresses covered the front porch. They started whooping and hollering for him to come closer before he'd even entered the street leaving the stockyards.

Two of them latched on to him as he entered the yard, one on each arm. Garth didn't bother shaking them off, two more would just have latched on. He'd known the ins and outs of whorehouses since birth. The two holding his arms wouldn't stop the other girls from continuing to call, blow kisses and bat their lashes in order to make a man believe he needed what they were offering.

The door was wide open and he marched over the threshold, barely pausing as one girl had to let loose to make it through the doorway. Piano music filled the air, and Garth drew in a deep breath in order to use his diaphragm to shout, "Elroy!"

An interrupted piano note lingered as temporary silence overcame the room. Garth took advantage of it and shouted again, "Elroy Williams!"

A thud sounded overhead. Mad enough to skin a mountain lion while it was still alive, Garth spun around and headed for the stairway.

"Hold up there, cowboy." A buxom redhead blocked his way. "We don't abide any fighting. If you got a beef with Elroy, you take it outside."

"I got a beef all right," Garth said before yelling, "Elroy!"

The woman waved a hand and Garth twisted, expecting to see a thug coming his way. All whorehouses had a burly character assigned to keep things from getting rough. Seeing nothing but more girls, he turned back around.

"I'm Willow," the redhead said. "The proprietor of the Crystal Palace." Glancing toward a girl, she said, "Perhaps you'd care for a drink. Nettie has several on her tray."

"No, I don't want a drink," Garth said. "I want to

climb those stairs, and that's exactly what I'm going to do."

"Oh, no you're not!"

That snarl had come from behind him, and the familiarity of the voice sent a shiver up his spine. Garth spun about and was too flabbergasted to even open his mouth, let alone speak.

"You can't even take the time to have a bath before you barrel into a whorehouse?" Bridgette shouted at the same time her hand smacked his cheek.

The sting knocked him out of his stupor. Somewhat. "What the hell are you doing here?" he shouted.

"Don't shout at me, you good for nothing—"

"Oh, no you don't!" He grabbed the hand she'd raised again. "I'm sick of you slapping me every time you see me."

"I haven't slapped you every time," she shouted, "but the times I have, you've deserved it!"

She struggled to get her arm from his hold, and others were helping her, including the buxom redhead who was shouting for him to leave. Which he had no intention of doing. Not without Williams or Bridgette. He bit back a curse. He should have known there would be trouble after he'd seen her.

"What are you doing here?" he shouted above the other noises while shoving the other women aside with his free hand. "In this place?"

Bridgette batted at him with her free hand. "I knew you'd changed, but I didn't expect this!"

"Expect?" he shouted in return. "I didn't expect to see you here, that's for sure!" Her nails snagged his whiskers as she batted at him again. He grabbed her other arm and pulled her closer to confine her from hitting him. "Will you stop that?"

"You make me so mad I could scream!"

"You are screaming!"

She kicked him in the shin so hard his back teeth stung. Done. So done. Garth lifted her off the floor and started for the door. Only to be stopped there.

By a man.

With a gun.

And a badge.

"Hell," Garth cursed. He'd left his gun with JoJo. Firearms weren't allowed within city limits. Not that he'd have shot anyone. Well, probably not.

"Put the lady down, sir," the man said.

"I can't," Garth replied.

"Why?" the man asked.

Bridgette had quit squirming and shouting, and the startled look in her blue eyes was almost laughable. Almost, because he was not in a laughing mood. "She'll hit me again," he said. "And I'm tired of being hit by her."

The shock in her eyes instantly turned into a stormy glare.

"Is that true, ma'am?" the man asked. "Did you hit this man?"

She huffed out air so hot it could have singed his beard. Never pulling her glare off him, she answered, "Yes."

"Why? Did he hit you first?"

Garth couldn't help but smirk at her while watching her entire face turn red.

"No," she snarled. "He didn't."

The man gestured toward the door with his gun. "All right then, both of you come with me."

"Can't we settle this here?" Garth asked.

"No, you can't," the buxom redhead piped in. "I don't

allow any violence at the Crystal Palace. None what-soever."

Garth turned to where she stood behind him, but his gaze landed on the man standing beside the redhead. It had to be Elroy Williams. "You," Garth said, singling the man out with a glare. "Are needed at the stockyard."

He nodded. "I'm on my way."

"Deputy Long, remove them from my property," the redhead demanded.

"I am, Willow, I am." The deputy once again waved his gun toward the door.

Garth lowered Bridgette enough for her feet to land on the floor, but kept a solid hold on one arm. She twisted and grunted, but walked out the door beside him. And down the steps, and along the boardwalk, all the way to the sheriff's office.

He let go of her there. Had to because they were put in separate cells.

"The sheriff will be in to question you both as soon as he arrives," the deputy said while locking the door on Garth's cell.

Bridgette was in the one next to his, holding on to the bars with both hands. "And when will that be?" she asked.

"Not long," the deputy said. "He just went over to the train station, and most likely stopped to eat."

Garth's stomach growled. He hadn't eaten since last night. After the stampede, and searching and finding no evidence for why it had started, he'd caught up with the herd, which they'd kept moving forward all day. The emptiness in his stomach was the least of his worries. He sat down on the bed and rubbed a hand against his forehead. Grit, whether on his hand or face, scraped his skin as he rubbed harder.

"I hope you're happy now."

Bridgette had moved from the front of the cell to the side, glaring at him through the bars.

"I wasn't happy before," he snapped, "so why should I be happy now?"

She spun around, and her long hair swayed across her back as she walked across her tiny cell. "Mrs. Kill-grove warned me I'd end up in jail if I kept hanging around you. I told her I wouldn't and that you wouldn't either." She'd reached the other side, where her cot sat, and spun back around to face him. "Just one more thing I was wrong about."

He could start spouting off things he'd been wrong about—especially when it came to her. "What the hell were you doing at that place?"

"Working! There was a woman there who needed medical attention."

A bit of his anger fizzled because he could believe that, and her.

"Until you came along and got us arrested!"

He could point out that she'd played the major role in that, but chose not to. Mainly because silence would irritate her far more than anything he said. And a bit of time behind bars might just show her how foolish working at the Palace had been. With a grin, he kicked up his feet and swung them around to lie down on the cot.

Bridgette growled like a mad cat before saying, "What are you grinning about? It's not funny."

No, it wasn't funny. He'd never been in jail before, and wouldn't be now if not for her. Garth pulled the front of his hat over his forehead. Out of the corner of one eye, he watched her grab the bars with both hands.

"This is serious, Garth! How are we going to get out of here?"

He folded his hands behind his head and crossed his ankles.

"Garth!"

And then let out an exaggerated sigh.

"Garth McCain, don't you lie there and act like you don't have a care in the world. I know better."

So did he. His cattle were bearing down on Dodge, set to arrive any moment, and he wasn't there to oversee it because he'd been caught bickering with her in a whorehouse. He almost said as much, but stopped himself. A smart man would just be quiet and wait for the sheriff—to whom he'd explain everything—then he'd be released and head straight for the stockyards.

She'd be released too, most likely, and could go wherever she wanted. There was no reason for her to be in Dodge—ill woman or not. Yet she was. Because she was as impulsive as ever. Had she forgotten about the tree? About falling out and dang near killing herself? He hadn't. It had taken him years to get the vision of her crumpled body lying on the ground under that tree out of his mind. He didn't blame that all on her. At the time his life had been turned upside down too. He'd lost his friends from the streets, his mother, and he'd been afraid he'd get blamed for her injury just like he had that little laundryman Bridgette had been the only thing about the orphanage he'd found tolerable. She hadn't been like the other kids. Her attitude and smart mouth had reminded him of the friends he'd lost.

Just as he'd thought, Mrs. Killgrove had thought he'd put Bridgette up to climbing that tree, to running away, and he'd been punished for it. Thankfully he'd finally outgrown that. Or gotten wise enough to know he didn't need to take the blame for others. That's why he'd decided to let her go when he let his past go, knowing she—actually no woman—had a place in the life he'd now made for himself. It had taken time for that to happen. Time, and others who helped him understand if he wanted a future he had to put the past behind him—and leave it there. He had. He was done with his past.

He was done listening, too. She hadn't stopped talking the entire time he was thinking. Flipping his legs over the edge of the cot and tearing off his hat at the same time, he barked, "Shut up, Bridgette. Just shut up!"

Her face turned bright red and she slapped at the bars. "Don't shout at me!"

"It's the only way you can hear me over your screeching."

Her glare turned stormy and cold. "You've changed."

"Yes, I have, and you haven't."

Indignation flared in her eyes. "Fine. Be that way."

"I am that way."

"Yes, you are, and you stink!"

He let her have the last word, mainly because he did stink. Dried cow dung was crusted to his britches from the stampede last night.

She plopped down on the cot in her cell. Back stiff and chin out, she stared at him through the bars.

Unwilling to let her take hold of him again, he stared back. He'd put up with weeks of whippings from Orson because she'd lived so strongly inside him. That wouldn't happen again. No one but him would live inside him.

Neither of them said a word. They barely blinked.

That's how the sheriff found them. Even as the man walked down the narrow walkway to the cell, neither he nor Bridgette moved.

"Mr. McCain?"

Garth broke their staring contest with a grin before

he stood and walked to the front of his cell. "Yes. I'm Garth McCain."

"Your bail's been paid," the sheriff said.

"Bail? You haven't heard our statements. We haven't been charged."

"I heard there was some commotion down at the Crystal Palace and stopped by there. Willow told me what happened. So did your cook, JoJo. He'd gone looking for you when you weren't at the stockyards. Ludwig Smith confirmed the rest. You're charged with fighting in public."

Garth waited for the man to unlock the cell and stepped out before he asked, "What about her?"

Bridgette bit her lips together so hard they went numb. She also sent up a silent prayer that Willow hadn't told the sheriff the name she'd called herself. Garth was borderline furious already. She knew the feeling. Seeing him with those girls hanging off his arms and shouting he was going up the stairs had made her see more colors of red than she knew existed.

"Her bail's been paid, too."

Relief made her shoulders dip, but she didn't release her breath. The only person who might have paid her bail was Willow. This was not going to be good. When the sheriff unlocked her jail cell, she marched out the door, passed Garth and continued down the narrow hall between the cells and a solid brick wall.

"Hello, Bridgette," JoJo said as she walked through the doorway. He added, "Hey, Boss," as Garth and the sheriff entered behind her.

Seeing no one but the cook, she released the air in her lungs. "Hello, JoJo," she answered. "It's nice to see you."

"Have the cattle arrived?" Garth asked.

"They were about an hour behind me," JoJo said. "If you hurry, you could get to the stockyard about the same time as them."

"Hold up a minute, Mr. McCain. I need your signature." Turning toward her, the sheriff said, "Yours too, ma'am."

She'd heard Sheriff Myers was a fair man, but she'd never met him. Almost as tall as Garth, he had shiny black hair and a friendly, clean-shaven face. "What is that?" she asked as the man slid a piece of paper toward where Garth stood near the desk.

"An affidavit that your bail was paid and that you won't cause any more disturbances while in Dodge City," he answered, sliding another one in her direction.

She stepped forward as Garth finished scrawling his name. Using the tip of the pen, he pointed at a number the sheriff had written on the form. "You owe me ten bucks."

JoJo cleared his throat. "Actually, I paid her bail with my money. Yours too, Boss. So, in all rights, you owe me ten bucks. Twenty counting hers."

Garth dropped the pen on her piece of paper. "You owe JoJo ten bucks." He tipped his hat toward Sheriff Myers. "Sheriff. It wasn't a pleasure, but good to meet you." Spinning around, he said to JoJo, "I'll see you later."

Bridgette's hand shook as she picked up the pen. If she'd had ten bucks, she wouldn't have been bartering her doctoring skills for room and board at the Crystal Palace. A place she surely couldn't return to now. After JoJo's visit, Willow would know Garth's name, and assume he was the McCain part of her Mrs. McCain name.

"Ma'am? Are you all right?"

"Yes, sheriff, I'm fine. Just reading this affidavit," she lied. Flat out lied. Garth was most definitely a bad influence. He'd only been back in her life less than a week and she'd already run away from home, taken on a false identity, gotten arrested and lied to everyone she'd met. Squeezing the pen tighter, she told herself, what's one more, but as she pressed the tip against the paper to sign the name that was printed on the top, her fingers stalled. Mrs. G. McCain. Had Garth noticed the name when he'd pointed out the amount written right beneath it?

"Just sign it and you can be on your way, ma'am," Sheriff Myers said. "There's not that much to it. It's really just a record for the bail money."

She nodded, wrote the name and dropped the pen before lightning could strike her. It wasn't storming, but in this moment a lightning strike wouldn't be uncalled for. Swallowing against the burning in her throat and blinking at the sting in her eyes, she turned to face JoJo.

He smiled, a crooked, missing-teeth smile that was the kindest she'd ever seen.

She trembled.

After putting his hat on his head, JoJo grasped her elbow and led her toward the doorway. "Thank you kindly, Sheriff."

Bridgette waited until they were several steps away from the sheriff's office before saying, "I don't have ten dollars."

Without missing a step, JoJo nodded. "That's all right."

"Garth won't pay you for my bail," she said.

"Won't bother me none."

"It'll bother me," she said. "I'll find a way to pay you. I promise."

"You have anything at that place you need me to fetch for you?"

She knew what place he meant, and so did he. That was the awkward part. "Yes. Everything I own is in a bag in the washroom off the kitchen."

"All right, I'll take you to the chuck wagon and then go fetch your belongings."

"Garth won't like that," she said. "Me at the chuck wagon."

"Well," JoJo said slowly. "I suspect he don't have a choice, now does he, Mrs. McCain."

Chapter Ten

It was good and dark, well after midnight by his guess, but clocks didn't hold much weight when it came to Dodge City. The town was just as busy after midnight as it was before. Some nights busier. That's how cow towns were. Grinning, Garth let out a pleasure-filled groan as he slid deeper into the steaming hot water. Nothing had felt this good for months. He'd taken a dip or two in rivers and ponds since leaving Texas, but nothing beat a tub of hot water. With or without a shot glass of whiskey. He'd forgone that addition tonight. Remnants of the aftereffects of Cecil's hooch were still too fresh.

"My mother used to tell me that someday I'd appreciate a bath, but I never believed her," Brad said from where he sat in a tub on the other side of the room.

Garth had handed out twenty-dollar gold pieces to each of his men. They'd get the rest, another eighty dollars apiece, when he got paid. That would be in a couple of days. After the buyers examined his cattle and the sale actually took place. Buyers were in town from not only Chicago packing houses, but New York ones, and they were eager. That was the buzz of town. How eager those houses were to buy up every cow hitting the yard. And his, the first of the season, would bring top dollar.

The other men in the bathhouse—it hosted six tubs, and they were all full of his cowboys—talked back and forth. Mainly about their plans for what they were going to do next. Garth heard the hum of the conversations, but wasn't listening to what they said. He'd already given them the talk about staying out of trouble, and keeping a portion of their money to see them back to Texas. Ultimately, it was all up to them now. They each had a job with him next year if they wanted it, and they were all welcomed to bed down near where JoJo had set up a camp in the tent city on the edge of town. Soon there would be more tents out there than buildings in Dodge. That's how it was in cow towns. Some tent cities lasted year round.

He hadn't seen JoJo since leaving him at the Sheriff's office, and wouldn't until tomorrow. Tonight, right after soaking off three months of dust and grime, he was going to the soft bed he'd already paid for and sleep until his eyes wouldn't stay closed any longer.

Bridgette came to mind, and Garth slid all the way down in the tub, dunking his head to wash her from his brain as easily as he washed away the dirt. When he came up for air, he grabbed the bar of soap and started scrubbing. After rinsing, and needing to keep his thoughts on something, he called for an attendant to bring him a razor and mirror.

Clean from tip to toe and wearing a new set of duds, Garth left the washhouse and headed for the hotel. He'd secured a room before hitting up the mercantile for clothes and then the bathhouse. That was another bonus of being the first drive in town. In a few weeks, there wouldn't be a room to be found, and men would be waiting for hours for a dip in hot water. An inch of sand would layer the bottom of the tubs then, because they were rarely completely emptied. That took too much time between customers.

Thoughts of Bridgette still hung in the back of his mind, but he refused to let them come forward. Tomorrow would be soon enough to learn why she was in Dodge. Cecil said the doctor farmed her out, but Garth doubted he'd have sent her to the Crystal Palace.

Garth chomped his back teeth together. He wasn't going to think about her. Not tonight. He needed sleep. Then, with a clear head, he'd contemplate the ins and outs of Bridgette, and how to get her back to Dr. Rodgers.

He entered the hotel, nodded at the clerk and climbed the stairs to the second floor. In his room, he removed little more than his boots and hat before dropping onto the bed. The image of Bridgette was there as he closed his eyes, but so was sleep, and it won out.

The sunshine, or it might have been a pesky fly that kept landing on his face, woke him. Stretching and yawning, Garth swung his legs over the edge of the bed. His stomach growled loud enough to be heard across town. Last night, he'd made the choice of a bath over food, so this morning he was hungry enough to eat one of his own cows.

He planted his hat on his head, pulled on his boots and left the room. Downstairs he ate enough for two men before heading over to visit the barber across the street to cut his hair and scrape off the whiskers he'd missed last night. All that done, he was fit and ready to face the day.

And Bridgette. Thoughts of her had hung with him all night, even while sleeping. He couldn't have that right now. He had twenty-five hundred head of cattle to get sold.

Two men met him less than a block from the barber shop. Wearing three-piece suits and string ties, they stood shoulder to shoulder, blocking his path.

"Garth McCain?" the one on the left asked.

They dressed like twins, but weren't. One was older and more hardened. "Yes, why?"

"Mr. Solstead, Nathan Solstead, would like to speak with you," the one on the left—the older one—spoke again.

"What about?"

"The cattle association. You brought in a herd of cattle yesterday, didn't you?" the one on the right asked.

"Yes."

"This way please."

His hackles were raised. There wasn't anything wrong with his cattle. Garth followed the men and entered a building two blocks up the walkway. *The Dodge City Cattle Association* was painted on the window out front, and a young man wearing a white shirt with black armbands waved them toward a door on the left. Garth moved forward as the older of the two men who'd led him here opened the door and then stepped aside.

"Thank you, Mr. Ellis, Mr. Harmes." A portly man whose black muttonchops connected to his mustache stood up on the other side of a long desk. "Close the door, please, Mr. McCain."

Although no animosity hung in the air, Garth would have felt more comfortable with his pistols hanging off his hips. Knowing others didn't carry weapons wasn't as comforting as it should be. Guns could be concealed in many places and he had a distinct impression that there was a gun in this room. Several.

The man walked around the desk. "I'm Nathan Solstead, Mr. McCain, and since yours is the first herd in town, I feel responsible to tell you what's coming down the wire." Solstead leaned a hip against the desk. "I can't lie. It's not pretty."

"I'm listening."

Solstead walked back around the desk. "Please be seated."

Garth stepped forward to an available chair, but didn't sit down until the other man did. The tension in the room had the hair on his neck quivering.

Flattening his hands on the desk, Solstead said, "You may have heard there are representatives from New York slaughter houses in town."

"I did."

"There are men in town from the railroad, too."

"There usually are." Garth hated men who beat around the bush. If something needed to be said, it should just be said. "And?"

"I'll get straight to the point."

Garth hoped so.

"Your cattle won't be auctioned for a couple of days."

Annoyed, for that was not news he wanted to hear, Garth asked, "Why not?" He'd expected to wait a few days after selling his cattle to get his money because it took time for the financial transactions to take place, but the cattle auction itself usually happens within hours of arrival. It's what he'd wagered on, why he'd wanted to be first to arrive. Buyers were always eager to get things started and they counted on word spreading about the fair prices they were paying.

"Because of the packing house agents." Solstead twisted his chair about to glance out the window behind him. "Feeding the metropolitan cities out east is big business. It's the cattleman's bread and butter, but it's expensive and there's no glory road." Turning back around, a serious glimmer filled his eyes. "We need a lot working in our favor to make it happen. The Eastman Packing House out of New York is attempting to option all the railcars leaving Dodge. They're claiming it's the wave of the future and that it's in the cattleman's best interest. That it'll make things easy all the way around. They'll pay dollar on the head as the cattle are loaded into their railroad cars."

As the underlying consequences took shape, Garth shook his head. "But that'll take out the market. Without additional buyers, there won't be any bidding, any negotiations."

"Exactly," Solstead said. "Eastman will set a price and that's what everyone will get. They know winter feeding all the cows being driven in would be impossible and that there's too much expense and risk in driving the cattle overland to another railhead."

"That may be true," Garth said. "But I just took on those risks and drove twenty-five hundred head of cattle six hundred miles, in order to get good prices, and that's what I expect."

"That's exactly what you should expect. And every trail boss behind you will expect the same thing, but if only one company rules the railcars—"

"They'll have us over a barrel."

Solstead nodded. "I plan on talking with the first few trail bosses and owners to arrive, hoping we can put a stop to it before it starts, but I have to tell you, the railroad is interested. Optioning railcars is guaranteed money for them. Other slaughter houses like the idea, too. They're already trying to decide which town they'll each claim. If played right, those slaughter houses could rule the cattle market, the entire business, and not just in Kansas."

"That's robbery," Garth said.

"I agree, and that's why I'm telling you about it. Asking you to stand with the cattle association."

"Of course I will. I didn't just spend three months eating dust to be cheated out of a decent payout."

"That's good to hear, Mr. McCain. We are going to have to band together."

"I agree. What can I do to help?"

Solstead leaned back in his chair. "Right now, I'm trying to catch every herd without fanfare. I don't want word spreading that we caught wind of and are opposing their actions. They aren't stupid, they know we will, but I don't want push to come to shove until we have enough on our side for a fair fight. I'm not even telling the stockyard agents. A bribe under the table could be too enticing for some men."

Always cautious, Garth asked, "If it's so secretive, how'd you hear about it?"

With a gesture toward the closed door, Solstead continued, "Dave Ellis and Scott Harmes are local ranchers, as I am. We buy up the two-year-old steers, pasture them for a year and sell them off the following winter, after the drives are long over. By then the slaughter houses are in need of a few rail cars of cattle to make it until the summer drives fill their houses again. An agent I've known for several years from a Chicago house was out to see me in February, to buy a load, and told me of this scheme. How it was in the makings. The arrival of the Eastman agents yesterday, men who have never ventured this far west before, tell me it's more than in the making."

Garth shook his head. Greed was a tough contender,

the basis behind many fights, and he wasn't about to let another man's dishonesty steal him of his rightful earnings. "What do you want me to do?"

"If you see a herd arrive, or know of one on its way, I'd greatly appreciate it if you would tell the trail boss to come see me. And if there are any you want to warn me about, think they might be tough to convince, that will be helpful, too."

"Can't think of a single boss who wants to be cheated," Garth said. "I have some cowboys we can trust. I'll send them back out on the trail. Tell them to find the bosses and pass along a message to look me up as soon as they hit Dodge."

"I'd appreciate that. Catching them before they hit town would be ideal. Once there are enough of us, we'll confront the slaughter houses," Solstead said. "Let me know if I can offer any assistance with catching the trail bosses."

"I will," Garth said. Another subject that hadn't left his mind had him saying, "And as long as I'm here, I'd like to mention a complaint about one of the stockyard agents."

Solstead nodded. "Elroy Williams. I heard about how you had to snag him out of the Crystal Palace, and I've already spoken to him about it. Firing him right now might not play in our favor, so I do have to tread lightly."

"As long as you've talked to him," Garth said, although he'd like a bit more punishment heading Elroy's way.

"Thank you. I do extend my apologies about that." Leaning forward and placing both hands on his desk, Solstead continued, "I'd also like to commend you for allowing your wife to assist the girls at Willow's place."

Garth went as stiff as a corpse. Couldn't even lift a brow.

"Willow swears Mrs. McCain saved Michelle's life and is disappointed now that you've arrived, your wife will no longer be staying at the Crystal Palace."

The night he'd told Bridgette he'd never pretended to be anything other than himself flashed across his mind. He wasn't pretending to be sober this time, he was pretending to know all about what Solstead was telling him. And it was damn hard. A hundred questions spun around in his head, all going nowhere, and the sting in his stomach was worse than a thousand hornets.

"Your wife must be a fine woman," Solstead said. "A spirited one. I'm looking forward to meeting her."

"She's spirited all right," Garth managed to say.

A shine appeared in Solstead's eyes. "That's the best kind."

Garth wasn't overly sure he appreciated the man's response.

"Oh, and I'll see that the sheriff returns your bail money," Solstead said, standing up. "Yours and hers."

Word certainly spreads fast in Dodge, but it did most every other place. Garth stood and shook the man's hand. "Keep it," he said. "The bail money. Put it toward something useful in the community."

"That's equally kind of you," Solstead said, nodding toward the door. "I know you're busy. I'll be in touch soon."

"I do have some things to see to," Garth said, more than ready to leave, and search down Bridgette.

"Where are you staying?" Solstead asked before Garth had reached the door. "I'd like to send an invitation for you and your wife to join my wife and me for dinner. It'll look less suspect if we all appear to be friends."

"The Dodge House," Garth said, pulling open the door. He tipped the edge of his hat at the men in the outer office, but that's where the pleasantries left him. Once outside, he gave the steam building inside him free rein as he headed for the tent city. Solstead had said Bridgette—or more specifically—Mrs. McCain was no longer at the Crystal Palace. That meant she was with JoJo.

Of course she'd be with JoJo. Where else would his wife be, other than at his camp. That conniving little wench.

Bridgette spotted a tall man storming across the grassy area between JoJo's tent and town as she draped the dress she'd just washed over the rope Bat had strung up, but it wasn't until she felt his glare that she knew for sure who the man was. He'd shaved and taken a bath, and… A chill as cold as a New York winter raced over her.

She spun around. There were few places to run, but she leaped over the rinse bucket and ran anyway.

Inside the tent JoJo had erected last night, she looked for cover. The four canvas walls would offer no protection. It was far more of a trap, so she turned and raced back out the door.

"Don't bother," Garth shouted. "I'll find you wherever you go, and I won't be any happier when I find you than I am right now."

She twisted left and right, searching for an escape. The open field, dozens of other tents, the chuck wagon. None of it would stop Garth. He hadn't altered his storming approach. It was a direct line to her. The rope with her freshly laundered dress didn't slow him. He didn't duck or walk around it, just swiped it aside with one hand as he barreled forward. The rope and her laundry hit the ground in his wake, and both her wash and rinse buckets toppled, splashing water across the ground as he came closer.

The air was tight in her lungs and her legs wobbled, but she planted her heels in the dirt and lifted her chin. He didn't scare her. Not much anyway.

"Now, see here, Boss—"

"Stay out of this, JoJo," Garth barked at the cook.

Both JoJo and Bat had arrived. They weren't blocking Garth's path, but they were at her sides.

"I'd like a word with my *wife*," Garth growled as he stopped directly before her.

Her heart crawled to her throat, where each beat cut off a bit more airflow.

JoJo and Bat both looked at her and the expressions on their faces said they'd stand up for her. Though she appreciated their sentiments, it would be like two squirrels fending off a grizzly bear. She gave them both a nod and balled her shaking hands into fists as her protectors scrambled away. Pulling resolve from Lord knows where, she asked, "What would you care to discuss?"

Running crossed her mind again as fresh anger snapped in Garth's eyes and he grabbed her arm. His fingers dug into her flesh as he twisted her about and shoved her toward the tent.

"You don't have to be rude," she snapped.

"I don't?" he barked. "Then tell me, *Mrs. McCain*, how is a man supposed to react to the woman's who's pretending to be his wife?"

They'd entered the tent and she wrenched her arm from his hold. "I can explain that."

"And you're going to."

"Stop shouting. Everyone can hear you."

"I don't care who hears me."

"Well, I do. And you should, too."

"Don't tell me—"

"Stop shouting," she said again, lowering her voice. He no longer frightened her. He hadn't before either, she just hadn't expected him to have found out this soon. Which had been foolish. Of course he'd have found out. Taking a deep breath, she calmly said, "I'm not going to tell you anything until you stop shouting." For her own benefit, she added, "And calm down."

"Calm down, I—"

"Yes, calm down. You nearly scared Bat out of his britches."

He opened his mouth, but snapped it shut. The action caused her heart to skip a beat. All his whiskers and dirt had hidden his extreme handsomeness. His features were certainly older and more defined, but clean-shaven, a hint of youthfulness as well as the Garth she used to know shone through. Despite the anger flashing in his eyes.

"Bat's seen me mad before," he said.

She huffed out a breath. "Everyone's seen you mad before."

"If people would quit irritating me, that wouldn't happen."

Sapped of her strength, she glanced around, but the tent offered no seating. Stacks of supplies lined the walls and the bedrolls she and Bat had used last night were rolled up along the back wall. JoJo had slept outside.

Watching her, Garth said, "Home sweet home."

She shot him a glare.

"Why would you leave a big house on the edge of town for this? Why would—"

"Why shouldn't I have left? It wasn't *my* house. It wasn't *my* family. I've lived with more different people the past nine years than I did at the orphanage."

Something that resembled tenderness flashed in his eyes, but disappeared as quickly as it had formed. "Bridgette—"

"What? It's fine for you to get on with your life, but not me?" She couldn't begin to explain how much that bothered her. How badly she hurt inside. A large part of her wanted him to hurt just as badly. "I'm supposed to stay in Hosford forever? Why? For what?"

"Gather your stuff," he said.

"No. I'm tired of waiting for my life to start." Once again anger flashed inside her. "I've spent years watching other people's families grow, helping them grow. It's time I start helping myself." Leveling a glare on him, she added, "No one else is helping me, that's for sure."

He waved a hand. "Gather your stuff."

Furious that he didn't seem to care, that he didn't even acknowledge his part in what was happening, she pointed out, "I can't. My things are wet, and you just threw them on the ground. Meaning I need to rewash them and then let them dry before I pack them."

He took off his hat and ran a hand through his hair, which had also been cut since yesterday. Her heart thudded. This version was older, bigger, stronger and angrier, but it was Garth, and in a very different way that unnerved her. He'd changed so much. Everything had.

"What were you hoping to gain by coming here?" he asked.

Her chin quivered and her heart tumbled, yet she

eyed him directly as an answer appeared. "Myself. My future."

They stood there staring at each other, neither blinking, much like they had yesterday in the jail cell. It was a showdown of who would give in first. It wouldn't be her. Silently, solemnly, she promised herself that she would never, ever, give in again. Not to him or anyone else.

And she didn't.

He did.

Without a word, he turned and walked out of the tent.

Bridgette let the air seep out of her lungs and closed her eyes. Drawing in another breath, she held it, forcing her insides to collect themselves. She'd told him the truth. She'd run away from Hosford, from the only home she'd ever known, in order to find herself, and there would be no going back. It was time for her to start living. And she'd show him that she didn't need him. Never had.

"You all right in there?"

She opened her eyes at JoJo's gruff voice. "Yes, I'm fine."

"Bat has more water heating and I hung the rope back up."

"Thank you," she answered. "I'll be out in a minute."

"Take your time."

She certainly could have ended up in worse places, with worse people. JoJo said she could stay with him for as long as needed. The tent wasn't a house, but it was better than Willow's place. At least from here she could hope to get a more presentable job. Perhaps with one of the doctors. She sighed. That could work except for the fact Dr. Rodgers was certain to hear about that. Dang it. Why hadn't she thought this through a bit more thoroughly?

As together as possible, she stepped forward and opened the tent flap. The first place her gaze went was the open span between the camp and town. She saw exactly what she'd expected. Garth's back as he walked away. A despondent sigh emptied itself from her lungs. Up until this moment she hadn't wanted to admit it, but that's what Garth did. He walked away.

Watching as he moved farther and farther away, she stepped out of the tent. *Not this time, Garth McCain. You won't get away that easy this time. This time you are going to see what you left behind, and be sorry.*

Feeling renewed, she smiled at JoJo and Bat, watching as their somewhat confused expressions softened until they both smiled in return. "Well, that laundry's not going to do itself, now is it?" she said, moving forward.

"Garth's a—"

"Stubborn, pigheaded bully," she said. "Always has been."

"That may be true," JoJo said, "but he's also—"

"Your boss." She flinched slightly at interrupting JoJo again.

"Yes, he is. But he's more than that. Bosses just boss people around and fill themselves up. Garth there is a leader. He shows people what needs to be done, allows them to learn how to do it and watches as it fills them up. Not him. Them. In a way they don't even know all he's just taught them." His gaze had gone in the direction of town where Garth was now nothing more than a smudge blending in with several other people. "People don't follow bosses, they follow leaders."

Bridgette shifted her gaze from where Garth had disappeared to JoJo. She couldn't agree, and didn't. "He doesn't care about anyone but himself."

Still looking toward town, JoJo said, "He's hard, and rough, and ornery, and shouts and cusses and stomps around, but that man cares more about others than anyone I've ever met." He turned to her then and asked, "Why else would he teach them how to get along without him?"

Chapter Eleven

Garth felt like a bird startled off its roost, aimlessly fluttering about with no place to land, no place to go. Usually, after bringing in a herd, he'd spend some time in the gaming houses and saloons. None of that held any appeal to him today.

After rounding up four of his best men, and sending them back down the trail to inform the trail bosses to come look him up before bringing their herds to town, he'd wandered about the stockyards, checking his cattle and grumbling about how every hour those critters remained penned up in his name cut into his profits. A couple of days could make that a deep cut, yet giving in to the slaughter houses would cut deeper.

Ludwig Smith, who was still a little pipsqueak of a man, wasn't so bad. Secretively, so no other ears could hear, he made mention the Eastman House representatives were whispering about offering a flat rate of four dollars a head. Four dollars! Criminy, on a bad day the worst he'd ever heard of was six a head. That was at the end of the season and old nags to boot. Four dollars a head was flat out stealing. He had half a mind to find those Eastman boys and tell them what he thought of their flat rate, but alone, that wouldn't mean much. Solstead was right. The cattlemen needed to band together.

That was an interesting concept to him; other than on a drive when everyone had to work together, he liked going about things singularly.

He could drive his cattle out of Dodge, take them elsewhere, Hays, Wichita, or one of the many smaller cow towns, but that would cost money he didn't have right now, and from the sound of things, the slaughter houses were trying to play their hands everywhere, not just in Dodge.

With no place else to go, Garth found himself on the boardwalk in front of the Dodge House. The cattle weren't the only things filling his head. Bridgette was there front and center. Trying to come up with a solution for the cattle was far easier than trying to figure out what to do about her. He didn't fault anyone for wanting to make something for themselves. Men that is. Women couldn't just go out and do that alone. She should know that. Her life couldn't have been that bad with the doctor and his family. Why couldn't she just have stayed put, or waited until he was long gone before coming to Dodge?

"Good afternoon, Mr. McCain. I have a message for you."

Garth hadn't even entered the hotel, still stood near the open doorway, but inside, the wiry, thin man wearing round spectacles behind the counter waved an envelope.

"It was delivered a short time ago."

Garth entered and took the envelope. "Thanks."

"You're most welcome. Just let us know if you need anything. The Dodge House doesn't have the reputation of being the best hotel in town for no reason."

Garth offered an acknowledgment by tapping the envelope on the edge of the counter before he turned about and headed up the stairs. Once in his room, he broke the seal and pulled out a slip of paper. He'd never considered himself a nervous man, but the words he read filled him with fretfulness like he'd never known.

> *Mr. and Mrs. Nathan Solstead request the pleasure of Mr. and Mrs. Garth McCains' company for dinner this evening*
> *7:00 p.m. at the Buffalo Run Hotel and Restaurant*

He set the note and the envelope on the table. *Mr. and Mrs. Garth McCain* was the part that gave his stomach a set of the jitters. Parting the curtain covering the widow above the table, he stared through the glass panes. Buildings blocked his view of the tent city, but it was out there, and so was she.

He shook his head. Dang it but she was making him think about things, remember things he didn't want to. She'd needed protection back at the orphanage. Years of being sickly had left her small and that alone had been a target for the other kids. He'd sincerely hoped the family that had taken her in had taken on that role. And that she'd let them, listened to reason and behaved. From what Cecil Chaney had said, and considering she'd come up with the idea to trade for the cow and calf, she still had a smart mouth and a head full of lofty ideas.

The click of the door latch had him turning about.

"Oh, I'm sorry. I didn't know anyone was in here." The young woman pointed at the bed. "I just came up to straighten the room and fill the water pitcher. Haven't had a chance before now."

Garth glanced at the bed. There was an indent where he'd slept, but he'd been so tired, he hadn't moved. The covers were barely wrinkled and he hadn't touched the water pitcher. "The room's fine," he said.

"Well, if there's anything you need, just let the front desk know."

She'd almost pulled the door completely closed before he said, "Wait."

"Yes?"

Fingering the envelope, he asked, "Where would I buy a dress? A little fancier than the one you're wearing." He didn't like admitting it, not even to himself, but for right now he needed Bridgette. It was her fault he needed her, but that didn't change the fact. Actually, keeping her close at hand for the next few days would be his safest bet.

"I'd hope it would be fancier than this one," the girl said with a smile. "Whicker's is just down the road and has some ready-made dresses, but Mrs. Owens has a dress shop just two doors up the road from us. She always has one or two outfits for sale, and they are much nicer than anything at Whicker's."

He'd never stepped foot in a dress shop, and wasn't too eager to do so now. "Do you think you could get me one? I'll give you the money. How much would you need?"

"Of course I can. I don't know for sure how much it would cost, but could have my father add it to your room charge."

"Your father?"

She nodded. "Hugh Franklin. He owns this place. Now what size will you need?"

"A bit taller than you, and…" His face heated up as he pulled his eyes off her. She was young, hadn't formed the womanly figure that Bridgette had, and it made him uncomfortable to compare the two.

"I understand," she said. "Will you need anything else besides the dress?"

Growing more uncomfortable, he said, "Sure. Whatever else goes along with it."

"When will you need it by?"

He picked up the invitation. "My wife and I are going to dinner at seven." The girl would know he'd checked in alone, so he added, "I'm going to collect her shortly."

"Oh, goodness, that doesn't give us much time. I'm sure she'll want a bath as well. Will you be back by five? I can have everything prepared by then, and that will give her time to get ready."

Two hours to get ready? It hadn't taken him that long to buy new clothes, wash off three months of dirt, shave, and fall to sleep, but women were different. No one had to tell him that. "That'll be fine." A bit of excitement at the idea of seeing Bridgette all gussied up had him adding, "A blue one."

"Excuse me?"

"The dress. Make it a blue one if possible."

"I'll see what I can do," she said.

Garth turned back to the window as the door closed and he drew in a deep breath. He'd best go see what he could do, too. Convincing Bridgette to join him for supper might not be as easy as it sounded. Most things weren't when it came to her.

Gathering gumption, he headed for the door.

The walk to the camp was uneventful. And short. He hadn't come up with a plan by the time he got there.

When he arrived, Bridgette was carrying a load of firewood from the trees that lined the riverbank, and despite the anger he'd harbored earlier, the sight of her sent things into a bit of commotion inside him. He wasn't used to that, and wasn't overly sure he liked it.

Without looking his way, she dropped the wood and then bent down to stack it in a neat pile. So much for wondering if she was still mad. "Gathering firewood is Bat's job," he said.

"Bat is doing something else right now." She still hadn't looked up.

Garth glanced around. "What?" Not spying hide nor hair of the boy, he said, "He can't be running around Dodge—"

"He's not."

"Then where is he?"

When she didn't answer, he glanced toward JoJo who stood near the back of the chuck wagon. JoJo didn't move, or say a word, but flashed his eyes toward the tent.

Garth listened for a moment, and what he heard surprised him. "You got that kid to take a bath?"

She glanced up then, and orneriness filled her eyes. "Not everyone is fond of walking around smelling like something a dog wouldn't eat."

That he could still appreciate: her quick wit. "Maybe not eat, but a dog would roll in it and then walk around thinking he smelled as pretty as cherry blossoms."

She sneered at him.

He laughed.

Standing up, she put her hands on the indents above her hips. "Is there a point to your visit?"

He hoped the dress that girl picked out would be blue, and that she'd get the size right. The dullness of Bridgette's gray dress didn't match her eyes or her personality. He gestured toward the chuck wagon. "Came to talk to JoJo. Find out if all the boys have checked in."

"They sure enough have," JoJo said. "Most laid their bedrolls here last night. The ones that didn't, most likely will tonight, along with their empty pockets."

Garth had already talked with most of his cowboys and knew the majority of them had bedded down near JoJo's camp. He trusted every one of his men, but a woman sleeping amongst them could cause temptation. JoJo, or Bat, wouldn't be any sort of protection against a liquored-up man. Surely she knew that. Most likely she did, but thought she could handle it. Which she couldn't.

"Willis staked out a section of ground down by the river for the horses," JoJo continued. "And Bat's been seeing to the mounts as usual. That kid sure does love those horses."

"I think I'll go take a look at them." Turning to Bridgette, Garth asked, "Care to take a walk with me?"

The shock on her face was worth smiling at, and he did. Just like Solstead said they had to tread careful with the slaughter houses, he had to tread careful when it came to Bridgette. He wasn't used to that. Being straightforward in demanding what he wanted suited him far better, and had never failed him.

She frowned. "Why?"

"No reason." He glanced toward the tent where splashing sounds still emitted.

Following his gaze thoughtfully, it was a moment before she nodded. "All right."

They started walking side by side. It wasn't uncomfortable. He'd always been at ease around her. After they'd covered a fair amount of distance, he asked, "How'd you get Bat to take a bath? I tried a couple of times along the drive."

"I simply asked him."

Garth shook his head. "No you didn't."

She cracked a smile. "It was a bit more than a simple request, but we came to an understanding."

He'd bet a new pair of boots the understanding she referred to hadn't come along as easily as she pretended it had. A twinge of compassion for Bat flashed inside his chest. "He's a good kid."

"Yes, he is. What are you going to do with him?"

"Me? He's not mine. JoJo's the one who took him in."

Her smile never waned. "So he did, and JoJo looks to you to steer them both in the right direction." Frowning slightly, she said, "Bat needs things, a home, a family, an education. Don't tell me you don't know that. I know you haven't changed that much."

Bat's future had crossed his mind, and he'd figured it would all work out in the end. Most things did. Knowing she wouldn't appreciate that response, he used their arrival at the rope that had been tied to various trees to pen in his remuda as an excuse not to answer. Lifting the rope, he gestured for her to duck under it.

The horses, used to human interactions daily, walked closer to greet them. She instantly started petting the elongated nose of the big roan mare he favored. Drawing a deep breath, he took a moment to contemplate where to begin. It helped that he knew her so well—at least the person she used to be. *That* Bridgette had a soft spot for helping people, and, he reasoned, so did this one. She'd never have put up with Cecil Chaney if she didn't. "I need to ask a favor of you, Bridgette."

"You do?"

Pretending as if checking over the horse held his attention, he said, "Yes, I do."

"If it includes me going back to Hosford, I can't do it. I plan on getting a job here in Dodge. Earning enough money in order to move on."

She'd never been a good liar. Still wasn't. He ignored that, although he had to smile inside himself. "Where you moving on to?"

"West."

"West?"

She stiffened and closed her eyes. "Yes. West."

"When?"

She let out a heavy sigh before turning to face him. "I'm not sure, but I won't tell anyone else my name is Mrs. McCain. That just sort of happened."

He certainly wanted to know more about that, as well as what had led up to it, but that would have to wait. She wouldn't supply the answers he wanted while her guard was up. "Well," he said, drawing the word out, "it's gonna have to keep happening. For the time being anyway."

Confusion and shock filled her eyes as she spun to look at him. "What?"

"Word spread that you're my wife." He ran a slow hand down the nose of the horse. "We've been invited to dinner."

She pressed a hand over her mouth, but then flayed both hands in the air. "What?"

Startled, the horse tossed its head and stomped a foot. Garth pushed the animal aside, but a second one immediately stepped into its place.

"Invited by whom?" Bridgette asked, quieter so as not to startle the other horse which she'd started to pet.

The sun shining on her hair was making the strands glisten and that made something inside him tighten and twist. He didn't want to think about how pretty she was. How pretty she'd always been. Looking away, he said, "Mr. and Mrs. Nathan Solstead. Nathan's the president of the cattle association. Dinner is at seven at the Buffalo Run."

Bridgette was shaking from head to toe and didn't know which reason to begin with in order to explain why they couldn't go out to dinner. What she'd told him was true. She was going to find a job and earn enough money to go West. Go anywhere that he wasn't. Coming to Dodge had been foolish. He didn't care if she got on with her life or not. He never had. "I—I can't go out to dinner with you."

"I have a girl at the hotel picking you up a new dress."

"It's not about a dress. I can't pretend to be your wife. I won't."

"It's too late for that. They already think it." He pushed aside a white horse that was vying for a bit of attention. "I really need your help with this, Bridgette."

Struck by the sincerity in his tone, she ducked under the horse's neck. "I can't help you, Garth." Although the idea it might actually happen no longer worried her, she still used it as an excuse. "I ran away from Hosford and someone might come looking for me."

"Who?"

Bridgette ran a hand along the horse's side as she walked beside it, mainly to keep Garth a distance away. He'd ducked under the horse's neck, too. "Dr. Rodgers. I was supposed to go to another family, help them until the wife had her baby."

"They'll have to find someone else."

"There is no one else." Learning that Rose Canton's mother-in-law still lived with the Cantons, and the fact that Mrs. Rodgers hadn't known that was Bridgette's next assignment had been the catalyst that had sent her to Dodge. Hearing she was being sent to a family who really didn't need the help confirmed she'd never been wanted at the Rodgerses' home and that there was no reason to stay. Knowing there was nowhere, no one, where she was truly wanted made her insides ache. The one thing she'd always wanted was further away than ever.

Garth grasped her elbow. Sapped by her own thoughts, the truth of her life, Bridgette didn't have the will to fight against him as he led her away from the horses. She probably didn't need to worry about Dr. Rodgers finding her. He was probably glad to be done with her. What she did need to worry about was telling the truth. She couldn't have the entire town thinking she was married to Garth. That would hinder her in finding a job. People wouldn't want to hire a liar and she couldn't blame them.

Together they ducked beneath the rope. He didn't say anything until they'd entered a small grove of trees near the riverbank and he'd tugged her down to sit next to him on a fallen log.

"Is there anything you can do about that?" he asked.

She closed her eyes as heaviness pressed down upon her shoulders. He was referring to leaving Hosford. That was Garth. He'd never depended on outsiders, only himself, and expected the same of others. "No, other than going back." Admitting that made her throat burn. "I can't do that, Garth. I can't go back there. I'll never leave again if I do." She knew that to be true, too. Hosford was the only home she'd ever known. She was already missing it, and wondering about the people who had been kind to her over the years.

Garth's elbows were braced on his knees as he stared forward, toward the muddy brown river. "If going back's not an option, what else could you do?"

Stung, she said, "There is no *if.* Going back is not an option."

He glanced her way, with one brow arched and a glint of humor in his eyes. "So what else is an option?"

"There aren't any," she pointed out.

"There are always options," he said. "You just haven't thought hard enough on it."

"Yes, I have," she argued. "Before and after I left."

"You mean before and after you ran away?"

Flustered, she glared at him.

He grinned. "If you'd merely left, you wouldn't be worrying about anyone coming to find you. There wouldn't be any need because you'd have told them you were leaving."

"It's not that simple."

"Why? Did you say you'd live there forever?"

"No."

"What did you say?"

Growing more flustered, she stood. "I didn't say anything. There was never an opportunity to."

"You mean you never made the opportunity."

Irritated by his calm attitude as much as she was by his words, she snapped, "And you would have? You would have made the opportunity. Told people that you were leaving. That you wouldn't live there forever."

"Of course. I always have. I've never just run out on anyone."

"Yes, you have," she argued. "You ran out the other night, when I told you to wait in the barn."

He shrugged. "I was drunk."

She ran her hands through her hair and squeezed her head at the frustration filling her system. Other than that night, he'd always laid out his plan far in advance of taking action. Even when it came to leaving the

Orphan Train. He'd prepared her for their separation weeks in advance of it happening.

"When that famer took me off the train, I told him I wouldn't be hanging around long, and I didn't. When Malcolm Johansson hired me, I told him I'd work for him until I had enough money to round up my own herd. When that happened, I offered him a couple of suggestions as to who he should hire to replace me."

She didn't doubt any of that, and it didn't make her feel any better. "Well, I'm not you, am I?"

He shook his head slowly. "Nope, you aren't. But you are the one claiming to be my wife, and we have to be at the restaurant in a few hours."

"You have to be at the restaurant. I don't."

His gaze locked on hers, but this time, it didn't feel like a showdown or a challenge. The disappointment in his eyes made her stomach gurgle and her chin kept trying to quiver.

Once again, he was the one to look away first. Slapping his thighs, he stood up. "All right then."

A shiver rippled her shoulders. "All right what?"

He started walking toward the camp. "You're right. You don't have to be there."

Hurrying to keep up with his long strides, she asked, "Are you going by yourself?"

"No, the invite is for me and my wife."

"So you aren't going to go?"

"I have to go," he said. "It's important for me to be there."

Marching along beside him, she said, "Well, I'm not going."

"You said that."

"And you said that you are going. And that the invite was for both you and your wife."

"Yep."

She stopped. They were getting too close to the tent city. Others might hear their conversation if they moved any closer. "So what are you going to do about that?"

He'd stopped beside her and his gaze went toward town before it settled on her again. "Not too many people have seen what you look like. There has to be another girl at the Crystal Palace who won't mind pretending to be my wife for the night." He flicked the end of her nose with one finger. "See you tomorrow."

Chapter Twelve

It was a full minute or more before the implications of what he'd said hit her brain. And another minute before the implications of those implications hit her stomach. Bridgette hoisted her skirt and ran to catch up with Garth. She didn't say a word, not even when he glanced her way with both brows lifted. He didn't need to know how dark and ugly her insides had turned a moment ago. Would never know, but if anyone was going to pretend to be his wife, it would be her.

She'd worry about the consequences later.

They walked in silence all the way to town. He took her arm as they crossed the road that led from the stockyards to town, and kept a hold of her as they started up the boardwalk. Bridgette kept her head up and her gaze forward as they walked past the Crystal Palace. Although JoJo had told her Garth had only gone there to find the stockyard agent, she couldn't help sneaking a peek out of the corner of one eye at him while the girls on the porch whooped and hollered.

"Aren't you going to wave to your friends?" he asked.

She ignored him.

A few blocks later, after crossing yet another busy

cross street, he guided her through the open doorway of the Dodge House. It was a huge white building, sporting more than twenty-five guest rooms—that's what she'd heard—and about the most expensive place to stay in town.

"Hello," the man behind the desk greeted.

"Hello, Mr. Franklin," Garth replied. "This is—"

"Mrs. McCain," the man interrupted. "I've heard about you, and it is so nice to meet you. My Chrissy has your bath ready." Turning to Garth, he asked, "Will you need the extra key to your room?"

"No," Garth answered. "One's all we need."

Mr. Franklin pushed his glasses up on his nose as he smiled at her again. "All right then. As I said, Chrissy has everything ready. It's a pleasure to have you staying with us, Mrs. McCain. A real pleasure." Almost as an afterthought, he added, "You, too, Mr. McCain."

Garth merely nodded as he guided her toward the steps. Bridgette didn't stumble, but should have. Her stomach was flipping and flopping as if she'd just tumbled all the way down an entire flight of stairs. Had the entire town heard she was Garth's wife? This was bigger and more convoluted than she'd imagined.

Her heart thudded painfully against her ribcage by the time they arrived at the second floor.

"Mrs. McCain," a young voice called as they turned the corner. "Down here. I have everything ready in the bathing room."

A bit of relief washed over Bridgette at hearing there was a private bathing room. The hotel in Hosford hauled a tub into the guest's room when a bath was requested, and she most certainly was not prepared to take a bath with Garth in the same room.

Her relief didn't last long. In her rush to catch up with

him, she hadn't collected any of her items. A bath didn't do much good when you put dirty clothes back on.

As if reading her mind, Garth quietly asked, "Is there anything back at the camp you need?"

Admitting there was annoyed her, but she had no choice. "Yes."

"I'll go get it."

"There's a bag—"

"JoJo will know." Letting go of her arm, he nodded toward the girl at the end of the hall. "Go take your bath."

She glanced down the hall and then back at him, wondering for a way to put a stop to all this.

"Go on," he said. "I'll be back shortly."

The twinkle in his dark eyes caught and held her attention, and moments later, full understanding hit her. Pinching her lips together, she growled at him like she used to years ago when he'd irritated her.

Stepping closer, to assure no one overheard, she whispered, "This would be a whole lot easier if you weren't enjoying it so much."

He didn't just grin, he laughed. It was deeper than she remembered, but still, it sent her back several years. She used to love to hear him laugh, and he used to do it a lot. At times, just to please her. She'd never told him she'd known about that.

Before she realized what he was doing, he grasped the back of her head and pulled her face close enough for him to kiss her forehead. The touch of his lips, warm and soft, sent a delectable shiver down her spine that burst into a pool of warmth at the bottom of her backbone, filling her insides. She'd loved him for so long. In all honesty, couldn't remember not loving him. They'd hugged and held hands, but he'd never kissed her. Thank goodness, because the touch of his lips made her want more. A whole lot more.

"Go now," he whispered, "before your water gets cold."

As he walked away, she drew in a ragged breath, one where tiny bits of air caught on invisible branches inside her, and hung there like pieces of fruit waiting to be plucked.

"Mrs. McCain?"

Bridgette had to pound on her chest to get the air moving before she could turn around. Garth's soft chuckle echoed in the hallway behind her as she put one foot in front of the other, walking toward the girl waiting for her.

"I'm Chrissy Franklin," the girl said. "My father owns the Dodge House. I have everything set up. Mrs. Owens had the most lovely blue gown ready for sale, along with a matching hat that is so adorable. I can't wait to see it on you. I thought we'd wash your hair right away so it can be drying while you finish your bath and get dressed. Then I'll curl it for you."

Bridgette's head was still spinning, along with other parts of her, so she merely nodded and followed the girl. The room was spacious, even with the large tub taking up a considerable amount of space.

"Do you need help undressing?" Chrissy asked.

Years ago Bridgette had gotten over the unease of seeing other women without any clothing, but this would be a first for things to be the other way around, and that was uncomfortable. "No," she said. "I can manage."

"I'll step out then," Chrissy said. "While you get undressed and climb in the tub. My mother is pressing the hem of your dress. I'll run down and get it. I have everything else up here already."

The girl gestured toward two benches that sat near the wall. Underclothes, right down to a new pair of stockings, were laid out across the tops of both seats. The door behind her clicked shut, and Bridgette crossed the room to run a fingertip over the delicate white lace trimming the camisole and pair of drawers. Always conscious of money, and knowing the prices in Dodge she muttered, "This must have cost a fortune."

Garth felt like whistling. He hadn't felt like whistling in years. JoJo had been full of questions, and though he'd provided the old man with enough information he wouldn't worry about Bridgette, Garth had kept most of his thoughts to himself. Those concerning her anyway. He'd known the idea of having someone else pretend to be his wife would get to her and that was exactly why he wanted to whistle. Walking down the boardwalk beside her had filled him in places he hadn't known had been empty, and kissing her, even though it was just a small peck on her forehead, had been even more fulfilling. He'd forgotten what it felt like to know someone cared about him.

He was almost back to the Dodge House when he spied one of the men he'd seen this morning across the street. Either Mr. Ellis or Mr. Harmes, he wasn't sure which was which. The man tipped his black hat and Garth copied the action in return, but then paused as his thoughts shifted slightly as the man continued on his way.

He'd purchased a new outfit for Bridgette, but never contemplated what he should wear tonight. Until now. Solstead would be wearing a suit, and therefore, he should, too. Not because he wanted to, but because that's what a cattleman would do. His heart thudded a bit harder as he wondered what Bridgette would think of him wearing a suit.

Convinced, Garth continued up the boardwalk and then entered the dry goods store where he'd purchased the clothes he was wearing before taking a bath last night. He'd never owned a suit, and wasn't sure what he needed, but the clerk knew. Right down to the hair oil he used to slick back Garth's hair.

A short time later, sporting a three-piece suit, complete with a white shirt, black tie and a new black hat perched atop his slicked-back hair, Garth made his way out of the store. His new black boots clicked loudly on the boardwalk, all the way to the Dodge House and up the steps to the second floor. Bridgette wasn't in the room when he opened the door, and that was a bit disappointing; he was hoping to surprise her with his new duds.

He set her bag on the bed, his old boots in the corner and then walked across the room to tuck the clothes he had been wearing in one of the dresser drawers. At the rate he was spending money, he'd have to cash in one of the bank notes in his leather purse long before he sold any cattle.

Other than while shaving, he rarely looked at himself in a mirror, but the image that flashed above the dresser had him looking up. The red vest beneath the black jacket was bright and attention getting. He wasn't so sure he liked that, but he did like the new black hat. He lifted it off to check out his slicked-back hair. Smoothing a stray hair into place, a noise had him turning about.

He'd left the door open, planning on going down the hall to check on Bridgette as soon as he'd emptied his hands.

There was no need to go down the hall. She was in the doorway, and he'd never seen anything like it. There were cute women, and pretty women, and then there were beautiful ones. He was looking at the most beautiful one ever.

The gown was blue, a pale blue, with tiny white lace at the hem, cuffs, and collar that stood up, encircling her slender neck. The white lace went down the front of the dress, bordering a row of buttons all the way to her waist. There was more lace on the skirt, trimming the layers of material that went clear to the floor.

His eyes shot back up, to her face that was framed by ringlets of golden hair that had been pinned up in a fancy fashion type of way beneath a dainty blue hat. On anyone else, he would have thought that hat silly. On her, it looked perfect.

Their gazes met, locked, and along with an intense heat that hit him below the waist, he felt a tinge of confusion at the humor sparkling in her deep blue eyes.

A moment later, he realized it was because his hand was still on the side of his head, where he'd been smoothing back his hair. She'd caught him preening in the mirror, and thought it funny. It was. Even to him.

Grinning, he planted the new hat on his head and stepped forward, arms held out at both sides. "What do you think?"

She giggled slightly. "Let's just say, I wouldn't have recognized you dressed like that any more than I had with your face covered in whiskers and one eye swollen shut."

He nodded, and turned about to glance in the mirror again. "That good, eh?"

She laughed louder.

He turned back around and let a long sigh exhale

while taking in her beauty once again. Grinning, he twirled a finger in the air.

Her cheeks turned pink as she spun around, showing him all sides of her dress.

Taking a step closer, he said, "I'd have recognized you if I'd at least had one good eye when I rode into the camp."

"No, you wouldn't have," she argued.

"Yes, I think I would have." His throat felt a bit thick, so he spoke quickly, "And I know I'd have recognized you if you'd been dressed like this. You are the very image of the woman I'd imagined you'd become. The very image."

A smile did a little magic act of now you see me, now you don't, before it settled on her lips. She pressed two fingers against her mouth and closed her eyes for a moment. When she opened them, she said, "You look exactly like the man I'd imagined you had become." She sniffled and blinked before adding, "A man I was afraid I'd never see."

The tears that welled in the bottoms of her eyes had him stepping forward and taking her hands. He curled his fingers around hers and squeezed them gently. "I'm glad we found each other, Bridgette. I sincerely am."

"Me, too, Garth. Me, too."

He might have kissed her right then; his face had been inching toward her, but a loud sigh had him glancing at the open doorway. Franklin's daughter stood there, with one hand pressed to her chest and stars in her eyes.

Bridgette pulled her hands from his and stepped toward the door. "Thank you, Chrissy. For everything."

"You're welcome, ma'am," the girl said with a sigh. "You two look so beautiful together. Like a prince and princess or a king and queen. I hope you have a wonderful time at dinner."

Brought back to his senses and the reason they were both gussied up, Garth asked, "Can you tell us where the Buffalo Run is located?"

"Several blocks north of here," Chrissy answered. "You take Front Street all the way to Third Avenue. Turn left and go two more blocks. It'll be on your right."

"Thank you." Turning to Bridgette he asked, "Are you ready to leave?"

She nodded. At least he assumed she did. All he really saw was her smile, and it nearly knocked him out of his new boots. Keeping his boots on, and attempting to clear his head, he took her arm and headed for the door.

He needed air. Fresh air. Cold air to cool off his loins which had grown sweltering beneath his new britches.

Mr. Franklin met them at the foot of the stairway. The woman beside him had to be Mrs. Franklin because she was an older version of Chrissy who'd hurried down the steps in front of Bridgette and him.

"We hope the two of you have a lovely evening at the Buffalo Run," the man said. "And please, if you're so inclined, do let your guests know we have a full-service dining room here at the Dodge House."

Bridgette must have had a clearer head than he did, because she spoke instantly. "Of course we'll let them know. As well as the other amenities you provide your guests. Chrissy's assistance couldn't have been better."

"You look beautiful, Mrs. McCain," the older woman said. "Simply beautiful."

Garth could easily agree to that, and did. "Yes, she does. Thank you, for all your assistance." Still holding

Bridgette's arm, and still needing air, he steered her away from the Franklin family and toward the door.

Once on the boardwalk, he paused to catch his bearings.

"North is that way," Bridgette said.

"I know," he answered, even though, still a bit off-kilter, he hadn't been exactly sure. "I was just giving you a chance to catch your breath."

"I don't need to catch my breath."

"I didn't either," he said, putting his feet in motion.

Before they reached the end of the block, she said, "If you keep walking this fast, we'll both need to catch our breath, or be breathing like we ran the entire way."

"Gotta cross the road while the coast is cleared," he said, hurrying through the intersection. Then he slowed his pace. "Better?"

She nodded. "Who did you say we are meeting for dinner?"

"Nathan Solstead."

"And he is?"

"The president of the cattle association."

"Have you known him long?"

Garth had never been one to lie or stretch the truth, so he said, "Since this morning."

"Is he new to town?"

"I don't think so. He has a ranch nearby."

"Then why haven't you met him before?"

It had always been like this between them, her asking questions and him answering. "I've only been in Dodge once before."

She'd stopped dead in her tracks and a frown twisted her face.

"Last year," he explained more thoroughly, "After

the drive, I visited Dodge before heading back to Texas. Wanted to explore the Great Western Trail."

She was still frowning. "Didn't your drive last year end here? In Dodge?"

"No. It ended in Wichita."

"Wichita?"

Feeling eyes on him, he glanced up and down the street. A few folks were looking their way, and he gave her arm a slight tug, to get her walking again. "Yes, Wichita. That's where Malcolm Johansson, the man I worked for, always sends his cattle to. But when it came to my own, I chose Dodge."

She'd started walking beside him, but her slowness said she was thinking hard about something or another. "So, you've never driven cattle past Hosford before?"

"No. Not until a few days ago. Why?"

"Just curious." With a wave of one hand, she said, "Here's Third Avenue."

They made the corner and kept walking. She'd grown solemn, and in an attempt to lighten the mood, he pointed out a few things that might catch her interest—the gas streetlights and pots of flowers on several corners. She responded, but her thoughts were elsewhere. So were his. "The topic is bound to come up, Bridgette."

"What topic?"

"How you came to be staying at the Crystal Palace. I don't want to get caught in the middle of something I don't know anything about."

She stopped again, and it was just as well. He could see the Buffalo Run, a three-story building, across the street less than a block away. Finely dressed men with women on their arms were strolling in and out.

"I believe you're already caught in the middle of it,"

she said, looking up at him solemnly. "We both are. And I'm sorry about that."

"So how'd you come to doctoring one of those girls? I'm assuming Dr. Rodgers didn't send you."

"No, he didn't. I accidently bumped into Ellen while she was looking for a doctor. She is the kitchen girl who works at the Crystal Palace, and said one of the girls was extremely ill. I went with her to see if I could help, and Willow ended up offering me room and board for my services."

That all sounded innocent enough. "Why did you tell them—"

"That I was Mrs. McCain?" She bowed her head regretfully. "It just slipped out when Willow said I could work for cash at her place. I told her I was married, and that was the name that just popped out."

"Popped out?"

"Yes. I didn't deliberate on it. I didn't mean to put you in this position. Mrs. McCain just popped out without any conscious thought."

The sincerity along with a glimmer of regret in her eyes tugged at him, made him want to pull her close and tell her it was all right. That no harm had been done, but harm had been done. He wasn't a liar, and pretending she was his wife was a lie. One that threatened to deny him all he'd worked so hard to gain over the years. The cattleman's association, the stockyards, even the slaughter houses wouldn't respect a man who lied, even about as unimportant a thing as being married.

He had half a mind to turn around, take her back to the hotel and then go to dinner by himself—tell Solstead the truth, but at that exact moment, Nathan Solstead waved their way before he assisted a woman, obviously his wife, out of a buggy.

"Come on," he said, directing Bridgette forward again. "That's Mr. and Mrs. Solstead entering the restaurant."

Bridgette started walking again, and willed herself to remain in control of her nerves. A moment ago she'd been ready to tell him that she couldn't go through with it. Couldn't pretend to be his wife. It had been one thing just to assume his name, but an entirely different thing to have to act the part. Knowing Garth hadn't been traveling through Hosford for the last eight years, that he'd been way over on the eastern side of the state, should have lightened some of the animosity she'd built toward him. But it hadn't. Wichita wasn't that far away. Not if he'd really wanted to find her.

He hadn't wanted to find her. All those years she'd spent waiting for him truly had been for naught. All her memories that he'd been the only person to care for her had been wrong, too. Knowing that increased her anger.

So did walking beside him. He'd had always been handsome, but dressed in the three-piece suit, he was downright striking. The most striking man on earth. Looking at him took her breath away, and she found it hard to think of anything else. Yet, she had to. She couldn't risk him taking a hold of her heart again.

She regretted saying her name was Mrs. McCain, but what she'd told him, how the name had just popped out of her mouth was exactly what had happened, and she knew why. From the moment he'd pretended to marry her back at the orphanage, that was who she had seen herself as, who she believed she'd truly become someday. Mrs. Garth McCain. She knew better now.

"We're here."

Bridgette grabbed Garth's hand as he reached for

the door handle. She'd never been this nervous. "I can't do this."

"We don't have a choice," he said quietly.

As she shook her head, he glanced around and drew a deep breath before saying, "It's about time you learned to face the consequences of your actions."

If they hadn't been in public, and if he hadn't grasped her arm to propel her forward, she'd have left him standing in the doorway. As it was, they were both in the entranceway where a man with black muttonchops waved them forward.

"Just behave," Garth whispered as he led her toward the couple.

At that moment, her anger turned into a desire for revenge stronger than ever before. Behave? Oh, she'd behave all right. She'd show him just how lucky he could have been if he'd kept his promise to her. Living with so many different families had shown her what perfect wives did and didn't do. She was going to be the most perfect one ever—and make him regret that she would never be his.

Chapter Thirteen

Although she'd never been out to dinner in a fancy restaurant—and this was certainly the fanciest one Bridgette could imagine—nor had she ever worn such finery, or pretended to be married, she was an adaptable person. Life had made her that way right from the start, and that helped considerably as they joined the other couple.

She smiled and used her manners, and made sure to look at Garth with an expression as close to the lovesick one Emma Sue had cast toward Cecil Chaney as she could muster.

It helped that the Solsteads were friendly and good people, and made her feel comfortable from the moment she sat down. They had five children, three boys and two girls, who had to be as pleasant as their parents. "Lydia sounds like a handful," she told Mr. Solstead as he finished a detailed and animated tale about their youngest daughter hiding a baby skunk under her bed.

"Oh, she is," Mrs. Solstead said. "She gets that from her father."

The way Virginia Solstead looked at her husband made Bridgette's stomach flutter oddly and made her question her acting abilities. Although the gazes she bestowed upon Garth were similar to how Virginia gazed at her husband, it was obvious that even though the couple had been married many years, they were still very much in love. Nathan returned his wife's gaze with a smile. Garth on the other hand, narrowed his eyes her way, telling her he knew what she was up to.

She lifted her glass and smiled over the rim at him. He might think he knew her, but he didn't. She was no longer the girl he'd left behind. She was the woman he'd never possess.

"Do you have any children?"

Caught swallowing, Bridgette merely shook her head at Virginia's question.

"We haven't been married long enough for children," Garth said.

She wouldn't call it disappointment, but there was a distinct tone in his voice that wavered on displeasure. She wasn't overly happy herself.

"They will come in time," Virginia said. "How long have you been married?"

"Over twelve years," Bridgette said.

The shock on all three of their faces made her giggle. "Garth and I grew up in the same town and pretended to get married when we were both just children."

A round of laughter encircled the table, before Virginia asked, "Did you travel to Dodge with the trail drive?"

"No," Bridgette started, "I—"

"Bridgette stayed with friends the past couple of months," Garth said. "The wife was expecting and needed help. She traveled to Dodge after the baby was born."

"Oh, are you a midwife?" Virginia asked. "We have

two excellent physicians, but they are kept busy. Your services would be most welcomed by many families."

Their food arrived right then, and Bridgette used the time it took to be served to contemplate what Virginia had said. Although never called one, she most certainly was a midwife. A tingle of excitement shot through her. Being a midwife would explain why she was at the Crystal Palace, considering Michelle's unfortunate miscarriage, and it was the perfect job for her to obtain. Following suit, she picked up her fork and knife, and began to eat while wondering how much she should charge for her services.

"How is your chicken?" Garth asked near her ear. Once again there was a distinct tone in his voice. And she didn't like it one bit.

Her hand paused briefly as she sliced off a piece of leg meat. Glancing up, she smiled at the scorn in his eyes. "Fine. How is your steak?"

"Excellent." His gaze left her. Smiling at Nathan Solstead, Garth said, "The steak is excellent."

As the man nodded, his wife said, "The Buffalo Run only serves beef from our ranch."

The couple shared another loving gaze. Bridgette poked another forkful of chicken into her mouth.

"If the beef is all this good," Garth said, slicing off another section of his steak. "I understand why."

The square table, covered with a white linen-and-lace tablecloth and hosting a single tapered candle in the center along with a vase of flowers, had them each sitting at a side, and Nathan Solstead leaned slightly toward Garth.

"Two of the men sitting at that table near the window are Jim Green and Howard Knight of the Eastman Packing House," Nathan said. "The other two are

Wayne Hammerman and David Latham of the River-side Slaughter House in Chicago."

Bridgette may not have followed Garth's gaze to-ward the men if she hadn't noticed the tick in his cheek. She'd forgotten about that. How the one side of his face would twitch when he was irritated. Considering how mad he'd been at her the past few days, it should have been twitching nonstop.

"They must be sampling the Solstead beef they will soon be purchasing," Virginia said.

Bridgette noted another significant sign. Nathan smiled at his wife, but this time there were no sweet nothings flashing in his eyes. With a tiny shiver crawl-ing across her shoulders, she turned to Garth. He was studying the men, as if memorizing exactly what they looked like and it wasn't because he was impressed.

As dinner progressed, an underlying current sur-rounded the table. Bridgette witnessed Virginia cast several curious glances at her husband and how Nathan ignored them. She'd lived with enough families to know there would be a discussion at the Solstead house tonight. There would be between her and Garth, too. There was far more going on here than he'd let on.

Despite the undercurrents, their meal remained pleasant, as did the company, and following a dessert that was topped off with ice cream that literally melted in her mouth, they all took their leave. At the door, Vir-ginia insisted they should have dinner together again soon, and invited them to visit the Solstead ranch to meet their children.

Garth nodded, but made no promises.

Withholding a sigh at his lack of manners, Bridgette smiled. "That would be lovely, and thank you again for the charming evening."

"Our pleasure," Nathan said. "Good night."

The other couple walked to their waiting buggy and Bridgette waited until she and Garth were a block away before asking, "What was that all about?"

The sun had set, but the gas streetlights lit the boardwalk, and provided plenty of light to see the scowl on his face. "What were you thinking ordering chicken?"

Stunned into a stupor, it was a moment before she could respond. "What?"

"You ordered chicken to eat."

"I like chicken."

"That's not the point."

His long strides were making her stretch each step to keep up. "Then what is?"

Without answering, he kept marching forward.

Flustered, she grabbed his arm. "Slow down."

He stopped and the scowl remained on his face. "We were having dinner with the man who supplies the beef to the restaurant and you ordered chicken."

A response to that simply wouldn't form, but one to the anger building inside her did. "Can I not do anything right in your eyes?" Not wanting to hear his answer, whatever it might be, she started forward, swiftly. "I know you were raised in an orphanage where no one cared if you lived or died, and that your mother ran off with a sailor, leaving you to fend for yourself on the streets of New York."

Garth grabbed Bridgette's arm to make her stop. This didn't have anything to do with his mother or how he was raised.

She spun around. "I know all that because I was there, too. No, my mother didn't run off, she died. Leaving me an orphan no different than you." Tears glistened in her eyes. "That's why we became family. Because we had no one else and promised we'd always be there for each other." She swiped at a tear on her cheek. "It worked for us. We were there for each other, and could be again. You'd see that if you'd quit being such an overbearing oaf."

The misery on her face made something inside him surrender; he wasn't sure what it was, but rather than anger, a softness overtook him, along with memories. He'd never forgotten about their pretend marriage ceremony. It had happened after she'd broken her arm and he'd been punished because Mrs. Killgrove was convinced he'd put her up to running away. Along with the memories and the softness inside him came a form of possessiveness he'd only known when it came to her. The appreciation other men had in their eyes when they saw her in the restaurant had filled him with pride. She was beautiful and the way she'd looked at him during dinner, almost as if he'd hung the moon just for her, had made him wish he had. It had made him wish for other things, too. Things that couldn't be.

That wasn't her fault, but grown men didn't need anyone. Not like kids did. Unwilling to address that, he said, "You've done a lot of things right."

With tears still dripping from the corners of her eyes, she said, "Name one."

Caught on the spot, his mind went blank.

She pulled from his hold. "Never mind."

He matched her steps and by the time they turned the corner, he'd conjured up an answer, "I don't know how many people you've taken care of, but—"

She held up a hand. "Stop. Just stop talking. It doesn't matter. We both know there's more going on than our past and me ordering chicken to eat. What's the deal with those slaughter house men?"

Of course she'd have figured that out. He hadn't been that upset that she'd ordered chicken, he was simply looking for a reason to be mad at her because he was afraid. Without the sale of his cattle, his plans would fall apart. He wasn't sure what that meant for him, and he wasn't sure what to do about her. She was making him feel things, want things, that he hadn't in a very long time.

"It's business," he said.

She swiped the tears off her face with both hands. "You mean it's none of my business."

"No, that's not what I mean."

"Well, it's what I mean," she said. "Your business is none of my business, and my business is none of your business."

On top of everything going on, that was enough to make his head spin. "What's that supposed to mean?"

"I'm sorry." Her pace had slowed, but she was still walking forward, and never glanced his way. "I'm sorry I ever said I was your wife. I'll let Mr. and Mrs. Solstead know it was all my fault. My mistake and—"

"But we are married," he said, trying to make light of things in order to give himself time to think things through. "The ceremony back at the orphanage that you told the Solsteads about."

"That wasn't real and you know it."

Garth stopped himself from grabbing her arm again. While she'd been talking with Mrs. Solstead about their family, Nathan had told him how happy he was to know Garth was married. A married man carries more clout than a single one. They're more established and have more to fight for in order to provide for their family.

He didn't like it, but had heard it before and Bridgette

had played the part of his wife well. Too well. Darn it. "I'll tell you what else I know."

She stopped and twisted about to look at him. "I'm listening."

Suddenly, so was he. Sounds he'd never thought much about one way or the other were filling his ears. The saloons that lined this section of Front Street were full. Noises made by men, women, pianos, roulette wheels and all sorts of other things, floated on the air, and he knew they'd get louder long before they became quieter. Things would get more bawdy, too. He'd lived through nights like this many times. She hadn't.

Taking her arm, he started walking again. "I'll tell you at the Dodge House."

If she'd been about to protest, she reconsidered as two men came flying out of a set of bat-winged doors. Fists flaying, they rolled across the boardwalk and into the street.

Garth quickly escorted her past the doors before others followed the men out of the saloon. A fight was a spectacle no one wanted to miss. Not even Sheriff Myers or Deputy Long, who ran up the street toward them.

Bridgette's speed increased and Garth didn't attempt to slow her until he had to pause in order to pull open the door of the Dodge House.

"Good evening, Mr. and Mrs. McCain," the proprietor greeted from his stance behind the desk. "I hope you had a lovely evening."

"We did," Garth replied, steering Bridgette toward the steps.

"I expected you shortly and lit the lamp in your room," Mr. Franklin said in their wake. "Let us know if you need anything else."

Garth held up his free hand in acknowledgment.

"Thank you," Bridgette said over her shoulder. "We will." Then as she turned forward again, she said, "There's no reason to be rude."

"I wasn't being rude," he argued.

"You didn't answer him."

"Yes, I did," he said. "I waved."

Her sigh was full of disdain. "You used to have manners," she said while heading down the hallway.

His spine stiffened. *Please* and *thank you* as well as *yes, ma'am* and *yes, sir* hadn't gotten him anywhere. Her either. The frustration of that sucked him in and made his mind go in several directions. Back on the street he'd been about to say he needed her in order to fulfill his plan of becoming his own cattleman. Tell her about the debacle the slaughter houses were instigating, but he didn't like how vulnerable that made him, and that had him double thinking everything.

By the time he stuck the key in the latch hole on the door of his room, steam was building inside him. He hadn't needed anyone in a very long time and didn't want to need her. Not to pretend to be his wife. Not for any reason.

"So what is it?"

She stood before the mirror, pulling out the pins that held her little hat in place. As his gaze went lower, to the places she'd blossomed, an entirely different sense of frustration bore down on him. What had he been thinking bringing her here to get ready for dinner? Now the Franklins thought she was his wife, too. Which meant this was where she needed to stay. All night. In his room. With him.

"Hell, no," he muttered.

"Excuse me?"

He'd paid in advance to stay at the hotel for the entire time he'd be in Dodge, but that wasn't about to happen. They'd both matured too much to share a room. Before he had a chance to second-guess himself, he tossed the key toward her. "Lock the door and don't let anyone in."

She'd caught the key. "Where are you going?"

Rather than make up a lie—the one they were living was enough—he said, "Out."

Taken aback, it was a moment before Bridgette reacted. The key in her hand brought her around. Nothing Garth did should shock her, but she clearly didn't know him anymore. Practically nothing he'd done was what she would have expected from the Garth she used to know. Which was fine because she didn't need the old Garth or the new one.

However, she'd been in Dodge long enough to know doors should be locked. After doing that, she walked back to the bureau and laid the key down beside the hat and pins she'd removed. Her gaze went to the mirror. She'd never had her hair curled before, and didn't want to disturb them by taking out the combs. If things were different, she'd have cherished this evening. The dress. The dinner out. How handsome Garth had looked. How beautiful she'd felt.

The breath she drew in was laced with remorse and that settled heavily inside her. As she turned away from the mirror a pair of boots sitting in the corner sapped the energy out of her. They were well-worn and dusty, and they tugged at her heart. She sat down on the bed, but her gaze never left the boots. "Why couldn't things between us be like they used to be?" she whispered. "Or like I'd imagined they'd be."

There wasn't time to contemplate the whys before a knock sounded. She stood and gathered the key off the dresser. Expecting Garth, she didn't open the door, just unlocked it and turned around. She was once again setting the key down when the knock sounded again. This time it was followed by a voice.

"Mrs. McCain?"

Recognizing it was Chrissy, Bridgette hurried back to the door and opened it. "Yes."

"I saw Mr. McCain leave and wondered if you needed any help taking off the dress," Chrissy said.

"No, thank you, I can manage."

"All right. Can I walk you out back?"

"Out back?"

"Yes. Our yard has a fence, but we still encourage female guests not to visit the outhouse alone after dark." She shrugged slightly. "Men from the saloon have been known to relieve themselves along the fence."

Bridgette could believe that. Men visiting the Crystal Palace didn't even walk around the side of the house. "In that case, yes, I'd appreciate your company." Noticing the clothing draped over the girl's arm was hers, Bridgette said, "Would you mind if I changed first?"

"Not at all." Chrissy handed her the clothing. "I had your clothes laundered and pressed."

"You certainly know how to take care of your guests," Bridgette said.

"Yes, we do. The Dodge House has an excellent reputation." Chrissy grasped the door handle. "I'll wait for you in the hall."

As Bridgette quickly changed, albeit being careful of her hair, she marked this down as another first. She couldn't remember a time when someone else had washed or pressed her clothes. It wouldn't be something she'd be getting used to, either.

The visit to the backyard was uneventful, other than

her disappointment of returning to an empty room. If this was Hosford, she'd walk to JoJo's camp without any worries, but walking about Dodge after dark was not something she was willing to do alone. She might be impulsive at times, but she was far from foolish. If that was the case, she'd have followed Garth out the door.

Huffing out a breath, she sat down on the bed. Wondering where he'd gone took up a good portion of her thoughts, as did the temperature in the room. She opened the window, and a short time later, removed her socks and shoes. After that, the softness of the bed encouraged her to lie down. It had been a long time since she'd slept on a real bed. There was one for her at the Rodgerses', and she remembered the first few nights she'd slept in it, how she'd compared it to sleeping on clouds it was so comfortable.

So was this one, and the pillow. And if she breathed deep enough, she could catch a hint of a spicy scent that reminded her of Garth.

Bridgette couldn't say what pulled her from sleep that held a dream so pleasant she didn't want to leave it. More frustrating than leaving it was how, in those brief moments between waking and opening her eyes, she couldn't remember what the dream had been about.

As her eyes opened, the sun shining in the window had her sitting up. The room was exactly as it had been when she'd fallen asleep. Empty.

After pulling on her socks and putting on her shoes, she walked over to look in the mirror. Sleep had destroyed the hairdo Chrissy had worked so hard on, but several curls remained. Bridgette removed the small metal combs from the mass and after finger-combing the long tresses, she pulled the sides back and reinserted the combs. It didn't look nearly as nice as it had last night, but looked nicer than the tight bun she normally twisted it into.

Her bag still sat on the end of the bed, and she dug into the bottom of it, retrieving the small satchel that held her meager coins. It pained her to part with any more, but she didn't want to be beholden to Garth for an amount beyond what was absolutely necessary.

She placed several coins atop the dress she'd neatly folded and set upon the bureau last night, hoping he would understand the money was for the underclothes. The dress shop would most likely take the dress back, but not the other items.

Upon unlocking the door, she took one final glance around, assuring she hadn't left anything out of order. She wondered what to do with the key, then concluded Garth would expect the room to be locked. Stepping out, she closed the door, locked it and slid the key under the door. The front desk had offered a second one, so there was no worry he wouldn't be able to get in.

Like last night when she and Chrissy had gone to the outhouse, she walked down the hall past the bathing chamber and used the set of stairs on that end. They led to a door that opened into the backyard. She also used the fence gate behind the outhouse. Once in the alleyway, she headed in the direction of the tent city. Garth would find her there; that was a given. She wasn't running away or hiding from him. There just was no place else for her to go, and she couldn't stay here.

She considered that aspect, of how she'd spent the night in the hotel room, alone, as she walked, and soon, each time she lifted a foot, it hit the ground a bit harder, a bit faster.

He had some nerve. Leaving her alone in a hotel room in the middle of Dodge City. Anything could have happened to her. For that matter, anything could have happened to him. What was she supposed to do then? Become Garth McCain's widow?

A shiver raced up her spine at that thought. Had he run into those men Nathan had pointed out at the restaurant? From the tick in his cheek, she knew something sinister was taking place.

She quickened her steps. Garth may not be willing to tell her, but JoJo would. He'd do anything for Garth.

Chapter Fourteen

Garth watched Bridgette cross the field, her carpet
bag swinging in one arm. He'd trusted her not to leave
the Dodge House last night, and she hadn't. It pleased
him to know she had that much sense.

"So how long will we have to wait?"

Brought back by Slim Jenkins, Garth shrugged.
"Can't say. Gotta wait for a few more herds to arrive
so we have something to bargain with." The trail boss
had taken the news pretty well, and Garth hoped the
others would, too. The cowboys would get paid relatively the same amount no matter how much the cattle
sold for, but the trail bosses, and the men who owned
the cattle wouldn't.

"Hank Black is no more than half a day behind me,
and Johnny Mac less than that behind him," Slim said.
"Could be less if they end up with a stampede like we
did."

Concerned for every cowboy on the trail, Garth
asked, "A bad one? Anyone hurt?"

"No. Happened last night, or this morning, however
you want to figure it. That's why I'm here so early. Got

them settled down quick enough, but I figured there was no use going back to the bedroll."

Stampedes weren't uncommon, but the coincidence between his experience and Slim's tickled Garth's nerves. "What set it off?"

"No telling. Doesn't take much at this point in the drive."

"No, it doesn't," Garth replied. "Lose any cattle?"

"Not a one. Just made us all that much more anxious to hit the end of the trail," Slim said. "Men and cows."

"I hear ya." Garth pointed toward the camp. "If I'm not here, I'll be at the Dodge House. Look me up when you get your cows in the yard. Tell Hank and Johnny Mac the same thing if you see them."

"Will do," Slim said. "Krebs, your cowboy, said he was riding down to tell them the same thing he told me."

"I asked him to," Garth said. "He tell you mum's the word?"

"Sure did." Slim slapped the tree they were standing under. "You know as well as I that old man Seacrest wants every dime he can get for these cows, and it's up to me to get it for him. My payday depends on it. I'm with you all the way. Can guarantee the same is true for Hank and Johnny Mac. The ranchers they drive for want the same as Seacrest."

"That's what we're counting on," Garth said. "I'll let the cattle association know you're in, and be in touch."

"Good enough." Gesturing toward the stockyard on the other side of the tent city, Slim asked, "How are the yard men?"

"Can't be trusted," Garth said. A twinge of guilt at including Ludwig Smith in with the others, had him adding, "The clerk's good—he makes sure it's a clean and accurate count."

"Good enough," Slim said. "Once I get Seacrest's cows in those pens, I'll be looking for you to buy me a drink."

Garth's eyes had gone to JoJo's tent, where Bridgette had disappeared a short while ago. He reached in his pocket and pulled out a gold piece. Flicking it with his finger in Slim's direction, he said, "I might be too busy, but buy one for Hank and Johnny Mac on me."

Slim gestured his thanks by tossing up and catching the coin again and then swung onto the horse that had been waiting patiently behind him.

Garth didn't have much patience. Never had and never would. The new boots he'd purchased last night had started to pinch his toes and he was anxious to get out of the suit pants and shirt. The coat and vest were still in JoJo's tent. He'd collect them, and Bridgette, and head over to the Dodge House.

He'd thought long and hard about it last night, and whether he liked it or not, he needed her to continue being his wife, at least until his cattle were sold. Then he'd drop her off in Hosford on his way south. She wouldn't like that, and he didn't blame her, but couldn't see any other way for things to be.

Halfway across the open space from the river to the camp, he saw her exit the tent. She didn't look his way, which was just was well. He could imagine how happy she'd be to see him.

She pulled down the back end of the chuck wagon and then picked up the pail she'd carried out of the tent and set it on the tailgate. He was about twenty steps away, give or take, when she turned around. If the anger that flashed in her eyes had been a bullet, he'd be dead.

A moment later, he wondered if he had been shot. Until he realized the potato rolling on the ground was what had hit him. As he glanced up, another one hit his shoulder. He ducked at the third one coming, but the fourth hit him in the chest again. She was pitching potatoes at him faster than he could dodge. Her aim was dead-on. As it always had been. He'd taught her how to aim and throw after she'd missed the constable his first day at the orphanage.

Ducking and weaving, he managed to avoid getting hit by a few, but several other potatoes met their target. Him.

"Bridgette," he shouted. "Stop it!"

"You stop!" she shouted in return. "Better yet, leave!"

If he hadn't ducked, the potato she pitched would have hit him square in the head. "Damn it, Bridgette!"

"You already said that!"

Another well-aimed potato caught his shoulder. He'd never been hit by potatoes before, and though they weren't deadly, they stung when they connected.

Crouching down, and weaving, he ran the last few steps. A potato knocked his hat off right before he dove forward.

She squealed, and spun about, but he caught her by the legs and dropped her to the ground. Anyone else, their ears would be ringing from the storm she was cussing up, but he knew her. She'd always had a smart mouth.

Her heels dug into his stomach; holding her down with his body, he shifted enough to crawl forward and grasp her waist. Then he rolled her over and pinned her on the ground by placing both hands on her arms and planting her skirt into the ground with his knees.

She screeched and hissed, called him names.

Glancing up, he noticed Bat and JoJo standing near the tent. "Bat, go gather up those potatoes."

As the boy took off, Garth leveled a glare on JoJo. With a nod, the old man said, "I'll go help Bat."

Leaning down, close to her face, Garth asked, "What has you so riled up this morning?"

"You left. Never came back. I didn't know if you were dead or alive."

Her squirming hadn't slowed, neither had the anger in her eyes. "More like you didn't know where I'd gone and that made you mad."

"Of course it made me mad. What was I supposed to do? Sit around twiddling my thumbs while you got yourself shot?"

Her beauty last night had awed him, but all riled up and flustered, she was adorable. Just like he remembered her. "You're much better at pitching potatoes than you'll ever be at twiddling your thumbs. And no one will shoot me. Guns aren't allowed within the city limits."

She wrinkled up her nose and growled at him.

He had a great urge to tickle her sides. May have if they hadn't had an audience. He didn't need to turn around to know JoJo and Bat, as well as a couple of his cowboys were watching.

"Get off me. You're getting my dress dirty."

The desire to kiss her was eating at his insides, but he couldn't do that any more than he could tickle her. At least, he shouldn't. Leaning down he gave her lips a quick smack. "I like your hair like that. You should wear it down more often," he said before bounding off her. He considered helping her off the ground, but she was already jumping to her feet, so instead, he took the hat Bat handed him and ducked inside the tent.

Grabbing his suit coat and vest, he left the tent. Then, hooking both garments with one hand, he flung them over his shoulder as he gave her wink and headed to town.

He felt like whistling again, and did so. Bridgette made him feel happy, relaxed, things he hadn't felt in a long time.

Town was quiet this morning, and he headed straight for the Dodge House, where he changed his clothes and ate breakfast. Of course he was quizzed as to where his wife was this morning, something that didn't bother him overly much. He'd grown used to explaining Bridgette's whereabouts long ago. Mrs. Franklin seemed to readily accept the fact Bridgette was at the tent camp with his men as she handed him a sealed envelope.

It was a simple message, and upon leaving the hotel, he went to the see Nathan Solstead as the note requested.

"It was a pleasure to meet your wife last night," Nathan said from behind his desk as Garth entered the room. "Virginia and I enjoyed ourselves."

"Likewise," Garth answered, taking a seat. Considering that enough pleasantry talk, he asked. "Any word?"

"Howard Knight, from the Eastman House, was in to see me this morning. He said two more drives will arrive in Dodge today or tomorrow."

"Three by night fall tomorrow from what I hear," Garth said. "I spoke to Slim Jenkins this morning. He's leading a herd for Bill Seacrest and should arrive later today. Hank Black is a few hours behind him, and Johnny Mac not far behind him."

Nathan leaned back in his chair. "Knight said he's ready to start loading cattle. Claimed the pens aren't large enough to hold three drives."

"They aren't," Garth agreed, "but unless he's ready

to pay top dollar, I'm not ready to sell, and neither are the other trail bosses." He drummed his fingers on the arm of the chair. "Did Knight say if he optioned all the cars?"

"No, and I spoke with Chuck Bolton at the depot. He confirmed no deal has been made. He's antsy though, wants to get those stock cars rolling. So do his bosses."

"The Chicago house boys aren't stepping up?"

"No."

Garth glanced around the room, mainly in order to give himself a moment to think. A large painting hung on the wall depicting a herd of cattle. He stared at it a few minutes, letting an idea form, before turning back to Nathan. "What if two of those herds hold back a distance? I could send a few extra cowboys out to help keep the cattle contained while the trail bosses come to town. That won't fill up the pens and it'll make four of us, along with you and other local ranches. Could be enough to make the slaughter houses know we won't take their deal."

"It could," Nathan agreed, "but I have to tell you, Garth, I think there's more behind this. I don't know what, but I have a gut feeling." With a glance toward a flag hanging in the corner, he said, "I think its Anthony."

"Anthony?"

Nathan nodded. "George Anthony. He was elected governor last fall, took office this year and he was on the state board of agriculture before taking office. Everyone knows the opposition between the cattlemen and the farmers in this state."

Garth had heard plenty about that. "Especially cattle drives."

"Anthony would love to see every acre of this state

growing wheat. He claimed the winter wheat crop last year surpassed all other states in the nation, and wants that to continue."

"You think he's using his political connections to put wheat above cattle?" Garth didn't have any experience in politics and couldn't think of a reason he'd ever want any, other than the twenty-five hundred head of cattle he owned. That was a reason whether he wanted it to be or not.

"Not connections," Nathan said. "Power."

"I don't like the sound of that," Garth admitted. "We'll need a whole lot more than four trail bosses and a few cattlemen to go against the governor."

"Yes, we will."

"So where do we find the help we need?" Garth asked. "Because I'm not giving up."

"I knew I liked you the minute you walked in the door." Nathan scooted his chair closer to his desk. "Can I give you a quick history lesson on the governors of Kansas?"

"If it'll help me sell my cows, I'll listen to a duck sing," Garth said, pulling his chair closer.

Concentrating on anything had been difficult ever since Garth's lips had touched her. She couldn't call it a kiss. There hadn't been any tender or loving actions associated with the connection of their lips. Yet, Bridgette couldn't get it out of her mind. Or the flash she'd seen in Garth's eyes moments before his lips had touched hers. That's where the tenderness had been, as well as a hint of something secretive and exciting.

It made her want to smile, and that confused her. She certainly wasn't happy about anything he'd done. Not how he'd tackled her, or pinned her to the ground or jumped up and walked away. Again. Her fate appeared to be watching Garth walk away.

No! Her past had been watching him walk away. Her future was finding a job as a midwife and leaving him behind. She'd do it, too.

Things hadn't worked out as she'd expected when she decided to come to Dodge, but she'd change that. JoJo didn't know much about the men from the restaurant, only that the sale of Garth's cattle had been held up for a few days, but JoJo had suggested she ask the owner of the mercantile about her midwife idea. Which made sense. Back in Hosford, Mr. Haskell knew more about the people living in the area than they knew themselves because they all visited his store.

"Let's go this way," she told Bat as they neared the alleyway she'd used this morning en route to the tent. Still cognizant of the fact she didn't want to be seen strolling along the streets—now because of those who thought she was Mrs. McCain—she added, "It won't be as busy."

Bat didn't say a word as he walked along beside her. It could be because he thought he was old enough to go to the mercantile by himself and was upset she had insisted on going with him. In that sense, Garth had been right. Bat couldn't roam the city alone. Not with a pocket full of coins. Furthermore, he'd need help toting back all the items JoJo had listed.

JoJo had offered to go with them, but most of the cowboys from the trail drive had set up sleeping areas near the chuck wagon and expected him to feed them, which he was in the midst of doing—using the potatoes she'd thrown at Garth.

The cowboys appreciated those spuds as much as they had her eggs and green beans back on the trail.

She'd only been there two days, but had noted JoJo served three foods. Beans, bacon and biscuits. Cheap and filling, he'd said.

They entered the alley, and she held in a sigh. She was thankful she and Bat most likely wouldn't encounter Garth on this route. At least she hoped she was thankful because she shouldn't want to see him.

The alley went past the back side of the Crystal Palace and when a muffled sound caught her attention, she paused. Mornings were the quietest time at the Palace, since the girls were sleeping after working all night. "Stay right here," she told Bat, and as an afterthought, handed him the basket she carried to tote things back to the camp.

Walking closer, she peered over the fence that surrounded the property. Seeing nothing, she followed the fence to survey the open space between the next building and the fence. Wondering if perhaps she'd heard a stray cat or other such critter, she turned to survey the buildings on the other side of the alley. There were few places for a critter to hide, other than perhaps between the three rain barrels set near the corner of one of the buildings.

She held up a hand, telling Bat to stay where he was as she crossed the alley slowly. An injured animal was nothing to rush up on. As she approached, her cautious curiosity turned into concern. Rushing forward, she knelt down. "Ellen, what are you doing?"

Squeezed between two of the barrels, the kitchen girl from the Crystal Palace lifted her head and pulled her hands away from her face. It was apparent she'd been crying. Still was.

"What's the matter?" Bridgette asked, brushing the girl's dark hair away from her face.

"Nothing."

"Something is or you wouldn't be out here."

Covering her face with both hands again, Ellen whispered, "I don't want to go back in there."

The very thing she'd feared since meeting Ellen filled Bridgette. Although Willow had said at twelve Ellen was too young, it was only a matter of time before that changed. Before Ellen would be old enough. "Did someone hurt you?"

Ellen shook her head.

"Don't lie to me," Bridgette said.

Removing her hands, Ellen said, "He didn't hurt me. I ran."

Bridgette needed no more of an explanation. "Come," she said, holding out her hand. "Come with me."

"No. I don't want to go back in there."

"Of course you don't, and you aren't. You're coming with me."

"To where?"

The fact it wasn't her camp didn't stop Bridgette. "To the tent city."

A hint of hope flashed in Ellen's big brown eyes before she shook her head. "They'll find me. Willow will send someone looking for me."

"They'll be sleeping for several hours yet," Bridgette said. "Now, come, hurry so we aren't seen."

Ellen wiggled her skinny frame from between the two barrels. "Willow will be mad."

"I'm sure she will, but I won't let her hurt you, or make you go back," Bridgette said, helping the girl to her feet. If she'd had anywhere else to go, Ellen wouldn't still be at the Crystal Palace. Her mother had worked for Willow, up until she'd died last year and her father had run off long before then.

"How will you do that?"

At the moment, Bridgette had no idea, but that would change. She'd think of something. "Don't worry about that." Taking Ellen's hand, Bridgette waved for Bat to join them. They walked between the two buildings, and then down the side street that led into the tent city.

Arriving at the camp and before JoJo could voice the questions on his face, Bridgette said, "This is Ellen. She needs to wait here, out of sight, while Bat and I go to town for supplies. We won't be long."

JoJo's whisker-lined lips clamped shut, but the questions in his eyes doubled. However, there was no animosity, just as she'd known there wouldn't be. He'd been the one to take in Bat, and surely wouldn't shy at helping another child.

"We'll be back soon," she said to him while leading the girl around the chuck wagon. "Ellen, you can wait for me inside the tent. JoJo will watch out for you."

"I don't want anyone to get in trouble," Ellen said.

"No one will be in trouble," Bridgette answered while opening the flap. "Just wait here. I won't be long." The repercussion of bringing Ellen to the camp made her stomach gurgle. Willow would not be happy to find the girl gone. Ellen had done almost all of the kitchen duties, including most of the cooking.

Closing the flap behind Ellen, Bridgette turned about. She didn't look at JoJo, just patted Bat's shoulder as she walked past him. "Let's hurry before the store gets busy."

"Still got my list?"

She knew JoJo would have to say something. "Yes. We won't be long."

"We'll be fine," he said. "No need to rush."

Relief filled her chest, as did warmth. His words

meant more to her than he could ever know. Glancing over her shoulder, she smiled. "Thank you."

He nodded, then bowed his head to give attention to the pan over the fire.

She took the basket from Bat, and this time steered him down the side street rather than the alley. There were people mingling about, going in and out of businesses and homes, but the side street wasn't as busy as Front Street and she didn't want to take the alley again, didn't want to chance being recognized by anyone at the Crystal Palace.

No one seemed to notice her and Bat, not even when they turned a corner and walked a block north to cross Front Street. The mercantile wasn't busy, and the proprietor was friendly, chatting about nothing of importance while filling her order. With Ellen at the camp, Bridgette decided to wait to ask about families in need of a midwife, and while thinking of Ellen and the bath the girl needed, asked for a bar of soap to be included with everything else.

After she paid the total from the money JoJo had given her, taking note of the amount of the soap so she could reimburse him for that from her few coins, she gestured for Bat to gather some of the items. The basket was full of eggs—JoJo had said the cowboys requested them after having the ones she'd given them—and because she'd have to carry the packets that held the pouches of coffee, sugar and bacon, she handed Bat the bar of soap. "Put this in your pocket."

He did so and then hoisted the large bag of flour off the counter. She thanked the proprietor and followed Bat toward the door. The eggs in the basket clicked together as she walked and she paused near the doorway to reposition a few amongst the straw. Even just one broken egg would be one too many.

Bridgette had to wait for two women to enter the store before she could exit. As she stepped onto the boardwalk, she noticed a man grab a hold of Bat's arm.

"Thief!" he shouted while pulling Bat into the street. "Someone get the sheriff! I caught a thief!"

"Let go of him!" Bridgette shouted. "He's not a thief! He's with me!"

A wagon had to swerve near the boardwalk to prevent hitting Bat as he struggled to get loose.

Bridgette had to wait for a wagon to roll past, but shouted, "Let go of him!"

"I caught a thief!" the man yelled. "He's with the cattle drive! Get the sheriff!"

Other wagons and horses stopped as the man held Bat by one arm in the middle of the street, yelling. "Get the sheriff!"

Bridgette marched forward. "He's not a thief! Now let go of him!"

Bony and dirty, the man spun around. "This here's a thief!"

"No, he's not," she insisted. "I just paid for that flour."

With a sneer that could make a coyote turn and run, the man stabbed something into the bag in Bat's hand. As flour poured onto the ground, he asked, "This flour?"

Bridgette was so appalled she couldn't speak.

"What's going on here?"

Of all the people who could appear right then, Garth was the one she most wanted to see, yet, at the same time, the one she truly did not want to see.

"Stay there," he said, pointing a finger at her.

Still a few steps away, she didn't want to stay, but

this was not a time to challenge him. Anger had his nostrils flaring.

"Sheriff's coming," the man said. "To take this thief to jail."

"Bat didn't steal anything," Bridgette told Garth, and the man. The misery on Bat's face as he held the now half-full bag with both hands, trying to stop any more flour from sifting out, increased her anger. "I paid for that bag of flour you just cut open."

"I ain't talking about the flour, girlie," the man said. "I'm talking about what's in his pocket." Pointing at Bat with the knife, he said, "He poked something in it. Look how it's bulging."

Garth grasped the man's wrist and Bridgette could see how hard he squeezed by how the man flinched.

"Let go of the boy," Garth demanded.

"When the sheriff gets here," the man said through gritted teeth.

People lined the boardwalk and others sat in their wagons or on their horses, but no one came closer.

"This is what happens when you cattlemen arrive," the man shouted for all to hear. "Thieves and hoodlums fill the streets. Even the youngest ones are no good! We shouldn't let a one of you in our town!"

Garth must have squeezed the man's wrist harder because with a growly whimper, he released Bat.

Everything happened so fast then. She'd been in the process of setting the groceries down in order to check to see if Bat was all right, when she saw the glint of the blade in the man's hand. He'd spun around and was thrusting the knife toward Garth. Without thought, she grabbed an egg from the basket and threw it. About the same instant the egg left her hand, Garth punched the man, and as he flew backward, onto the ground, the egg, still in route, hit another man who'd just arrived.

The sheriff.

Her well-aimed egg hit him square in the face.

And shattered. Leaving a good portion of the shell hooked on his nose as the yolk and white dripped off his lips and chin.

The entire street went silent.

The entire town.

Chapter Fifteen

〜〜〜〜

Frozen by dread or fear, or a mixture of the two, Bridgette didn't move as the sheriff plucked the shell off his nose and tossed it aside. Her airway plugged as she lifted her gaze from the eggshell on the ground to the fury in his eyes. This was not going to end well.

"You have to quit throwing things at people."

Turning to Garth, who was at least partly to blame, she pointed out, "He was going to stab you."

"I saw him," Garth growled, "and didn't need your help."

The man was still on the ground. Not moving. Yet, she felt inclined to ask, "How was I supposed to know that?"

"By thinking," Garth barked.

Fury danged near snapped her spine in two. Turning her attention on the sheriff, who waved for two men to come closer to gather the man off the ground, she said, "Bat didn't steal anything."

Not responding to her directly, Sheriff Myers asked Bat, "What's in your pocket?"

Shifting the half-full flour bag to one hand, Bat dug in his pocket and pulled out the bar of soap.

His hand shook as he held the soap for all to see. Stepping forward, Bridgette placed a hand on Bat's shoulder. "I asked him to put it in his pocket after I paid for it," she explained. "Our hands were full."

Garth took the small white brick out of Bat's hand and smelled it. His dagger-throwing gaze shot to her. "Soap?"

"It's an essential to some people," she said with clear implications.

Sheriff Myers stepped between her and Garth. "That's enough."

"She paid for the soap and everything else," the store proprietor said as he joined the fray. "Wiley had no cause to accuse the boy of anything."

"All right, folks," Sheriff Myers said to the people still watching, "go on about your business." He then told the two men who'd lifted the accuser off the ground, "Take Wiley to the jail." Turning to her, he said, "Gather your stuff. Let's get out of the street."

"Come with me, young man," the shop owner said to Bat. "I'll replace that bag of flour with a new one." Looking at Garth, he added, "Free of charge."

Garth's nod, how he thought that was enough acknowledgment, added fuel to Bridgette's anger. "Thank you, sir," she said. "That's very kind of you."

"Come on," Sheriff Myers said, "out of the street."

They all complied, and as Bridgette paused to pick up her basket, she had every intention of completely ignoring how Garth bent down to pick up the other packages she'd been carrying.

Until he hissed, "Do you have to cause commotion everywhere you go?"

She grabbed the basket off the ground. "I didn't—"

"Move!" the sheriff shouted behind them.

Snapping her teeth together, she marched to the boardwalk.

"I'm sorry for what happened here, Mr. McCain," the shop owner said. "Wiley's had a beef against the cattle drives ever since his wife ran off with a cowboy a couple years back, but the rest of us, most everyone in Dodge, welcome the cattle drives, and the business you provide. I hope this incident won't stop you or your wife from doing business with my store." Without waiting for an answer, he said to Bat, "Come along, son, I'll get that new bag of flour for you."

Now standing on the boardwalk, Bridgette made no attempt to move, but did bite her tongue at how Garth merely nodded to the store owner and Bat as the boy looked for permission. Would it hurt him to actually speak? To verbally acknowledge people and their actions with a kind word? She was going to point that out to him, let him know just how rude that was, once the sheriff was no longer standing beside them. She had no desire to revisit the Dodge City jail. Which was a possibility considering how the sheriff had smeared yolk across his cheek while wiping his face with the back of his hand.

The small amount of patience Garth had ever admitted to owning had long ago worn thin, but even the last hint had completely disappeared when he'd stepped out of Solstead's office and seen Bat being dragged into the middle of the street. He couldn't put all the blame for that on Bridgette, but the egg on Sheriff's Myers's face was all her fault.

He dug into his pocket and pulled out several bills. Taking two off the top, he held them out to the sheriff.

"Are you trying to bribe me, Mr. McCain?"

"No, just paying her bail in advance," Garth said.

"My bail?" she piped loud enough to echo off the building. "You're the one who knocked a man out in the middle of the street."

She clamped her lips tight as both he and Sheriff Myers looked her way. If a few hours in a jail cell would actually do her some good, Garth might consider letting the sheriff haul her off. But this was Bridgette. Sitting behind bars would only give her time to fathom up some other irresponsible scheme, and he didn't need that. Who knew how far-fetched it might be.

"Put your money away," Sheriff Myers said. "I'm not going to arrest either one of you. Harvey Whicker is right. Jud Wiley always was ornery and has gotten worse since his wife run off." Shaking his head, the man continued, "Now, I normally don't step in where I don't belong, between a man and wife that is, but Mr. McCain, your wife's been causing commotion ever since she stepped foot in town, and—"

"I have not," Bridgette spouted.

As Garth slid the money back into his pocket, he chose to ignore her, as did the sheriff.

"Her living over at Willow's set quite a few tongues wagging," Sheriff Myers said. "Even though most folks didn't believe…"

"She was my wife," Garth finished as the man looked at him with a brow lifted.

The sheriff shrugged. "Women have been known to claim to be married when they aren't."

This was his out. His chance to set the record straight, but Garth wasn't sure he wanted it. There was a challenge in Bridgette's eyes, one that dared him to take it, and a part of him wanted to prove a point, but the other part of him couldn't do that to her. And not just because he needed to continue the farce for his own sake. Truth be, if there ever had been a time when he'd thought about a future that included a wife and children, she'd been a part of that thought. He hadn't wanted to admit it, but it was true.

She didn't need to know that.

No one did.

Garth nodded, letting the sheriff know he'd heard him. "I apologize about the commotion, Sheriff," he said. "I expected to have already sold off my herd by now and be on my way back to Texas."

"Folks are questioning that, too," Sheriff Myers said with a nod. "The first herd of the season has never stayed in the pens this long. Businesses are ready to see money start flowing through town."

The storekeep arrived then, along with Bat carrying a new bag of flour. Garth noted the man's actions with a nod—despite what Bridgette thought, and she was thinking it again, a nod was more than enough between men. He nodded to the sheriff, too, as he took her elbow. "I'll keep her close at hand, Sheriff."

Conceding their conversation was over with a nod of his own, the sheriff replied, "See that you do, Mr. McCain." He didn't sound as if he thought that was possible when he repeated, "See that you do."

Garth was inclined to agree, but that was one more thing he'd never admit to Bridgette. Tightening his hold on her arm as she attempted to pull it away, he growled, "Keep walking and don't say a word."

She kept walking, but said, "I have nothing to say to you."

"Then why'd you open your mouth?"

"Because I can."

"Because you know it'll irritate me further," he corrected. "Do you not think I have enough problems without you stirring up dirt at every corner?"

"I'm not stirring up dirt at *every corner*," she said. "We were in the *middle* of the street."

No one had ever been able to drive him to the very edge of his sanity, and then keep him from jumping over like she could. He'd hauled her out of plenty of scrapes back then, and it had always been just like this—she'd point out some tiny little detail that despite all his anger and frustration would make him want to smile at her wit. And shake his head that he was falling for it.

"What?" she asked. "We were in the *middle* of the street."

"I know where you were," he said. "Just keep walking."

She did, but after a few steps said, "Thank you for arriving when you did. And for offering to pay my bail." With a sigh she added, "And for keeping me from getting arrested."

"Just keep walking," he repeated before stating, "Once the sheriff takes a look in the mirror, he may change his mind."

"I didn't mean to hit him. I thought that Wiley man was going to stab you."

He lessened the hold on her elbow, but didn't completely let her loose. "I know."

After a few more steps, she said, "Go ahead, say it."

Garth bit his lips together, mainly to keep from smiling again.

"Bridgette," she said in a stern and mocking tone. "You need to think before you act." Shaking her head, she said, "Actually, it's more like, *Damn it, Bridgette, you need to think before you act.*"

"You're right. You do. And for the life of me I can't figure out why that hasn't sunk in."

Head up, chin out, she said, "You don't scare me, Garth McCain. Never have and never will."

This time he chose not to answer. He didn't want her to be afraid of him. Never had and never would.

He steered them all to cross Front Street and then continued down a side road so they wouldn't have to walk in front of the Crystal Palace. Bat didn't need to see the girls on the porch whistling and shouting encouragement to come closer.

As they took the next corner, walking toward the open field they'd cross a couple of blocks ahead, Bridgette looked over at him. "Why haven't you sold your herd yet?"

"Politics," he said. Solstead had given him a history lesson all right, and in the end thought their best bet was to contact the former governor of Kansas who had been more favorable to the cattlemen. Garth wasn't convinced of that, and had told Nathan waiting around for an answer or the man to arrive only left his cows penned up that much longer.

"What do you mean?"

"The slaughter houses are trying to play their hand. One house is attempting to option all of the rail cars out of Dodge, leaving no opportunities for the other houses to bid on the cattle."

"So it would be sell to them or nothing?"

"Yes, and they're lowballing the prices as well."

"What are you going to do about that?"

"We're still working on it," Garth answered.

"Well, you best work faster," she said. "You heard the sheriff say the businesses are waiting for money to start flowing. Dodge City depends on the cattle drives. For the men," she glanced his way, "to empty their pockets before heading south again."

Her statement, though she'd emphasized it with a bit of intolerance, struck a chord inside him. Solstead wanted the slaughter houses' plans to be kept quiet for a while yet, but maybe that wasn't the right way to play this out. The townsfolk had expectations, depended on certain things, namely the money the drives brought to every one of their businesses. Knowing that was in jeopardy—the amount every cattleman, owner or cowboy had to spend—would not settle well.

As the thoughts continued to swirl in his mind, he gave her elbow a gentle squeeze. "Sometimes that pretty little head of yours does amaze me."

She frowned.

He grinned. "That was a compliment."

The smile that arose on her face made her eyes shine. "A first."

He was fairly certain he'd never paid her a compliment years ago. Most kids don't think along those lines, but he clearly recalled last night. He hadn't been able to get how pretty she'd looked out of his mind all day. Solstead had even commented on how beautiful she'd looked. "I complimented you on how nice you looked last night."

"After you fished for one of your own."

He clearly remembered that, too, and laughed. "I'd never worn a suit before."

She giggled, but stopped and looked him square in the eyes. "You did look very handsome."

"And you were the most beautiful woman in town," he answered with utmost honesty. As her smile formed, he reiterated, "Are. Not were."

A blush tinted her cheeks pink. "I wasn't fishing for another compliment."

"So I don't have to say your aim is pretty good, too?"

Her laughter floated on the air like a bird's song, and he liked the sound of that.

"I can't believe I threw an egg at the sheriff," she said, shaking her head.

"I can. It's exactly what you would have done nine years ago."

"And you would have saved me from getting arrested." She leaned slightly, bumping her shoulder against his arm. "Maybe we haven't changed that much. You or me."

They had changed, there was no denying that, but that was expected; it happened to everyone as they aged. At the same time, they were still the same people. Bridgette Banks and Garth McCain. Two peas in a pod. That's what Mrs. Killgrove said every time they got into trouble together. Actually, every time she got into a scrape and he bailed her out. Bumping her in return, he laughed. "Maybe," he said. "Maybe."

A light and carefree mood accompanied them the last leg of the journey to the camp. Several of his cowboys, Lowell, Thomas, Gil and Brad, were sitting around; Akin and Trace were down by the horses.

"Boys," he said in greeting.

"Boss," they replied in unison.

He caught how they glanced at one another and at him and Bridgette. There were bound to be questions, several of them. "Tired of town?" he asked.

"Broke," Gil answered. "It didn't take long."

"Usually doesn't," Garth answered as he set the packages he'd been carrying on the tailgate of the chuck wagon. Bridgette set the basket of eggs beside his items and he noted the weighted glance JoJo gave her before glancing at the tent. The tiny quiver that tickled Garth's neck had him looking at Bridgette, and frowning.

"Thanks for carrying these back for me," she said, opening the packages and hastily setting the coffee and sugar in the cubbyholes of JoJo's cabinet. "I'm sure you're busy. Have things to do."

He did, but got the sense there was something here he should know about. Especially as the cowboys, one by one, started drifting away from the camp. An inner sense told him he'd find whatever it was in the tent. Pulling the brick of soap that had caused such commotion in town out of his pocket, he tossed it in the air and caught it again. "I'll put this in the tent."

"No." Bridgette jumped in front of him. "I'll need it out here."

"For what?"

"Washing of course. What else do you do with soap?"

"According to you, I don't know."

With a glare that said she didn't appreciate his humor, she reached for the soap.

He pulled his hand away and held the soap out of her reach. "What's in the tent, Bridgette?"

"Give me the soap, Garth."

Keeping it away from her as she jumped to reach it, he said, "Tell me what's in the tent and I'll give it to you."

Bridgette clenched her teeth together as Garth held the bar of soap out of her reach. "Just give me the soap," she growled. He couldn't find Ellen. Not right now.

"Not until you tell me what's in the tent."

She jumped for the soap again, but then realized that while she'd attempted to get the soap from his hand, he'd maneuvered around to be standing right next to the tent flap, and before she could stop him, he pulled it open.

She managed to get a hold of his arm and the soap, but it was too late, he was already staring at Ellen. He let go of the flap and turned to give her a glare that was as hard as the one in the street earlier. "Who is that?"

"Ellen," Bridgette answered. He didn't frighten her, just as she'd said, but she was tired of disappointing him. A sigh left her chest. "She's an orphan."

He hissed and cursed beneath his breath. "This isn't an orphanage, Bridgette. It's a cattle camp."

She pulled on his arm, forcing him away from the tent. Ellen, nor the other dozen sets of ears tuned their way, didn't need to hear what she had to say. Once they were a distance away, Bridgette said, "I know this isn't an orphanage, but I couldn't leave her. Willow will put her to work soon. Upstairs. Not in the kitchen."

"Willow?" His eyes widened as understanding hit. "That's Willow's kitchen girl?"

"Was," Bridgette corrected. "I won't allow her to go back."

"You won't allow?" He took off his hat and ran a hand through his hair and then slapped his hat against one thigh. "You don't have any say in it."

"Yes, I do." She squeezed at her temples, wishing a plan would pop in, one that made sense and that he'd agree with. Of course that didn't happen. Miracles were as elusive as rainbows in this country.

"She can't stay here," he said.

"I know that," Bridgette hissed. "I'll think of somewhere for her to go."

"Think?" He shook his head. "When are you going to think before you act?"

"I do think—"

"Not about the consequences. You didn't think about that before you ran away, before you claimed to be my wife, before you pitched that egg."

Leave it to him to point out every time he'd been disappointed in her actions. "Fine, I didn't! There wasn't time, and there wasn't this time, either. You know as well as I that Ellen can't go back to Willow's. She's just a child, and you can imagine why she ran away. It's no different than why you let Bat join the trail drive."

He slapped his hat against his thigh again and paced in a circle, pausing every now and again to glare at her and mumble a curse.

"I'm not budging on this, Garth."

"You aren't budging," he repeated. "*You* aren't budging. You—" He stopped walking and stared at her intently before he nodded. "I wouldn't expect anything less."

"What do you mean by that?"

He shook his head as he started for the campsite. She ran after him, but only as far as the tent, where Ellen stood outside, wiping tears off her cheeks.

"It's all right," Bridgette said softly.

"No, it's not," Ellen said. "I'll go back. I didn't mean to get you in trouble with your husband."

Eyes still on him as he marched toward the cowboys, Bridgette sighed. "You didn't get me in trouble with him." To herself only she added, *I've been in trouble with him since the day I laid eyes on him.*

"He seems awfully mad."

"He's just in a bad mood," Bridgette said. "Has been for a long time."

"He's got a lot on his mind," JoJo said. "Over yonder are fifteen men he can't pay until he sells his cows.

He's worked hard the past decade and has his life savings tied up in this trip."

Bridgette flinched inwardly. She hadn't considered how heavily the sale of his cows could be affecting him.

"Driving twenty-five hundred head across open range for six hundred miles isn't easy or cheap." Looking at her, JoJo said, "The end of the trail is supposed to be the easy part. No man wants trouble or problems there. No man deserves that."

A ball of guilt landed in Bridgette's stomach. She'd been trouble for Garth since he'd arrived in Dodge. No, she wasn't all of his problems, but she'd contributed to them. Maybe he truly hadn't changed over the years. He'd always been tall and big and tough on the outside, but gentle and thoughtful on the inside. The kind of person who wouldn't mind taking a child on a cattle drive, or buying a woman a new dress. Heaving out a sigh, Bridgette said, "I'll be right back."

Garth told himself it was for the best as he watched two of his best cowboys walk toward the remuda. He couldn't blame Bridgette for taking Ellen away from the Crystal Palace. That's what she did best. Took care of others. And that's where she belonged. Back in Hosford taking care of people. As much as he knew that to be true, a part of him didn't want it to be.

"I'm sorry."

A grin teased his lips at the sound of her voice. Anger no longer filled him, rather, his insides held a touch of sadness. It came from knowing she had to leave.

He turned around. "I know you are. I'm sorry, too." Taking a couple of steps closer to her, he continued, "And you're right. The Crystal Palace is no place for a young girl, but I can't provide the protection she needs. Not with everything else going on."

She laid a hand on his arm. "I didn't expect you to."

Maybe not, but he did. That was one of the things he'd thought he'd put behind him, but hadn't. Couldn't. It was in his nature. Here too, she was right. That was why he'd allowed Bat on the trail drive, and why he'd pushed himself to become a trail boss in order to protect the other men riding with him.

As much as he'd thought he'd changed, he hadn't. He hadn't changed when it came to her, either. Taking off his hat, he scratched his head. "You know what you have to do."

"What?"

"Go back to Hosford." Before she could protest, he continued, "I can't keep worrying about you. There's too much going on here. Even if there wasn't, this still isn't the place for you. Hosford is. You can take Ellen there. The Rodgers family treated you well, you said so yourself, and it would help with our other problem."

"Our other problem?"

"Yes, us being married. I'll say you had to go help another family. It corroborates with what we told the Solsteads. Once I sell my cattle and go back to Texas, no one will even remember." It would mean he'd have to find a new market for his cows next year, but so be it. He took a hold of her hands. "You don't belong here, Bridgette, living in a tent, or the Crystal Palace. You belong in a big house, with trees and a garden, and rainbows. The things you always wanted." His throat tightened as he said, "Pretending to be my wife won't get you those things. It won't get you nothing but trouble. Mrs. Killgrove was right. We are nothing but trouble for each other." With a sting in his jaw, he added, "Go home, Bridgette. Go back where you belong."

Chapter Sixteen

Used to being ridden several miles a day, the horses never slowed their pace. Though their gait was merely a walk, the animals traveled the miles between Dodge City and Hosford in what seemed like minutes rather than hours. The ride to Dodge had taken much longer, at least in Bridgette's mind it had. Of course the stagecoach had stopped several times, and each time the driver had looked at her, she'd shaken her head, letting him know it wasn't her stop. She'd ridden on the stage several times before, in order to be dropped off within a few miles of whichever family she was to assist. When she'd left, she'd thought she'd never have to think about that again.

She'd been wrong.

Trace and Gil, the two men Garth had instructed to take her to Hosford, followed on the horses behind the two she and Ellen rode. During the past four hours, she'd gone from sad to mad to sad again. As well as a plethora of other emotions. Garth was right. She hadn't wanted to live at Willow's place or JoJo's tent, but what he didn't know was that where she lived didn't matter to her as much as being somewhere she knew she was wanted. That's all she'd ever desired. To be wanted.

He didn't want her. It was time for her to admit that and stop chasing rainbows.

As the buildings of Hosford came into sight, she turned to Ellen. "You'll be fine here. Dr. Rodgers won't put you in a home that isn't safe. He lays down a firm set of rules before offering assistance, and he'll check up on you regularly."

"How long did you work for him?" Ellen asked.

"Nine years," Bridgette said.

"I bet he'll be happy to see you."

Bridgette held her breath rather than answering. Dr. Rodgers would probably be as happy to see her as Garth had been.

As if thinking about him could make him appear, she had to blink at the buggy that rounded the corner, driving directly toward them. Nothing like being tossed in water over her head.

Bridgette pulled her horse to a stop and turned to look over her shoulder. "Wait here, please."

"Is that him?" Ellen asked.

"Yes, that's Dr. Rodgers." Bridgette squared her shoulders and urged the horse forward.

Garth stared at the shadows dancing across the ceiling of his room at the Dodge House. The weight on his chest was so heavy it hurt to breathe, as if an elephant sat on his chest. A flashback occurred at the thought. On the train shortly after they'd left New York, many of the children had been guessing what they'd see next. When Bridgette said it was his turn to guess, he'd used a saying he'd heard on the streets. People heading West had often said they were going to see an elephant. They hadn't meant they'd actually see an elephant, just something new and different.

She'd laughed when he'd said an elephant, and he'd been shocked when the train had rolled into one of the many stations along the way and there, parked next to their train full of children had been one carrying a circus, complete with an elephant.

He'd said, *I told you so!* to all the others, while being as stunned as they had been. Bridgette hadn't been stunned. She'd been proud. Of him. And she'd told him so.

He'd been right to leave her on that train all those years ago, and he was right to have sent her back to Hosford today.

Telling himself that again didn't help. He sat up and swung his legs off the bed. At the window, he stared into the night sky. Trace and Gil should be back by now. Probably already bedded down near JoJo's tent. He'd said he'd talk to them tomorrow.

He would.

Spinning around, he returned to the bed. Rather than lie down, he grabbed his boots.

He'd talk to them tonight instead.

His walk through town was anything but uneventful. Girls catcalled from the upper stories of the buildings as men stumbled out of the saloons. As scheduled, Slim Jenkins had driven his herd of Seacrest cattle into the pens this afternoon—shortly after Bridgette had left—and Slim's men had thrown themselves into the life at the trail's end with all the vigor and gusto the town had expected.

The man walking toward him touched the rim of his hat. "You're up late."

"You, too," Garth answered, stopping to lean against

a light post. After making the suggestion that had been
put in his head by Bridgette to Solstead, the two of them
had visited Sheriff Myers. A cordial visit had been a
welcome change for both him and Myers.

"Dodge is a town that doesn't sleep. Not this time
of the year," the sheriff said. "Therefore, neither does
the law."

"I suspect not," Garth said.

Nodding towards two cowboys bustling out of one
saloon and into the next, Myers said, "Word's spreading."

Garth nodded. "Slim's men are telling every bartender, card dealer and woman they encounter that this
will be the last time they visit Dodge."

"I hope this works."

"Me, too."

Myers kicked a rock with the toe of his boot. "Word's
spreading your wife left town. Had to go help a family."

Garth bit the inside of his mouth as he nodded. He
hadn't said a word, but news of Bridgette's leaving had
still spread.

"She sure kept things hopping around here for a few
days," Myers said with a chuckle. "Life with her must
be fun."

Garth felt inclined to admit, "It's not dull—that's
for sure."

Myers laughed. "Gotta respect a woman with that
much gumption, and appreciate them." He then tipped
his hat. "Well, I gotta continue my night watch. Promised my wife I'd be home early tonight."

"Take care," Garth said as the sheriff stepped into
the street.

"You, too," Myers replied.

Garth turned about and started for the tent city again,

thinking harder about Bridgette. Life wasn't dull with her around, and he did respect her. And appreciate her.

Just as he had years ago. If he'd used his savings to buy a piece of property and a house, rather than cattle, he'd have something to offer her. But, he hadn't. He'd bought cattle, and if the plan to hamper the slaughter houses didn't work, he wouldn't be able to afford a shack. It would be years before he could buy a real house. Without selling his cattle, he'd not only lose the money he'd invested in the herd, he'd have to use up a good portion of his savings to pay off his cowboys for the cattle drive they'd just completed.

A heavy sigh left his lungs. From the day he'd entered that orphanage, Bridgette had filled him with all the things life was supposed to be full of. Sunshine and laughter. Escapades and arguments. He didn't want to admit it, but having her around again had been fun. Leaving her on the train all those years ago had hurt. Hurt more than when he'd been put in the orphanage, more than when he heard his mother had left, and he'd sworn he'd never be hurt like that again. Never care what happened to someone ever again.

That hadn't worked out as planned. There was a reason he'd been grumpy all these years. Because try as he might, he couldn't help but care about others. He cared about his men, and about JoJo and Bat. And he cared for Bridgette. Hadn't ever stopped caring about her, and probably never would.

But he'd learn to live without her again. He'd done it once, and the second time around would be easier. That's how most things in life were. She had everything she'd ever wanted back in Hosford. She'd realize that if she stopped long enough to notice it.

The noise of town faded as he started across the field.

Fires burned near many tents, mainly to keep nighttime visitors away—bugs and four-legged critters, as well as two-legged ones. Although JoJo would have protected her with his own life, the tent city had been no place for her, and his hotel room certainly hadn't either. Which is where people would expect her to be staying, with him. Her going back to Hosford was best all the way around. She surely had to understand that. He did. The life of a cowboy gave him everything he needed, and would for years to come. That had been his goal for a long time, and nothing was going to change it. Not the slaughter houses and not a girl from his past.

A neigh had him turning toward the river, where the horses were kept. That was the big mare he favored. The two of them made a good pair. She broke up disputes and kept the horses in line much like he did the men. That neigh was her welcome-back-to-the-herd call. It must have taken Trace and Gil longer than he figured. Garth headed in the direction of the horses, glad in a sense that he wouldn't have to wake them to ask about how the trip went.

He hadn't yet arrived at the roped-off area when he recognized the rider climbing out of the saddle. He cursed and kicked his speed into a jog.

Bridgette must have heard his approach because she spun around and the carpetbag she'd just untied from the saddle slipped from her hold.

Garth took a hold of her waist with both hands. "What are you doing here?"

"Why aren't you at the hotel?"

"I came—" He let out a curse. "Never mind what I'm doing, why aren't you in Hosford?"

"Because you need me." She held up a hand. "Don't start cussing and telling me you don't. Just, for once in your life, admit that you need help. That you can't do it all alone. You're letting Solstead help you, so why not me?"

Garth wasn't sure what overcame him at that moment, but whatever it was, it twisted his insides. She was right. Solstead was helping him, but he was also helping Solstead and all the other cattlemen.

The thudding of hooves had him twisting about.

With a final hop, a horse and rider stopped beside them. "Want me to wake the others?" Trace asked.

Utterly irritated and confused, Garth asked, "Why?"

Trace looked at Bridgette. "Didn't you tell him?"

"I haven't had a chance to," she answered.

"Tell me what?" Garth asked.

"We think we found who started our stampede and Slim's," Trace said. "Actually, *she* did. Not more than five miles south of here. Gil is there, keeping an eye on them." Nodding at Bridgette, he added, "We rode to town to tell you."

"Who is it?" Garth asked before he twisted to her. "What did you do?"

"I just saw some men that looked suspicious and pointed them out," she said.

"She did. Don't know who they are, but from the looks of things, they plan on visiting another herd tonight," Trace supplied.

"Wake the boys," Garth ordered. "And send someone to town to find Slim. Try the Bottomless Glass."

Trace spun his horse around and Garth looked down at Bridgette. Running his hands up and down her arms, he asked, "How many are there?" A thousand other questions were floating around in his mind, but the cattle had to come first. "Where'd you see them?"

She glanced in the direction of the tent city. "I don't know. Your men made me wait on the road."

Using one hand, he turned her chin so she had to face him and lifted both brows.

The look in her eyes told him she had ignored their instructions. "I don't know how many there are," she said. "We'd stopped for…" Her eyes snapped at him. "For me to relieve myself, and while I was in the bushes I noticed four men on horseback, riding fast. We followed them to a rundown farm, a lot like the Chaney place. They didn't see us, but Trace and Gil think they're rustlers. Trace and I rode here while Gil stayed behind. Trace went to the hotel to find you and I came here so you'd have your saddle." She twisted to remove the bridle. "This horse is tired. You'll need a fresh one."

Getting mad at her for following Trace and Gil wouldn't do any good. The deed was done and telling her she should have stayed put when his men had told her wouldn't prevent it from happening again. "Did you see any cattle?"

"No, but as it was growing dark, Trace and I stayed off the main road so it took us longer to get here."

"Why didn't you stay in Hosford?"

"I already told you. Because you need me. Now unfasten the saddle." She pulled the bridle off the horse. "I didn't come here to make trouble for you, Garth, not the first time and not this time. I—"

"Bridgette—"

"No, let me finish. I'm not exactly sure why I came here the first time, but I know this time it's because I want to help you."

"I don't need—"

"Yes, you do." She grinned. "You need a wife, and that's me."

He couldn't stop how her sass made him grin. Maybe he didn't want to keep from smiling. If she hadn't needed to stop, Trace and Gil may not have seen those men, so maybe, this one time, she was right.

As if reading his mind, she said, "Whether you want to admit it or not, you know I'm right. Let me pay you back for all you've done for me, and then we can go our separate ways, just like you said." Without waiting for him to comment, she added, "Want me to go get the sheriff to ride with you?"

"No." Garth adjusted the stirrup on his saddle. She was right, but he wasn't going to admit it. Not aloud anyway. "Sheriff Myers has his hands full in town."

Men carrying saddles and bridles hurried across the field. Garth quickly adjusted the other stirrup and then stepped beside her. "And you are going to stay—"

"Right here." She stretched onto her toes and planted a quick kiss against his lips. "With JoJo and Bat." She grinned, knowing full well that was exactly what he'd been going to ask of her. "However, I expect you to tell me everything as soon as you return."

Her kiss had stunned him so thoroughly his mind went blank for a moment. When his wits returned, he asked, "What happened with Dr. Rodgers? With Ellen?"

"I'll tell you all about that right after you tell me everything." She walked around him and the horse.

He followed.

She picked up her carpetbag and jiggled the bridle she held in her other hand. "I'll give this bridle to Bat."

"Bridgette…" He wasn't sure what he wanted to say.

She nodded toward his men throwing saddles on their horses. "You'll be careful?" she asked as another cowboy handed him the reins of his big mare.

Hoisting his saddle onto the mare, he figured having her around for one more night couldn't hurt anything. "Always am."

"I'm serious, Garth."

"So am I."

She glanced toward the men running across the open field from town. "You better be."

She started walking toward the tents and he didn't pull his eyes off her, even as Slim shouted for him to give them time to mount up.

Garth saddled the mare while keeping one eye on JoJo's tent. He watched Bridgette enter the tent and then exit. She stopped near the chuck wagon, and remained there after he'd swung into the saddle. When she lifted a hand, waving at him, he copied her actions. That was the first time they'd ever waved goodbye to each other.

He'd never done that before because he'd never wanted to say goodbye to her. Not ever. For some reason, doing so tonight didn't feel like goodbye, not really. It felt more like *I'll see you again soon.* An odd tenderness filled him so completely it made his throat swell. Then it made him smile.

He turned the horse around, and waved at her again, then led his cowboys a short distance downriver, to where Slim and his men were saddling their horses.

Bridgette couldn't describe all the things happening inside her, or why she had to blink aside a few tears. It could be because Garth was riding into a dangerous situation, or because she'd expected him to be angrier at her for returning. He didn't like when his orders weren't followed. For once, he was going to have to get used to it.

"He'll be back."

Smiling, she glanced at JoJo before looking back at

the group of men riding out. "I know." It would take more than a few rustlers to get the best of Garth McCain. She also knew she'd returned for the right reasons this time. Garth needed her help and she would give it, and then she'd get exactly what she wanted in return.

"How'd things turn out for that little girl?"

"Very well. Dr. Rodgers was happy to have a new apprentice, and Ellen was delighted at the prospect. The Rodgerses are good people." In all the years she'd lived with them, she'd never thought of them as she did now. They had treated her very well over the years, just as they would Ellen. She just hadn't wanted to admit that, mainly because she hadn't wanted to think of them as family. But they were her family.

"That's good to hear," JoJo said. "You hungry?"

"No, we ate at the Rodgerses' house." Saying goodbye after eating had been hard. Both Shelia and Mrs. Rodgers had cried. Tears had formed in her eyes, too, but she'd told them she'd be back. And she would be. Right after her job here was through. That's how she was looking at this now. No different than all the other families she'd lived with.

"You want me to add some more wood to the fire?"

Bridgette dropped her gaze from where the men had been swallowed up by the darkness and shook her head. "No, it's late, and sitting around waiting won't make them return any faster."

"No, it won't."

Twisting, she handed him the money in her hand. "Thank you for this."

"What's that?" JoJo asked.

"The money I owe you for bailing me out." Unbeknownst to her, the Rodgerses had saved the wages she'd earned over the years and had presented her with a tidy sum while saying goodbye.

JoJo shook his head. "Garth already repaid me." With a lopsided grin, he added, "Even if he hadn't, I wouldn't take that from you."

Her heart swelled and she kissed his rough cheek. "Thank you."

He coughed into his hand while rubbing his mustache and then gestured toward his bedroll. "I—I'll be right outside the door, so don't be worried about any noises."

"I won't." As she opened the flap, she turned about. "He's lucky to have you, JoJo."

"Ya, he is, but he's luckier to have found you again."

She shook her head. "I'm the lucky one." That was the truth, and it was time she appreciated that. Seeing Garth again after all these years may not have been as she'd imagined, but it had made her take a hard look at herself and the things she wanted.

With a smile on her face, she entered the tent and sat down on the extra bedroll JoJo must have laid out for her. She hadn't thought of it before, but the extra bedroll must be Garth's, and she closed her eyes to send up a prayer of safety for him.

Careful not to wake Bat who hadn't stirred during the rousing of the cowboys, she removed her shoes before lying down.

Worries attempted to filter into her mind, but she wouldn't let them. As sure as the sun would rise, Garth would be back, unharmed and as ornery as ever. She could count on that.

Bridgette was in the midst of a dream that had her surrounded by rainbows when a familiar voice made her eyes pop open. She sat up and grabbed her shoes, but had yet to pull one on or flip her hair away from her face when the tent flap opened.

"It's about time you woke up."

"I—" She stopped herself from saying more and returned the smile on Garth's face. Sunlight lit all four sides of the tent, and put a shine in his eyes. "Did you catch the rustlers?"

He sat down beside her. "Yes." Brushing her hair away from her face with one hand, he said, "They are in a place you're familiar with—the Dodge City jail."

She eyed him closely. "No one was hurt?"

"No." He frowned. "Are you disappointed? Did you want me to shoot someone?"

"No." She readied a shoe to pull on her foot. "Don't forget who you are talking to. I know all your gruffness is for show. You wouldn't have shot one of those rustlers just like you wouldn't have shot that calf."

He took the shoe from her hand and set it aside while leaning closer. "I wouldn't have?"

She was counting on that being true. "No, you wouldn't have."

He lifted a brow, but was still grinning. "Thank you. Trace and Gil claim they would never have seen those rustlers."

She grinned. "I told you—I'm here to help. Nothing more."

His eyes took on a smoldering tint that caused her heart to thud. Without looking away, he leaned closer.

"You have," he whispered. "And I'm going to kiss you."

Fully unprepared, she had no response.

Allowing that to happen was a huge risk, but the moment his lips touched hers, she knew it was the right decision. An expansive thrill raced through her system and she looped her arms around his neck.

Her lips parted at the first flick of his tongue and the battle was on. Her tongue against his, and it was the most dedicated fight they'd ever had. It went on until they were both winded, and their lips separated by some mutual consent.

However, as their eyes met, winded or not, their lips met again. The first kiss had immediately become an exploration of unfamiliar ground, but this time it was a gentle journey of territory already discovered and appreciated. She'd known him for years, yet hadn't experienced the depth of that right now. And just as she'd imagined, kissing him was utterly amazing. The desire for more had her scooting closer.

Slowly, without ever breaking the kiss, he eased her backward until she was lying on the bedroll with him beside her. Eyes closed, she accepted the wonderful sensations washing over her as his hands explored her sides and then leisurely covered her stomach with languorous circles. Deep beneath his hand a fantastic heat welled inside her and began to pulse. She arched into his touch, silently begging his tender ministrations to continue.

His lips slipped off hers, but continued to place soft, affectionate kisses over her chin, along her neck and then back up the side of her face. The heat inside her grew until it turned fiery, telling her she wanted more than tender kisses. Much more.

As if he read her mind, Garth pressed his hand more firmly against her stomach before he whispered in her ear, "Come on, sleepyhead, we have to ride out to the Solstead ranch."

She heard him, but had no desire to go anywhere, and she let that be known with a soft groan.

He chuckled, then grasped her arms and pulled her upright in one swift movement. After planting a solid kiss upon her lips, he said, "JoJo will make you some breakfast while I saddle the horses."

Protesting was first and foremost on her mind, until she opened her eyes and remembered they were inside a tent with a dozen cowboys mingling around outside. She also remembered she had a job to do. Sighing, she said, "I'll need to wash up and change my clothes."

"I'll get you a bucket of water."

Pretending to be his wife might be her easiest—and also her most difficult—assignment ever. "You're in a good mood this morning."

He tapped the tip of her nose. "Hurry up and I'll tell you why."

Chapter Seventeen

Garth laughed at how swiftly Bridgette grabbed her shoes. He knew her almost too well. Coaxing her into compliancy was too easy. But that's what he had to do. Make her see that no matter what she thought, he knew better. Dodge was no place for her. There was no future for her here. Not the one she wanted, or the one he wanted for her.

He'd thought about that last night while rounding up the rustlers, and her being here. As much as he appreciated her sentiment, her supposed reason for being here—to help him—he knew better. He hadn't needed anyone before, and didn't now. He just needed to prove that to her.

"Don't just sit there," she said. "Go fetch me a bucket of water like you said you would."

As Garth pushed off the bedroll, the desire to kiss her again struck. That hadn't been part of his plan. Kissing her. It had just happened. Hair tumbling about and sleepy eyed, she'd just been too irresistible. Few things got to him like she did, and he needed to remember that.

After delivering the bucket JoJo had set outside the tent flap, Garth went to saddle a couple of horses. Having only gotten a few hours of sleep, he should be worn out, but there were too many parts of him alive and well to be tired today. Things had gone splendidly last night, and though he'd always instructed his men to be careful, he'd been more insistent that no one got hurt. Not a single shot had been fired, and catching those rustlers red-handed meant things were starting to go in the right direction.

By the time he led two horses to the tent, Bridgette was standing near the chuck wagon, forking scrambled eggs into her mouth. She'd changed out of the drab grey dress into a white blouse and blue skirt. Her hair had been pulled back on both sides, but the rest hung in soft waves over her shoulders and down her back. She'd stirred something inside him since the day she'd delivered those eggs and beans to his campsite, and kissing her this morning had brought it a bit closer to the surface.

She set down her plate and walked toward him. "JoJo says things went well last night."

Of course JoJo would have told her that. The old coot was smitten with her, and claimed Garth was too, if he'd just admit it. There was nothing to admit. He'd been smitten with her for years, and he'd lived without her for years. He nodded to the horse. "Mount up so I can adjust your stirrups."

She complied and held her feet out of the way while he shortened both stirrups. Then he swung onto his horse and as they rode past the chuck wagon, told JoJo, "We'll be back in a few hours."

Rather than riding through town, they rode around the stockyards. Taking in the full pens, she said, "Another herd arrived."

"Yesterday," he answered. Looking at the pens full

of hearty beef, he said, "You can't beat Texas cattle. Don't ever let someone tell you differently."

"What makes them so special?"

"They're hardy, but more importantly, they're mine. I rode deep into Mexico to gather some of those critters."

"You like being a cattleman, don't you?"

"Yes," he admitted, and then glanced her way to point out what she liked. "How did things go with Dr. Rodgers?"

Shaking her head, she said, "Oh, no, you have to answer my questions first."

"Sounds like JoJo already told you."

"No, he just said things went well."

Limited as to what he would tell her, he started before she could ask again, "The men we hauled into town last night weren't rustlers. They're farmers. At least that's what they call themselves, but none of them have produced much of a crop."

"Why?"

"They blame it on the cattle drives. Say the cows tear up their fields on the way to Dodge, killing their crops."

"Do they?"

"Some might," he answered honestly. "But most trail bosses are careful not to cross tilled ground. Jud Wiley was one of the men we brought in last night."

She snapped her head so fast his way her neck should have popped. "Why wasn't he still in jail? He had no cause to accuse Bat the way he did."

Garth had harbored plenty of anger toward Wiley over the Bat incident. No grown man should accuse a child in such a way without solid proof. He personally understood the full consequences of that. Had lived with them most of his life. Yet, a part of him could understand Wiley's anger at cattlemen. He wouldn't appreciate his wife running off with some other man. "Sheriff Myers didn't have any cause to keep him in jail." After a moment, he added, "Then."

"He does now?"

He nodded. "Wiley and his sons, as well as a couple other dirt farmers, already started two stampedes. They snuck up on the cattle at night and used slingshots to fire rocks at the cows until they got them stirred up enough they started running amongst themselves. Both my men and Slim Jenkins got the cattle settled down without too much trouble. Wiley and his crew were planning on doing the same thing to Hank Black's herd last night."

"Why would they do that?"

"Stampeding cattle would tear up a field in no time. Then they'd have proof, reasons for others to join them in their hatred of cattlemen."

"But cattlemen are what Dodge City thrives on."

He grinned. "Sure are, and because of you, they are all talking about that."

"Me? I didn't do anything." Panic flashed in her eye as she said, "Honest, Garth, I didn't talk to anyone about—"

"I know you didn't. You gave me the idea yesterday that people need to know it's the slaughter houses holding up the sale of cattle, and how the cowboys feel about it."

"I did?" A smile formed and she nodded. "I remember now, while we were walking back to camp after the soap incident. Will it help?"

"Already is. That's why we're riding out to Solstead's ranch. It's Saturday so he's not at the office in town." Her sincere interest captured his attention. He talked to other people regularly, but it wasn't the same. When he talked to her, she listened, not because she had to, because she wanted to. Her expressions told him so. More than that, they told him she cared. Cared about what he was saying, whether it was about seeing elephants or standing up against the slaughter houses.

He cared about what she had to say, too, always had, which made him change the subject. "Your turn."

She nodded. "All right."

He waited, and discovered he was holding his breath. Going back to Hosford couldn't have been easy for her. When she glanced his way again, and the smile hadn't fallen from her face, a tingle rippled over his shoulders as he questioned if she'd gone all the way to Hosford or not. There hadn't been a chance to ask Trace or Gil about it.

"Dr. Rodgers hadn't told anyone I was gone." Shifting in the saddle so she could look at him as they rode, she shrugged. "All these years I assumed they didn't care, but they did. They do. Even Mrs. Rodgers."

Garth transferred the reins to his other hand in order to prop one on his knee. "Of course they did and do. You're a likable person."

She laughed. "Likable?"

He shrugged.

Lifting her chin, she said, "They were all glad to see me and to know I was all right."

"I'm sure they were."

She bit her bottom lip as her thoughtful gaze settled on him for a moment. "He said he wasn't surprised when I left."

"He figured you would eventually?" Garth asked, suspecting it had always been on her mind.

A glimmer appeared in her eyes as she said, "He figured you'd find me. He and Mr. Fry wrote to each other regularly over the years, and that night he heard it was you in the barn at Cecil Chaney's, he knew I'd leave." She shook her head. "Mr. Fry didn't lie to you. At one time Dr. Rodgers had planned on going to Wyoming, but Mrs. Rodgers didn't want to leave Kansas, so they didn't. He said that he asked Mr. Fry not to tell you that, because he was afraid you'd arrive before I was old enough to know what I want."

Garth shook his head. He'd been set on searching for her years ago, but had decided to take the advice that had been given to him. Leave her alone. Let her grow up. She'd matured. That was for sure, and he had to wonder if he had, inside, where it truly mattered. He stopped his horse, and she pulled hers up beside him. "You've always known what you want. A big house with trees for shade, a yard big enough for a garden and windows so you can see the sky."

"Don't forget the rainbows," she said with a teasing glint.

The draw was there again to kiss her, and was too strong to ignore. He leaned across the open space between them. "I never have." He kissed her. Briefly because the horses pulled them apart by stomping sideways.

She laughed as she steered her horse straight.

Once they were walking side by side again, she said, "Dr. Rodgers didn't tell his wife and daughter because he didn't want them to worry about me. And he said Rose Canton didn't need my help. He'd been hoping another assignment might keep me from leaving. I told him it was time. Time for me to make my own life. I introduced them to Gil and Trace, said they were two of your men, and that you were busy with your cattle. I told them all about Ellen. They were more than happy to take her in, and then we all had supper together."

He was certain there were a lot of things she left out, yet said, "It wasn't as hard as you thought it would be, was it?"

"No, it wasn't. Once again you were right." She shrugged. "I should have told them before I left."

Gesturing to the Y in the road, he explained the Solstead place was to the right, little more than a mile away. As they veered with the road, the plethora of emotions dancing around inside him had him asking, "Why'd you come back?" She had everything she wanted with the Rodgerses, and he'd been prepared to let her go back to that life.

"I told you last night. To help you. And don't tell me you don't need it. I know better. There are a lot of men who won't get paid if this sale doesn't happen." Glancing his way, she continued, "A married man carries more clout, and as I see it, you need all the clout you can get."

He should have known she'd heard Nathan tell him that.

"I'm your clout right now. I'm the one who started that rumor and I'll be the one to finish it."

His spine tingled as he wondered what she meant by that. With the cattle sale held up, he hadn't thought much beyond it, but should have. The ride all the way to Texas wasn't so bad. For a man. It sure would be for a woman. She could travel in the wagon with JoJo, but that would be a long and rough ride. And once they got to Texas, it wouldn't be any easier. He had no place for her to stay. No place to live. He hadn't needed one other than Malcolm's bunkhouse now and again, but she couldn't stay there. What the hell was he thinking? He had no intention of taking her back to Texas. No intentions whatsoever when it came to her.

"Go left!"

Caught not paying attention, Garth snapped his head up in time to see a steer barreling up the road. Two cowboys on foot chased after it. Bridgette had already spun her horse around and was veering far to the right of the steer.

"Go left!" she shouted again.

Garth spun his horse around and went left to cut the cow off and turn it about. The steer turned, but then attempted to cut out again. It bawled and bounded back the other way as Bridgette bore down on it from the right. Caught between his horse and hers, the steer had no choice but to head back up the road toward the ranch.

The entire episode had lasted no more than a couple of minutes. About the same amount of time it would have taken him and one of his men to cut a stray back into the herd.

Winded from its escape, the steer slowed, and both he and Bridgette slowed their mounts to keep the critter corralled between them.

"Where'd you learn to ride like that?" he asked.

"I stayed with a lot of families over the years," she answered. "And learned something from each one of them."

"I guess you did," he replied, more in awe than he cared to admit. By the way the two cowboys who'd given up the chase stared at Bridgette, he'd say they were in awe, too. "Get the gate," Garth told them.

As they ran ahead, sending gaping stares over their shoulders, Bridgette said, "In truth, all I had to do was hold on. The horse did most of the work."

She was riding an excellent cutting horse, yet simply

knowing how to let the horse work took skill. "Maybe," he said. "But you held your seat like a seasoned rider."

"Thank you," she said with a nod that made him laugh.

Her face was glowing, almost as brightly as his insides. She had a right to be proud of herself, and he had a right to proud of her. Life was good today, and that made him remember life had always been good with her. Even while living at the orphanage, being with her had made it all tolerable, and not nearly as bad as it could have been.

The steer entered the pen like that had been its plan all along, and both cowboys waved their thanks.

"Look at this place," Bridgette said as they steered the horses toward a hitching post. "It's beautiful."

Besides numerous pens, there was a barn, hay shed, bunkhouse, and a single-level but long sprawling house. It resembled several ranches he'd seen, but he had to admit, it was a nice-looking spread. And that made a ball form in the pit of Garth's stomach.

"That was some mighty fine riding there, Mrs. Mc-Cain," Nathan Solstead said as he walked toward the hitching post. Looking at Garth, he added, "Two of my best men couldn't have rounded up a steer that fast."

Bridgette was about to express her thanks for the compliment when she noticed the shine had left Garth's eyes. A chill zipped her spine. Maybe she'd said too much. Garth wasn't one to want help whether he needed it or not. She couldn't let that hamper her plan. Giving Mr. Solstead a nod, she climbed off her horse.

"Glad you got my message so fast, Garth," Mr. Solstead said while taking the reins of her horse.

"I didn't get a message," Garth said.

"I sent a man to town about an hour ago to ask you

to ride out. Tom Osborne will be here shortly." Turning to her, Mr. Solstead said, "Virginia was hoping you'd ride along. She ran into the kitchen to brew a pot of tea as soon as she saw you on the road. Go on in—we'll put the horses up."

Bridgette turned to Garth. He certainly had left out a lot of information while telling her about what was happening. Tom Osborne was the previous governor of Kansas. He'd lost the seat to George Anthony last fall. Osborne had also been a US marshal, and was a director of the Atchison, Topeka, and Santa Fe Railroad. She knew all this because she'd delivered Marybelle Crane's baby last year, and Marybelle was one of Osborn's cousins,

"Go on in the house," Garth said to her as he led his horse around her to follow Mr. Solstead toward the barn.

There had been a time when she'd known all there was to know about Garth. His hopes and dreams and promises. He was no longer that boy, and it was a good thing she realized she was no longer that girl, either.

"Bridgette, it's so nice to see you again."

She turned to where Virginia Solstead waved from the front door.

"Come in. I have tea brewing."

Bridgette walked around the hitching post. "It's good to see you, too."

While they waited for the tea to brew and then cool—cold tea was far more refreshing in the heat of the summer than hot tea—Virginia introduced her daughters, both Lydia and the older one, Rayanne. The girls were pleasant and polite, but hurried off to occupy themselves when Virginia gave them permission to do so.

"I've so looked forward to talking to you again,"

Virginia said. "I'm just tickled to have you here. I was afraid you'd be staying in Hosford."

"I just had to take some supplies there," Bridgette answered, hoping that would be enough of an explanation. "Your home is beautiful." The spacious kitchen not only held all the necessities, there was a pump at the sink, a rarity for most farm homes, and of course there were windows and real wood floors.

"It's come a long way since Nathan and I first moved out here," Virginia said. "The thriving cattle business has made all the improvements possible. I do hope they get all this hullabaloo with the slaughter houses taken care of soon. It's keeping Nathan up at night. And Lord knows, when a man can't sleep, no one else gets any either."

Bridgette laughed along with Virginia, but her smile froze when Virginia spoke again.

"I'm just dying to know how you convinced Garth to let you work at the Crystal Palace."

"I didn't work there," Bridgette declared. "I was providing medical services."

"Oh, honey, I know that!" Virginia fluttered a hand. "I most certainly never thought elsewise. But do tell, did he know you were there? It didn't sound like it from what Martha Long told Gladys Adams. Martha is Deputy Long's wife. We all belong to the same recipe exchange group, but sometimes we don't get around to exchanging a single recipe."

Bridgette's first instinct was to clamp her lips tight. She hadn't known the deputy was married, but had a good idea of what he'd told his wife about Garth finding her at the Crystal Palace, and could imagine the amount of gossip that sent through all sorts of groups.

"You can tell me," Virginia said. "We wives have to

stick together, and if we can't talk to each other, who can we talk to? No matter how kind and loving our husbands may be, men just don't understand some things."

The excitement, rather than contempt, in Virginia's eyes dissolved Bridgette's fears and the way the other woman grasped her hand and gave it a squeeze told her she'd met a friend.

"That's true," Bridgette answered.

"Oh, dear me, I've been married long enough to know it certainly is. And to know that men aren't always the smartest grape in the bunch." Fluttering her hand again, Virginia went on, "Now my Nathan, he is a smart and a wonderful man, I love him with my very bones, but sometimes, he's not very wise. Take this whole cattle fiasco. I tried to talk to him about it. He thinks he can handle it all by going to the governor, when in truth, things get settled a whole lot faster when we take them into our own hands. We know what we need far more than any governor. Oh, but listen to me, I'm getting off subject, and I'm just dying to know what the inside of the Crystal Palace looks like."

It took a minute for Bridgette's mind to switch subjects, but then she said, "Well, there's not any crystal in it."

"I don't doubt that," Virginia said with a laugh.

Bridgette then told Virginia how Ellen had begged her to help Michelle shortly after she'd gotten off the stage. Although she left several things out, she also told Virginia about taking Ellen to Dr. Rodgers, merely explaining she'd known the doctor for years. After that subject, they moved on to many others, like the best places to shop in Dodge—those where the wives actually ran the business, but the husbands thought they did—ways to keep dirt from seeping in around window frames and a plethora of other things important to women that men never take notice of. Their visiting never slowed, and Bridgette gladly assisted Virginia with preparing a lunch through most of their conversations and laughter.

Bridgette followed the other woman's lead and didn't participate in the conversation the men brought with them to the table when the lunch was served. But she wanted to. She could tell Virginia wanted to, too.

Nathan Solstead and Tom Osborne were doing most of the talking, and though he hadn't said much, she could tell Garth wasn't completely agreeing with all they were saying. As much as he said she was the impulsive one, he wasn't one for talking things through. Actions were what he went for, but he also had a knack for knowing which action was the right one. That, at times, she lacked.

The conversation so far had explained far more than Garth had offered previously. It appeared that besides the slaughter houses attempting to rule the sale of cattle, the government was talking about quarantining all of the cattle coming out of Texas.

"The legislature has suggested pushing the quarantine line all the way to the Colorado border," Tom said. "Nebraska is all for that. They've already established a good-sized stockyard at Ogallala. Ran over fifty thousand head through there last year alone."

"Dodge has surpassed seventy-five thousand head shipped out every year," Nathan said. "This quarantine talk is a farce."

Tom shook his head. "Texas fever is real, and those cattle are infecting others."

"Not every cow leaving Texas is sick," Garth said.

"Every measure is taken to make sure of that. There's not a single longhorn in my herd."

Bridgette bit her lips together, but did lay a hand on Garth's knee beneath the table.

The former governor held up his hand. "I'm on your side, Garth. Cattle are what's building Kansas from the ground up, and I want to see that continue. That's why, as governor, I offered a compromise, a quarantine line down the center of the state, let the eastern farmers have their crop land, and the west have their cattle ranches. I couldn't get it passed though, and now Anthony is leading the crusade. But he's on the farmers' side. He's planting rats in communities all across the state, getting farmers worked up and protesting against the ranchers. Dodge is the most important city on this side of the state. The men you spoke of starting those stampedes are all part of Anthony's plan, and it's only just the beginning."

"You think he's behind the slaughter houses and their standoff?" Nathan asked.

"I can't say yay or nay," Tom said. "But, if they drive down the prices so the cattle drives go elsewhere and then they come back and offer the local ranches top dollar, it's a win-win for Kansas. The farmers no longer have their fields trampled, and local ranchers have far less competition in selling their cattle. Anthony's smart—he doesn't want to completely rid the state of the cattle trade—there's too much money behind it."

"The slaughter houses haven't said anything about giving locals a higher price," Nathan said. "And we depend on the cattle drives to replenish our herds."

"The slaughter houses aren't going to play all their cards at once," Tom said. "This isn't all going to play out overnight. But mark my words, gentlemen, I've been in enough closed-door meetings to know something along those lines is bound to happen."

Bridgette was watching Garth and the tick in his cheek. Her own frustration was growing, but it was all for him. He'd worked so hard driving cattle north for others, and just as his dream of doing it for himself was about to come true, it was being taken away.

Therefore, she couldn't stop herself from pointing out the one thing that hadn't been mentioned. "What about the Atchison, Topeka and Santa Fe Railroad? It seems to me that they shouldn't allow any one slaughter house to option all the railroad cars."

The silence that instantly overtook the room pressed heavily on her shoulders. The only person looking slightly pleased that she'd spoken was Virginia.

Clearing his throat, Tom Osborn said, "The A.T. & S.F. has many railcars, Mrs. McCain. No one company could option them all."

She knew that as well as she knew he hadn't answered her question. "I'm sure they couldn't," she said, never pulling her eyes off him. "But they could option a select number. Say those running in and out of Dodge specifically."

"I'm not aware of any such transaction, but have already assured your husband and Nathan that I will check into it."

"That's good to hear." She used her napkin to wipe her mouth before adding, "Considering you're on the cattlemen's side."

The scraping of chair legs echoed in the silence that once again filled the room. Garth laid his napkin on the table. "Gentlemen, I don't mean to cut this fine lunch short, but Bridgette and I need to get back to town."

His tone told her she'd done it again. Irritated him. So be it.

They bid their farewells and Bridgette gave Garth time to brood. For a mile or two, then she asked, "What's your place like in Texas?"

"I don't have a place." His answer was accompanied by a deep scowl.

She'd mainly been trying to drum up a conversation. Confused, she asked, "Where do you live?"

"I spend a night or two in Malcolm's bunkhouses when I need to get out of the weather, and pay him rent to store my cattle on his pastures." His gaze was solemn when he said, "I don't have a house. I don't have any trees or gardens or rainbows." He shook his head. "All I have are a bunch of cows that nobody wants to pay me for."

Bridgette was taken aback. She'd never, not even when they'd lived in the orphanage with next to nothing to call their own, heard him say anything so demoralizing. Telling him all would work out in due time wouldn't help, not right now, so she held her silence the rest of the way to town. And contemplated exactly what could be done to solve the issues he faced the entire way. Virginia's comment about taking things into your own hands entered her mind, as did something Dr. Rodgers had told her on her first assignment. *When someone needs your help, you don't offer, you act. You do what needs to be done.*

Chapter Eighteen

Garth left Bridgette at JoJo's tent and went in search of Slim. He'd left for Solstead's ranch full of optimism and hope, and returned empty. A void sat inside him, leaving him so hollow he couldn't even muster up anger. That had never happened before.

He'd never lost everything before. Because he'd never had anything to lose. Not like he did now. He hadn't lost yet, but it was imminent. He'd almost had it all, too. Still could if he got full price for his cattle, but from what Tom Osborne said, that wasn't going to happen. Solstead might think the former governor was on their side, but Garth hadn't gotten that impression.

He cursed. He was tired. Tired of dusting himself off and going on. Straightening his shoulders, he drew in air all the way to the bottom of his stomach, and held it there for a moment. This all might be easier if not for Bridgette. Sitting at Solstead's table had made him understand something. He wanted to be successful for her. Show her how hard he'd worked the past few years. Not just dreaming as they used to, but doing.

He found Slim on the other side of the tent city, sit-

ting on an overturned bucket and whittling on a stick
of wood.

"Boys spread the word," Slim said, "but it's not helping. Making this worse actually. A bunch of plowboys
are saying the end of the cattle drives is a good thing."
Tossing the stick onto the ground, he stuck his knife
into the dirt. "To boot, one of the slaughter house men
was just out to see me. Said he'd wired old man Seacrest
about the trouble my cowboys are causing. How they're
trying to start a feud with the farmers."

"Maybe he was bluffing," Garth offered.

Slim shook his head. "I'd let you read Secrest's reply,
but I threw it in the fire. He told me to get the boys in
check, and that we'll all answer for it when we get back
to Texas."

Garth considered telling Slim the rest of what was
happening, the quarantine line, but held off. There
wasn't anything either of them could do about that.
Instead, he nodded toward the stockyards. "Another
herd arrived."

"Yep, and three more are held up on the trail. I told
them to look you up."

"Are they in town or should I ride out?" Garth asked.
No matter how discouraging things seemed, he wasn't
going to give up. There had to be a way to make the
slaughter houses back down, at least this year. The dis-
mal outlook for the cattle drives would need to be taken
into account before next year.

"Ride out," Slim said. "You know cowboys, if the
boss ain't there, they'll be sneaking into town, especially when they are this close."

"I'll go mount up," Garth said.

"I'll ride with you," Slim answered. "Nothing for
me to do here."

He and Slim spent the rest of the day talking with trail bosses. As a whole they hashed around several scenarios and though not one of them held a lot of hope or weight, Garth promised he'd talk with Nathan tomorrow morning and told the bosses to ride into town midafternoon to see if anything had changed.

Garth was hungry and tired by the time he unsaddled the mare. Upon delivering his gear to Bat, he glanced around before asking JoJo, "Where's Bridgette?"

"Don't know," JoJo admitted. "Been gone all day. I figured she was with you."

"I dropped her off here before I rode out with Slim," Garth growled. Hell, he shouldn't have to make her promise to stay put every time he left.

"Her bag's not here," Bat said. "Maybe she went to the Dodge House."

"Now, see there, she probably did," JoJo said. "That's most likely where she is, waiting on you to arrive."

The cook was trying to cover his own ass, and that didn't settle any better than him not knowing where Bridgette was. "She better be," Garth barked. "She damn well better be."

As he started across the open field, the anger boiling in his belly had him glancing over his shoulder. He stumbled slightly and then spun around, trying to figure out what was out of place. Nothing. The tent, the chuck wagon. JoJo and Bat going about their business.

Going about their business as if nothing was wrong. That's what was out of place. They'd both be searching high and low if Bridgette was really missing.

Garth spun around and started walking toward town again. The Dodge House was safer for her than the camp. He'd thought about her today, and her safety, and while talking with the other trail bosses he'd come to admit he wasn't in as dire straits as he'd made himself believe. He still had a pocket full of bank notes, money he'd saved over the years, and even a bad sale would give him enough funds to pay off his hired hands. Things not turning out as he'd expected bothered him, but it wouldn't consume him.

Bridgette did that. The couple of kisses they'd shared had hung with him all day. Forgetting her this time might prove to be harder than the last time after all. That had him wondering if he even wanted to forget her. The idea of her waiting for him at the Dodge House had him walking a bit faster. The streets weren't busy yet, mainly because the sun hadn't set. Once that happened and the cowboys who had driven their herds into the stockyards got cleaned up, and liquored up, the streets would be full.

Nothing slowed his trek to the Dodge House like the laugh he heard walking through the doors. Turning his steps away from the staircase, he entered the dining room. Bridgette sat at a table with Mrs. Franklin and a few other women he didn't know, or care to. She didn't look his way as she nodded and apparently answered whatever question someone had asked.

It struck him then how beautiful she was compared to the others, and how proud he was to have those others believing she belonged to him.

Mrs. Franklin noticed him at the door and directed Bridgette to look that way. She smiled as her eyes met his, and then hurriedly walked around the table. His heart picked up speed the closer she came.

"There you are," she said upon arrival at the arched doorway. "Where did you go?"

"I had to ride out to meet the drives held up on the

trail," he answered, trying to sound normal despite his insides. "What are you doing?"

"Oh, just visiting. Have you eaten?"

"No. You?"

"No, I was waiting for you."

That was Bridgette. She'd waited for him to eat years ago, often saving her meager portions to share with him. Glancing over her head, he noticed all the women had stood. As they gathered slips of paper off the table, he continued to try and act normal. "What was all that?"

"Recipe sharing."

His spine quivered at the innocence she attempted to display. It too took him back years. "Bridgette," he said slowly.

"What?" she asked, wide-eyed. "Mrs. Franklin puts honey in her corn bread. Not on top afterwards, but in the mixture before she bakes it. It's delicious. You'll have to order some."

The women were filing past them, saying farewells, and when one made mention of a cake recipe, he had to conclude she was telling the truth. There was no reason for her not to. He nodded toward the dining room. "I will order the corn bread," he said. "I'm hungry."

They sat at a table for two near the window, across from each other, and he couldn't help but notice how the setting sun caught on her hair, making each honey-colored strand sparkle and shine. When Mrs. Franklin took their order, and Bridgette ordered the roast beef, a hint of humility burned his cheeks. "You could have ordered chicken," he said after the owner's wife had walked away.

She smiled. "I don't feel like eating chicken tonight, I feel like eating beef. The Dodge House gets their meat from the Wagners. They own the butcher shop on the north end of town. The Wagners buy their beef from several local ranchers, and guarantee its freshness."

Thoughts were circling his head, the past and the future, and every one included her. "Oh? How do you know that?"

"Adele Wagner just left."

"She was part of your recipe exchange?" Talking with her, even about things as silly as lady's groups, was enchanting. She was enchanting, and maybe it was time he realized just how much she meant to him.

"It was not my recipe exchange. The women gather regularly to exchange recipes—I just happened to be here at the right time." She unfolded her napkin and laid it on her lap. "I'll share some with JoJo. It wouldn't hurt him to broaden his basics b's."

"Basic b's?"

Tilting her head sideways, she lifted both brows. "Biscuits, beans and bacon."

Garth had to chuckle. "He does include beef every now and again."

"Will wonders never cease?"

They both laughed, and far more relaxed than he had been earlier, he asked, "What did you do all afternoon? Besides exchanging recipes?"

She glanced out the window. "Nothing really."

Onto her again, he said, "Bridgette."

She snapped her gaze back to him and leaned across the table. "How can you do that?"

He leaned over until they were almost nose to nose. "What?"

"Say my name in such a way it gives me the chills."

"Only when you know I know you aren't telling the truth."

She sat back and huffed out a breath of air. "I came

here to return the dress you had purchased for me, but I couldn't."

"Good. It's yours," he said. "I bought it for you." And deep down, he wanted to buy her more than a dress. Always had. Years ago, she'd made him want more out of his life, and now he understood why. Because he wanted to see her dreams come true. That was his dream.

"But it was so expensive."

"I'm not broke," he said a bit defensively.

"You don't have a house," she said quietly, bashfully.

"No, I don't. Because I haven't needed one. When I wasn't rounding up cattle of my own, or taking care of them, I worked for Malcolm, just like I had for years. It made no sense for me to buy a house, buy land."

"But you will someday, won't you?"

He'd contemplated that a bit today, during their silent ride back from Solsteads. The man did have a fine spread. Close to the stockyards, too. "Yes. When I figure out where I want to live."

"You don't want to live in Texas?"

"I don't know." He picked up his glass of water and took a sip before asking, "Where do you want to live?"

It was like watching a sun rise, how her face started to light up and then grew brighter and brighter. Her smile was enough to drop him to his knees if he'd been standing.

She closed her eyes for a moment, and there was a hint of moisture on her lashes when she opened them, and the blue of her eyes was darker, brighter. A smile still curled her lips as she said, "Wherever you live."

If they weren't sitting at a table in the middle of a restaurant he'd have kissed her. Instead, he reached across the table and wrapped his fingers around hers. "I want to live wherever you want to live." Squeezing her fingers gently, he added, "I couldn't buy a place in Texas when I figured on going to Wyoming some day."

"Why?"

"I heard that a girl I used to know lived there."

She licked her lips as if she was going to say something, but Mrs. Franklin arrived with their food.

He thanked the woman, out loud so Bridgette could hear it, and ate, although he couldn't say he tasted much. Not even the honey corn bread. The way Bridgette kept looking at him, and smiling, even the way she took a bite of food and chewed, made it impossible to think of anything but her. Verbal conversation was nonexistent, but they communicated silently throughout the entire meal, and that had his blood hammering inside his veins.

They laid down their forks at the same time, and their napkins. Their eyes remained locked on each other as they stood and met at the edge of the table. Once again, if they hadn't been in public, he'd have kissed her, and not stopped.

Her eyes said she'd have let him. No, that wasn't what her eyes told him. There was no "letting" when it came to Bridgette. Her eyes said she'd have kissed him back, and not stopped.

He took her hand, and without a word, they walked out of the dining room.

"Good night, Mr. and Mrs. McCain."

"Good night, Chrissy," Bridgette said.

Garth nodded. He wasn't about to waste a breath of air. He'd need it in a few minutes. As soon as they entered their room. Their room. That's what it would become in a few minutes.

Each step he took increased the thudding inside him, pushing at the desire that was already consuming him.

They walked down the hall, slowly, sharing knowing glances that made him want to pick her up and run.

She giggled as if reading his mind, and when they stopped near the door, she ran a hand up and down his back while he dug in his pocket for the key.

In the room, he shut the door and locked it. Bridgette had entered before him, and as he turned around, she stood no more than a foot away, waiting. Fighting the desire to pull her into his arms and kiss her until neither of them could breathe, he lifted a hand and ran the backs of his fingers over the softness of her cheek.

"You know what's going to happen," he said quietly.

Her eyes searched his face, slowly, as if considering the ins and outs and unknown ways of the world thoroughly. His lungs were locked tight by the time she folded her fingers around his and pulled his hand off her cheek.

She kissed the back side of his hand before she whispered, "Yes, Garth, and it's been a long time coming."

Leave it to her to point that out. She was being coy, teasing him, that was clear, and he couldn't help giving back a bit of his own. He leaned back against the door. "Well, if I've made you wait too long…"

She laughed. "Changing your mind?"

He wanted this woman and every teasing little move she made increased the agony of that want. "No, but if you are…"

She shook her head. "Don't put this off on me."

"I—" His thought stopped.

With a brazen, slow sway of her hips, she moved forward and wrapped her arms around his neck. "Kiss me, Garth," she whispered. "Kiss me like a man kisses his wife."

"I intend to," he managed to say before his lips found hers.

He covered her face with kisses, every curve and crevice, and slid his hands up and down her arms, over her shoulders, down her back, around her waist. The need inside him grew beyond cognition. All he knew was this was Bridgette, a part of him that had been missing for too long. Much too long.

Picking her up by the waist, and capturing her lips completely, he carried her across the room. They fell onto the bed as one, and bounced. The springs creaked and the headboard bounced against the wall.

The sounds made them both laugh. Garth rolled onto his back and pulled her with him so she was lying atop him. Brushing her hair away from her face, he bit the inside of his cheek in an attempt to keep in check all the emotions and desires racing inside him. He'd never told her how much she meant to him and wasn't sure how to go about doing so. Flowery words and compliments weren't his way, but he had an inkling she'd like to hear them.

He swallowed. "Bridgette, I—"

She pressed a finger against his lips, and while shaking her head, leaned closer, until her lips took the place of her finger. Softly and slowly, she kissed his lips, his chin, his neck and the hollow of his throat. By the time she worked her way back up to his lips, he was as close to the edge as she'd ever taken him.

Bridgette had never known such freedom. She didn't have to pretend, didn't have to hold back, or even imagine. This was real. This was Garth. Finally, completely, hers. Exactly what she'd been waiting for her entire life.

Her heartbeat increased as Garth took control of their kissing. While his hands ran up and down her back, his tongue parted her lips and swept in to catch hers. The thrill was beyond comprehension, and she joined the sweet tussle of their tongues and lips with all she had.

New and fascinating sensations washed over her, and she welcomed each one. Tremors of delight ran up and down her spine as his hands continued to caress her back, pressing her entire length more firmly against him. And something she could only imagine was pure ecstasy erupted inside her breasts as they pressed against his chest.

The desire that flowed inside, filling every nook and cranny, encouraged her to end the kissing and push herself off him. She jumped off the bed before he could stop her.

"Where—"

"Stay right there," she said, stopping him from getting up. Grinning at his frown, she walked to the foot of the bed and grasped one of his boots. "I think this is accomplished more easily without clothes."

"Bri—"

"Uh-uh," she said while pulling his boot off. "You knew what was going to happen as much as I did. Don't try to say you didn't." Tugging the other boot off and tossing it to land near the first, she added, "And don't tell me you don't want it to."

He sat up. "I can't deny that. Neither knowing nor wanting."

"Good." She started unbuttoning her blouse. "Me either." When he started to move, she waggled a finger at him. "Stay put."

"Why?"

Withholding the excitement zipping around inside her was almost impossible, but she tried to keep a straight face. "You'll see."

The smile on his face made something in her very core leap with anticipation. She drew a deep breath to contain it, and waited as he propped the pillows and leaned back against them.

"I'm watching."

Anticipation leaped again deep in her belly as she undid another button. "Then keep watching."

"I am."

She laughed, but then as she unbuttoned the last button and was about to pull the blouse out of the waistband of her skirt, she realized she still had her shoes on. Holding up a finger, she said, "Hold that thought."

"What thought?"

"You know." She plunked down on the nearest chair to remove her shoes. Excitement had her fingers fumbling and she managed to twist the laces in a tight knot on the second shoe. "Hold on," she said.

"I'm not going anywhere, but do you need help?"

The laughter in his voice had her cursing her shoes. Her first morning at the Crystal Palace when she'd heard the doves discussing *things*, she'd made mental notes to try a few someday. Especially upon hearing how much it excited men. And now it was happening.

Her fingers paused as the laces let loose. This was what she'd always wanted, but after tomorrow, she may never see Garth again. Once he sold his cattle, he'd head back to Texas, so tonight might be her only opportunity to truly love him.

"Bridgette?"

"There," she said, kicking off the shoe. When it came to all or nothing, she'd take all even if it only meant one night.

She stood again, and quickly removed her blouse. Tossing it on the table, she took a deep breath to get her rhythm back, and then started unbuttoning the waist-band of her skirt.

Slowly, she pushed her skirt down, over her hips, and watching him as it fell into a pile around her feet, she pinched her lips together at the appreciation on his face. When their eyes met, he lifted a brow, and she had to squeeze her thighs together against the bubble of delight that burst inside her. No matter what happened tomorrow, this was the right choice for her today.

Turning around, she almost tripped before remembering to kick aside her skirt. She wasn't very good at this, but hoped he wouldn't notice. As she untied her camisole, she wondered which to remove first, the top or bottom of her underclothes. Determining it really didn't matter, she untied her drawers and as they fell to the floor, she pulled the camisole over her head. She let it drop and remembered to step out of the drawers before looking over her shoulder to smile at him. "Are you ready?"

He shrugged and pointed. "You forgot your socks."

"Damn," she muttered.

"What did you say?"

Bending over to pull off one sock and then the other, she said, "Nothing." Straightening, she caught her own reflection in the mirror and remembered when she caught Garth preening in the mirror. The glow of the setting sun was also in the looking glass, and in the far corner, she could see him staring at her. His eyes were full of rainbows. They always had been when he'd looked at her just so. Happiness burst inside her and she turned about, holding both arms out to her sides.

"What do you think?" she asked while completing a slow pivot.

He was standing before her when she made the full

circle. Gently, he cupped her cheeks as his gaze trailed a long appraisal from her head to her toes. "I've never seen anything more beautiful."

"I hoped you'd say that," she whispered, just barely because merely breathing was growing impossible.

He kissed her, thoroughly, leisurely, before he swung her into his arms and carried her back to the bed. "Where did you learn that?" he asked.

She lightly nipped on one ear as he lowered her onto the mattress, slowly this time so the spring didn't squeak or the headboard clang. "I've stayed with many families over the years and learned something from every one of them."

He'd stood and was unbuttoning his shirt, which drew her full attention. "I don't believe a family taught you that."

"It wasn't a family, per say." She climbed onto her knees and pushed the shirt off his shoulders and down his back. "But a place I stayed nonetheless."

"I wonder if there's anything left for me to teach you," he said, unbuckling his belt.

Running her hands over the hills and valleys of his firm chest, she said, "You've always taught me the best lessons."

He had, and did so once again as soon as he was as naked as her. With slow, tender kisses that practically made her delirious, he pointed out every place he could kiss her, caress her, stroke her. She followed his lead, exploring his body as thoroughly as he did hers, and when they finally came together, flesh to flesh, the joy of becoming one overshadowed the snap of pain that had surprised her.

"It's over," he whispered in her ear.

On that, she knew he was wrong. "No, it's just begun," she whispered. "We've only just begun."

She was right, and he told her so, many, many times throughout the night, before, during and after they'd both reached unexplainable heights. Once hadn't been enough, not for either of them. Loving Garth with her body was as amazing as loving him with her heart. He'd not only shown her the pleasures, driven her to a point when she'd thought she couldn't take any more, where it had become almost too much, he'd taken her further, into a world full of rainbows that created a kaleidoscope around them.

The brilliance of those magical rainbows still danced inside her when she awoke snuggled in the crook of Garth's arm. Refusing to open her eyes, Bridgette concluded she'd never been so content, so at home. She could happily stay right here forever. They could request food when needed. Mrs. Franklin would—Bridgette's eyes flew open, and the sunshine filling the room had her jumping off the bed.

Chapter Nineteen

❦❧❦❧❦❧

Garth's fingertips brushed her back as she hurried toward the foot of the bed, searching for her clothes.

"Where—" He sat up, looking around. "What's wrong?"

Stepping into her drawers, she said, "I have to get to church." How could she have forgotten? It was obvious why she'd forgotten. Garth, and loving him had filled her mind, but that was also exactly why she shouldn't have forgotten. As she was pulling her camisole over her head, he gripped her waist and spun her about.

"Church?"

"Yes." She couldn't look him in the eye; if she did, she'd be back in bed beside him and that couldn't happen. "Do you see my socks?" she asked while scanning the floor, looking everywhere but at him.

He caught her face with both hands, giving her no choice but to look at him. Her heart skipped several beats. Maybe last night had been the biggest mistake in her life. If possible, she loved him more than ever.

"Because of what happened last night?" he asked. "To me, we are married. We—"

"No, not because of last night." Stretching on her

toes, she kissed him quickly. "We've been married for years. Since the orphanage." Glancing around for her clothes, she said, "I promised the ladies from the recipe exchange I'd be at church this morning." That was the truth.

"You did? Why are you getting so friendly with women you just met?"

"What's wrong with that? Hosford is only a short ride away. It'll be nice to have friends so close." That much was true, although she doubted she'd ever see any of them again. After today she'd no longer have to pretend to be his wife.

He let her loose and she quickly grabbed her socks.

"I guess so," he said quietly.

Sitting on the chair to pull them on, guilt rolled across her stomach. "All the ladies attend church, and I couldn't not accept their invitation. It would have been rude. Especially for the wife of a prominent cattleman."

Gathering his clothes, he started getting dressed too. "About that—"

Suddenly scared, she insisted, "You don't have to attend with me."

His brows furrowed as he looked at her.

"Well, you could—I just figured you wouldn't want to. Said it would just be me." She was holding her breath. Her plan would be crippled if he went to the church.

"Where is this church?"

"On the corner of First Avenue and Spruce Street." Because they were near, she put on her shoes. "It's the only church in town, but different denominations use it at different times." Shoes tied, she crossed the room. "I promised to be at the first service, so I must hurry. We're meeting for tea beforehand." Picking up the blue dress he'd bought her that was still neatly folded on top of the dresser, she asked, "Do you mind if I wear this?"

He'd put on his pants, but not his shirt, and the sight of his bare chest had her swallowing hard.

"It's yours," he said. "You can wear it whenever you want." He took a hold of the dress. "Hold up your arms. I'll help you put it on."

She complied and had to hold her breath and bite her tongue as the insides of his wrists brushed over her breasts as he slowly lowered the dress. The glint in his eyes said it was on purpose, but she already knew that. Desire flared inside her.

Leaning close, he whispered, "I guess I can't hold you hostage all day." His kiss was excruciatingly slow. "And we have tonight."

She bit the tip of her tongue knowing she couldn't promise that.

He stepped back so she could button her dress. "Where's your hairbrush?"

Drawing a deep breath, she answered, "In my bag." She watched as he collected her bag and set it on the table. In a few hours he'd be mad at her. So mad. It was a chance she'd been willing to take in order for him to sell his cattle and go back to Texas. That's where he belonged, and Hosford was where she belonged. With people who loved her, wanted her, despite how she'd never given them a chance over the years.

Garth had wanted her last night, and she had wanted him, but she also knew it wouldn't be enough for him. She could never put the shine in his eyes like his cows did. She couldn't fault him for that, either. He'd found what he'd wanted just like she had. His family was cattle, and hers was back in Hosford.

Spinning around, she finished buttoning the dress

and kept herself from glancing in the mirror until he'd laid the brush on the dresser. Then, while running the brush through the snarls in her hair, she watched him cross the room again. He poured water into the basin and then carried it and the towel to the dresser.

"Do you want me to walk you to the church?"

"No, that's all right, but thank you. It's Sunday morning, and the church isn't far. I'll be fine." After twisting her hair into a bun and securing it, she pinned on the little hat and then used the washcloth to scrub her face.

"I'll probably go to the stockyards while you're at church," he said.

"I assumed as much." She set the cloth on the dresser and hurried for the door. Luckily, the key was still in its hole. After unlocking it, she pulled it open, but stopped shy of bolting out of it. Turning around, she said, "Last night, here with you, was the best night of my life."

She ran then, all the way down the hall and the steps. There wasn't even time for her to catch her breath. Victoria Franklin stood at the bottom of the stairs.

"Hurry," Victoria said. "Or we'll be late."

Garth took his time getting dressed, and thinking. Thinking about Bridgette and how she'd always been there for him. Not just at the orphanage, or now, pretending to be his wife, but all the years in between. She'd always been there, in the back of his mind, encouraging him to continue on, reminding him that every day his future, his dream, was one step closer. She'd always been in his heart, too.

He didn't want to go back to living without her. But completely. In the flesh.

Dressed, he left the room and had no sooner entered the street, when Nathan Solstead rolled up in an awning-covered buggy.

"Jump in," the man said. "I'll give you a ride."

"Where to?" Garth asked as he grasped the awing brace to step up into the buggy.

"The stockyards," Nathan answered. "Figured I might as well check over the new herds while Virginia's at church."

"Don't you attend with her?"

"Usually, but she said there was a special ladies' meeting happening before services today. They do that at times, plan holiday gatherings or events, but mostly they exchange recipes and gossip."

Settled on the seat, Garth nodded, glad he hadn't tried to convince Bridgette not to leave earlier. She'd been excited to go, and now he could understand why—sort of. No special meeting or recipe would have made him leave their bed this morning. During the quiet hours of the night, while holding her close, he'd come up with a plan that might be an answer to all his issues, and he was now ready to put it in place. Bridgette was his future, with or without a solid cattle sale.

"Jim Green and Howard Knight were out to see me yesterday," Nathan said as he flayed the reins over the horse's backside. "Shortly after you and Osborne left."

"They ready to buy some cattle at decent prices?" Garth asked.

"No. They told me they know several other drives are holding up outside of town, and wanted to know how long I thought the stockyards could continue to feed all the cattle penned up there."

"I've been wondering the same thing," Garth replied. "Every day is costing me money I don't have until those cows are sold. I've got half a mind to buy me a piece of land around here and put mine back out to graze."

"That's not a bad idea, Garth—no matter which way this fiasco turns out, you'll be ahead. Maybe not this year, or next, but it won't take long. I guarantee it."

Garth glanced at the other man. Cattlemen were a tight-knit group, but they were still in competition. Especially the owners.

"I can't say it'll happen as fast as Tom made it sound," Nathan said, "but I do agree that the cattle drive days are numbered. That quarantine line will happen, and railroads are working their way down into Texas—soon quarantine line or not, cattle won't need to be driven to Dodge to be shipped. You buy a piece of land around here, sell off some stock, but keep the young ones to sell off over the next couple of years as well as a few breeders to keep the line going—before long you'll have a herd as big as the one you drove here."

Garth held his silence. What Nathan was describing was directly in line with what he'd been thinking last night. It would give him the home Bridgette wanted. Where she could stay busy exchanging recipes with all her new friends.

"Those folks out East don't know they're buying Texas cattle. They think it all comes from Kansas, and will continue to think that way." Glancing his way, Nathan added, "Soon it will be that way. Ranchers here will be raising enough cattle to feed the nation, at least a good portion of it. We already have the railroad and the reputation. A smart man would take advantage of that."

"You have a point," Garth said.

Nathan had stopped the buggy in the middle of the street and turned his way. "Got an hour before we go check the cattle?"

"Why?"

"Because I know of a nice chunk of property and the price isn't so terribly bad, either."

Garth gave a single head nod.

Nathan steered the buggy around and headed west. "A fella from out East—Boston or Baltimore, or was it Buffalo? Don't rightly matter, he was a bit standoffish. So was his wife. It was understandable that they didn't fit in. Even had a couple former slaves who cooked and cleaned for them. Anyway, they built the house and barn and stuck it out for a year or so before they packed up and went back East."

They rolled past the church as the bell in the tower started clanging. Garth grinned, glad Bridgette hadn't been late. "Why hasn't the place sold?"

"Because it's big, lots of acreage. Would make a fine ranch. That's what the fella had plans for, but he didn't like cows." Nathan laughed. "He thought he was going to bring sheep into this area. That wasn't about to happen—there were too many of us against it. Anyway, when they went back East, he left the deed with the bank, along with specific orders it was to be sold as is, no breaking it up into smaller chunks."

Garth had a notion to tell Nathan to turn around. He couldn't afford a place that big.

"Turns out, he's getting a bit anxious to sell," Nathan continued. "And Ruford Potter at the bank told me just the other day that the price has dropped considerably. The owner still wants to sell the entire lot, but the price is more reasonable. Ruford said it's full of furniture, beds, a stove, even pots and dishes."

Nathan talked the entire time they rode west, and Garth thought of Bridgette. He heard Nathan talking, but his mind was on the little exhibition show she'd provided for him last night. It had not only been tantalizing, it had been adorable, and he could imagine she'd give him the same show when he told her about a house.

"You've got a mighty big grin there."

Shifting from looking inward to outward, Garth nodded toward the buildings growing before him. "I like what I see," he said. Truth was, what he saw as Nathan drove into the yard amazed him. If Bridgette had drawn a picture of her dream home, this would be it. There were even trees. Small ones, only a couple years old, but in time they'd grow to shade the two-story house.

"Looks like we aren't the only ones here." Nathan wrapped the reins around the buggy handle. "That's Ruford's rig. Don't know who the saddle horse belongs to."

The banker was there, so was another man from Colorado. Garth held his silence, watching the other potential buyer's interest grow as all four of them explored the barn, sheds and house, which was furnished with fixtures and doodads that Garth hadn't known a home needed.

"I'll need to have my wife look at the property," the other man said. Josh Gibbs was middle-aged and dressed in a suit that suggested he had the money to buy the property. "She's arriving on the train in Cimarron tomorrow."

"I'll need to have my wife look at it, too," Garth said, trying to hide the excitement building inside him. "And sell a few cows."

"Fair enough," the banker said. "I'll be glad to accompany either of you back out here. Just let me know when."

Garth nodded and walked back toward Nathan's buggy, mentally adding up how many bank notes he still had and how many cows he'd have to sell in order to pay off the cowboys and have enough left over to live on. It would be tight. Especially not knowing how long it might be before he sold his cows, or for how much.

Nathan climbed in on the other side. "Gibbs said his wife's family lives in Cimarron and that this house might be a bit too far away for her."

"When did he say that?" Garth asked.

"In the house, I overheard him talking with Ruford." Nathan set the horse and buggy in motion. "I also told Ruford we'd meet him a mile up the road."

Garth didn't reply; his mind was too busy. Something this important needed thought, plenty of it, and he needed to talk to Bridgette. She was the impulsive one. Not him.

Before today that was. By the time he and Nathan rolled into Dodge, Garth had far fewer bank notes in his pocket and a meeting set up with the banker to complete the mortgage tomorrow. His mind was hopping between disbelief at his hastiness and anticipation at telling Bridgette.

"Looks like something big is happening at the stockyards," Nathan said, urging the horse into a trot. "Half the town must be there."

"The entire town," Garth said. People filled the open area while several were making their way up the platform. The crowd made it impossible to see exactly who. "Think they're ready to start auctioning cattle?"

"Knight didn't say anything about that," Nathan said. "But it sure looks like it."

Nathan parked the buggy as close as possible. They both climbed out and started working their way to the front of the crowd.

Garth made it all the way to the front line, where JoJo stood. Having noticed the cook, he'd kept his gaze locked on him while working his way through the crowd. "What's happening?"

The way JoJo grinned and nodded toward the platform had a tightening happening inside Garth's stomach, and as he turned to settle his gaze on the people lining up on the platform, his stomach fell. "What the hell is she doing up there?" he hissed to JoJo.

Bridgette wasn't the only one. The entire platform was full of women, including Nathan's wife and Victoria Franklin from the Dodge House. Garth's hands balled into fists as Bridgette stepped up beside Willow from the Crystal Palace, and then he noticed who else was on the platform. "Damn," he muttered.

The four main men from the slaughter houses were there, too, along with the women.

"You should have seen it," JoJo said.

"I am seeing it," Garth growled. "And I'm going to stop it. What—"

"No, you ain't." JoJo gripped his arm with a solid hold. "Just listen to what they have to say. It took six of them to haul that bigger fella up there."

Garth looked at the men again, and then gawked. The slaughter house agents weren't just sitting in chairs, they were tied in them—wearing little more than their drawers. "Is she trying to get herself arrested again?"

"Could be."

Recognizing the sheriff's voice, Garth's stomach sank as he turned toward the two men standing on the other side of Nathan.

Sheriff Myers shrugged. "But I can't arrest them all. My wife's the one in the yellow." Grimacing, he tilted his head toward his deputy. "Right next to Deputy Long's wife."

"I don't even know what to say," Garth admitted.

JoJo still had a hold of one arm and while jerking on it, hissed, "Hush."

"Good afternoon!"

Garth's teeth clenched as Bridgette's voice carried across the crowd.

Chapter Twenty

Seeing Garth standing in the front row scared the dickens out of Bridgette. It shouldn't. The storm on his face was exactly what she'd expected.

Filling her lungs with air, she willed her nerves to hang with her a bit longer. "Good afternoon," she repeated. "The women of Dodge City have a few things to say today." While waiting for the mumbles and grumbles to die down, she purposely didn't look at Garth. Her plan, as she'd modestly called it in the beginning, had taken on a life of its own. One that had started as soon as she walked in the back door of the Crystal Palace yesterday.

Willow hadn't been that upset about Ellen, actually, she'd been glad to hear where the girl was and that she'd be taken care of. Since Michelle was still healing, she'd taken over the kitchen duties. What Willow had been angry about were the rumors the cowboys were spreading around about this being their final cattle drive to Dodge. When Bridgette confirmed they weren't rumors, Willow insisted something had to be done, that without the cattle trade, Dodge City would shrivel up and blow away. Bridgette had told Willow she planned on asking a few of the merchants to join her in talking to the slaughter house men and the railroad agent, but also that simply talking wouldn't be enough. They'd put their heads together and in the end, Willow said she'd round up the slaughter house men while Bridgette rounded up the wives of merchants, including the railroad agent, Chuck Bolton's wife.

The *recipe exchange* last night had gathered a few women, and the others had been recruited at church this morning.

Taking another deep breath, she said, "Dodge City is a thriving community because of the cattle trade. The season that is just starting could see more than two hundred thousand cows being sold here. That number could grow next year, and the year after, and again, for years to come. If the community allows it to!"

Mumbles and shouts filled the air.

She hadn't practiced what to say exactly, and took advantage of how *allows it to* was repeated several times. "Yes! Allows it to. The men you see on this platform are trying to put a stop to it."

"No—"

Willow stopped Howard Knight from saying more by slapping a hand over his mouth. She also waggled a finger at the other men.

"These men are from two of the slaughter houses," Bridgette explained. "There are more men from other houses in town, but these four are leading a crusade that will not only cheat the cattle owners, it will take money out of every business owner's pocket." As the grumbles started again, she shouted, "But the women of this community are here to put a stop to it."

"Paying less per head isn't going to hurt the farmers none!" someone shouted.

Eleanor Kane stepped forward. She'd told Bridgette she had ten kids and could call them from a mile away, and used that voice while shouting into the crowd. "How much of your grain is sold to the stockyard, Mr. Hollings? A large portion of our grain goes there. To feed the cattle brought into town for sale. Yes, I'm a farmer, not a rancher, but I have the good sense to know if cattle prices fall, if cattle sales fall, so will the price and sale of grain. It's that simple. And if that happens, my family will have a lot less money to spend at the stores in Dodge. It's the same for every person in this town!"

Grumbling and mumbling spread through the crowd before someone shouted, "She's right!"

"You're only saying that because she's your wife!" someone else yelled.

A tall man pushed his way through the crowd. "Yes, she's my wife, and she's right. Every person here depends on the cattle drives to bring money into Dodge and therefore has a stake in the sale of cattle here!" Eleanor Kane's husband kept walking toward the platform. "Look at what happened in Abilene. As soon as the cattle drives went elsewhere, the fields dried up. The town dried up. It's barely half of what it used to be!"

"He's right!" Abigail Myers, the sheriff's wife, stepped forward then. "The wives, mothers, and women of this community are united here today to let everyone know the people of Dodge City will not let that happen to us! We will stand together against oppression. We will not allow any of our citizens, of our businesses, to be coerced. If these men aren't willing to pay full price for the cattle they purchase, then we are prepared to put them on the train and ship them back to Chicago and New York!"

"In their underwear!"

That was Deputy Long's wife Martha, and considering the young woman had been quiet up to now,
Bridgette had to glance at the deputy. He was as red in
the face as Garth, which caused Bridgette to tremble
slightly.

"Mr.—" She had to cough slightly to make her voice
loud enough to be heard over the shouts while pointing
toward a man standing near Garth. "Mr. Bolton of the
A.T. & S.F. has railcars ready to roll, unoptioned ones
and if these buyers are willing to pay fair prices, to follow all the rules and regulations duly overseen by Mr.
Ludwig Smith…" Bridgette then pointed to the nervous stockyard agent. He'd been wringing his hat in his
hands ever since she'd asked him to follow them onto
the platform. He also had a pocket full of her money.
The money Dr. Rodgers had given her. She'd told Ludwig he was to add it to the total of Garth's cattle sales,
knowing Garth would never accept it from her. He was
too proud for that. "…they may participate in the cattle
auction that is set to begin immediately."

"Might want to let them put their clothes on first!"
That shout from the crowd was followed by laughter.

Bridgette glanced toward the four men. Their dignity
had to be hanging on a thread. Being hauled out of the
Crystal Palace by the very girls they'd spent the night
with had just been the beginning. Put on display for all
to see—which had been completely Willow's idea—
and forced to participate or be shipped home had to be
enough to let them know they'd chosen the wrong town.

Cheers from the crowd had Bridgette turning around
again, and watching as several men, led by the sheriff and Nathan Solstead, walked up the stairs and onto
the platform.

Garth wasn't among the men and she didn't expect

him to be. He was still standing in the crowd, glaring at her. She squeezed her eyes shut to keep the tears at bay. If only he'd understand that she'd done this for him. But he wouldn't. That wasn't his way. She'd known that from the beginning and shouldn't be disappointed.

"These women are the epitome of what Dodge City is made of," Nathan Solstead shouted. "We can't let our petty differences divide us or our community!"

The cheering of the crowd lasted for an extended length of time. When it died, Nathan turned to the men in the chairs. "Are you prepared to play the Dodge City way?"

The crowd erupted again when the men nodded.

Smiling, Nathan nodded toward her. "Then, as Mrs. McCain said, let the first sale of the season begin!"

While the crowd cheered, a great deal of hustle and bustle happened on the platform. Sheriff Myers and Deputy Long started herding the women off the platform in order for the other men to deal with the slaughter house agents still tied in their chairs. Bridgette was herded down the stairs along with the others and braced herself as Garth appeared.

He took a hold of her arm and pulled her a few steps aside. "Were you trying to get yourself killed?"

"No, I was getting your cattle sold so you can go back to Texas. That's why you came to Kansas, isn't it?"

"Yes, but—"

"But nothing." The pain in her heart said this plan had been as flawed as her first. She'd set out to do what she wanted, help him sell his cattle, and that's what she had to focus on. Someone shouted his name just then, and she drew a deep breath. "Go see to your cows, Garth."

"Where are you going?"

Stretching onto her tiptoes, she kissed his cheek. "Home, where I belong."

She turned around and ran toward the other women before he could stop her. All pleased by how well their plan had worked, they were gathered a short distance away from the platform, congratulating each other. They had a lot to be proud of, and excited about.

"Everyone is welcome to join us in the Dodge House," Victoria Franklin invited over the general chaos of the men organizing the opening of the sale while purposely including Willow with a wave of her hand. "We'll celebrate there. It's too loud here."

Being herded forward by the women around her, Bridgette tried to keep her gaze forward, but had to shoot one final glance over her shoulder, searching the crowded platform. Garth was easy to spot. Tall. Broad. Commanding.

Knowing she was the one walking away this time didn't make her feel any better than she had watching him walk away. Her plan had been to show him she was capable and could create plans that worked just like he could. That she'd be fine without him. That he could go back to Texas and never have to worry about her again. The part she hadn't considered was that she'd lost her heart to him again.

Actually, she'd lost it to him years ago, and never got it back.

Torn between selling his cattle and following Bridgette, Garth turned around and immediately found her in the group of women. The same instant, his instincts had him looking past her, to where the sunshine caught on the barrel of a gun. An agonizing, fear-filled bolt of terror shot through him like a bullet. He shouted her name, and ran across the platform. Shoving people aside, he shouted her name again. The sharp report of the gun ricocheted through the air, into his ears, and hit his heart with more pain than if the bullet had struck him.

Running down the stairs, across the dirt, horror compiled with helplessness as he watched Bridgette jerk backward. It was worse than a nightmare. He was running but couldn't get there fast enough, couldn't catch her as she fell to the ground.

In that instant, he went deaf, numb, and focused on nothing but getting to her side. There, he dropped to the ground. Blood already marred the blue dress he'd bought for her and as he cupped her face with both hands, a cold and excruciating darkness flooded him.

In all his years, he'd never witnessed the depth of shock or fright that filled her blue eyes.

"Garth." Her voice cracked as she gasped. "I. Can't. Breathe."

He struggled to maintain control. His eyes were stinging. His heart was wrenching. "I got you, honey." The blood was coming from just below her left shoulder and he refused to think what that meant. "I'm here."

Tears fell from her eyes and each one of her gasps tore harder at his insides.

Her face contorted as she whispered, "I. Love. You."

"I know, honey, I love you, too. But don't talk. Save your breath." He wasn't certain if she sighed or if the gurgle he heard was her letting out her last breath. Fear and rage, a rage so fierce he felt it to his very soul, tore his insides apart. "No! No!" He picked her up and stood. "Where's the doctor? Where's the damn doctor?"

"This way."

Garth blindly followed, holding on to a thread of

hope that Bridgette was still breathing. Her eyes were closed, her body limp in his arms, but with every step he took, he kept believing he could feel her breathing. She couldn't die. Not Bridgette. Not Bridgette. She was too full of life. Of love. Of sweetness and kindness and all the things that made the world go round. He was proof of that. Without her, he was nothing more than a shell of a man, existing on anger and resentment. She made him whole. Made him feel. And love. He loved her more than anything. Always had.

"Lay her down."

Lost inside and out, Garth barely realized he'd entered the doctor's house, or that the man was standing over the table, waiting to examine Bridgette. Feeling more vulnerable, more scared and panicky than when he'd been a child living on the streets in New York, he said, "She's not dead. She can't die."

"Just lay her on the table, son. Let me take a look-see."

Garth didn't want to lay her down. He didn't want to let go of her, as if that might make her stop breathing.

"Mr. McCain," a woman said softly. "She'll be in good hands. Just lay her down so the doctor can examine her. You can stay right here beside her."

He knew he wasn't the child he'd been years ago, hadn't been for a long time, yet, he felt as if he was only a shadow of a man. He had only ever been a shadow of man until she'd made him whole. She'd stood by him as a child and as a woman. A proud beautiful woman who he couldn't lose. They belonged together. Through thick and thin.

Garth eased her onto the table and then took a step back so the woman could start cutting away the blood-soaked dress. When the damage to her flesh was revealed, reality returned with full force. Torn between staying beside her and learning who was responsible ravaged his insides. Staying beside her won out, as it always would.

"She's lost a lot of blood, but will be fine. The bullet's lodged in her collarbone," the doctor said within minutes.

"What do you have to do to get it out?" Garth asked, rubbing a hand along Bridgette's shin. He couldn't stop touching her. Had to feel the life in her.

"Surgery," the doctor replied. "You'll need to step out."

"I'll—"

"No," the doctor said. "You can wait in the front room. My wife will come get you as soon as we are done."

It was the worry in the wife's eyes, a woman who moments ago had been standing with Bridgette on the stockyard platform, that Garth conceded to. With a nod, he left the room with Bridgette's blood on his hands and retribution for her injury on his mind.

He was crossing a second room, heading toward the front door when two men jumped in front of him, blocking his way. Ready to toss them both aside, his steps faltered when two women stepped in front of the men.

The sheriff nudged his wife aside at the same time Nathan moved his wife out of the way. In no mood to be stopped, Garth started forward again.

"He's in jail, Garth," Sheriff Myers said. "He's in jail and not going anywhere. Deputy Long is standing guard."

Iron bars weren't going to stop him.

"Bridgette needs you here, Garth," Virginia Solstead said. "Not behind bars yourself."

Garth had to suck in air as her words dowsed his

branding-iron-hot nerves. Virginia had been in the other room up until the doctor told him to leave. Letting the air out of his chest, he asked, "Who was it?"

"Luke Wiley, Jud Wiley's youngest boy," Myers answered. "I figured he'd show up sooner or later, with his pa and brothers in jail, but I didn't expect this. He's only thirteen."

A bit more of the fire inside Garth died down at discovering the boy's age. Thirteen. A kid. Not much older than Bat. Who, Garth noticed for the first time, was on the other side of the room, standing next to JoJo. Both of them had red eyes.

Despondent rather than angry, he asked, "Why Bridgette? Why'd he shoot Bridgette?"

"Wiley's wife ran off with a cowboy who had come to town with a cattle drive a couple of years ago, leaving Wiley and their five boys to fend for themselves," Myers said. "That was their farm you captured Wiley and the others at. The oldest son left not long after their mother, but the rest of the boys have been following Wiley's footsteps, hating every drive, every cowboy, more than the last."

"Then he should have shot me," Garth said.

"No," Myers said. "He wanted to take away the thing you loved the most. Just as that cowboy had done to him."

Chapter Twenty-One

$\mathcal{B}$ridgette had never been sick or hurt, not severely. The pounding in her temples, the ache in her arm and chest and the churning in her stomach said that had changed. She didn't want to open her eyes. Going back to sleep, where she hadn't felt so awful, was a much more agreeable choice, and she was almost there, drifting back into numbness when she heard it again.

It wasn't her name as much as the person who said it that made her open her eyes. The brightness of the light hurt, but she kept her eyes open long enough to see Garth before closing them again.

"How are you feeling?" he asked.

"Terrible." The fog inside her head lifted inch by inch, allowing her to recall the events up until she was walking with the other women away from the stockyard. She opened one eye, just to measure the pain and her ability to look around. Nothing was familiar, other than Garth. Pinpointing her gaze on him until the pain was too much and she had to close her eye, she asked, "Where are we?"

"Dr. Austin's."

"Why?"

Garth's hand squeezed hers. "You were hurt."

Additional memories came, along with a shiver of fear that increased her heart rate. Garth had shouted for her and then… "I couldn't breathe." She couldn't recall why. "What happened?"

"Shhh." Garth kissed her forehead. "Don't worry about it. You're fine. I'm here. Go back to sleep."

The way he nuzzled her forehead and ran a hand over her head was comforting and calming. Pain still throbbed in her head and her shoulder. "How bad was I hurt?"

"You're going to be fine, honey. Just go back to sleep." His kisses trailed down the side of her face and then he snuggled his head against hers.

Comforted by his nearness, she gave in to the heavy cloak of sleep that slowly settled around her again.

When Bridgette awoke the next time the room was dark, but Garth was still there, holding her hand. Knowing that once again eased the pain now centered on her shoulder. She tried to remember what had happened, but all that she could recall was Garth shouting her name and then running toward her. Her heart started racing again. He should have been selling his cattle. She tried harder to remember, but her mind wouldn't work.

The next thing she knew, it was light again, and Dr. Austin was standing over her. So was Garth, and she asked him the first thing that came to her mind. "Did you sell your cattle?"

His smile was cajoling and that made her heart beat fast again.

"Is that why you're still here and not—" Her train of thought shifted instantly at the sight of his shirt. Fear shot through her. "Why is there blood on your shirt?"

"I sold plenty of cattle for top dollar," Garth said, lifting her hand to his lips. "And I'm here because of you."

She shook her head slowly. "You're supposed to be on your way back to Texas."

"The blood on his shirt is yours, young lady," Dr. Austin said. "You were shot. Luckily, it lodged itself in your collarbone and didn't do much damage. Besides being very sore for a few weeks while the break heals, you're going to be fine."

Bridgette heard what the doctor said, but her mind was once again on Garth. She knew him so well, and his temper. "You didn't shoot them back, did you?"

"No," he replied. "Who would keep you out of trouble if your husband was in jail?"

"Let me take a peek at the wound, and then I'll leave the two of you alone," Dr. Austin said.

That happened relatively quickly, and though the examination wasn't pain-free, it wasn't nearly as bad as it could have been. Because Garth was there. A dozen questions danced about in her head concerning what had happened, but in truth, how he'd called himself her husband was what lingered in her mind.

"I'll be back with some soup in a little bit," Dr. Austin said.

Bridgette had never been uncomfortable around Garth, but the way he shifted from foot to foot teased her nerves. He hated fidgeting and never did it. "You don't have to stay," she said. "I'm sure you have things to do."

"I do, but I can do them later."

Her throat felt thick, but it was nothing compared to her injury. "The doctor said I'll be fine, and I will be. I'm sure your cowboys are ready to head south. You, too."

He sat down on the edge of the bed. "Why do you want me to leave so badly?"

She tried to muster up a smile. "Because that's what Garth McCain does."

"Maybe Garth McCain has changed."

Tears stung her eyes as she shook her head. "Not the one I know." He hadn't. He'd always been a bit ornery and grumpy and stubborn, but also kind and caring, dependable and protective, smart and determined. And handsome. Love wasn't blind as she'd thought; it was forgiving, and all encompassing. He'd taken a hold of her hand, and she squeezed his fingers. "I don't want him to change, either. I came back to help you sell your cattle so that you'd know I'll be fine without you. So you'll never have to worry about me again. You can go back to Texas knowing I'm happy living in a big house with my family."

"Is that what you want? Me to go back to Texas and you back to Hosford with your family?"

Her heart sank, yet she nodded. "Yes."

"Well, that's too bad."

"No, it's how it has to be."

"Why?"

"Because that's what you want. If being a cattleman wasn't what you wanted, you wouldn't be one. You've never done anything you didn't want to do."

"You're right, I haven't, and that's why I'm not going back to Texas. Because I don't want to."

"You're just saying that because I'm hurt and you feel responsible." She wiped aside a tear burning her cheek. "It wasn't your fault."

"I know it wasn't my fault, and I know it wasn't your fault. We were in it together, just like we always were, and that's all that matters. That we were together." He kissed the back of her hand. "And I'm not going back to Texas."

"But if you sold—"

"I sold cattle, plenty of them, and I have the money you gave Ludwig."

"I wanted you to get top dollar."

"I did. I made enough money that I bought a house. It has everything except for a rainbow. We'll have to wait until it rains for that."

Although he was serious, the shine in his dark eyes was bright. So bright she could see all the colors of a rainbow in them. Those were the rainbows she'd always been looking for. They had clarity and depth. The ones in the sky always looked faded, as if covered in dust. He was her rainbow, and her heart couldn't take much more. "What are you talking about? What house?"

"Your house. My house. *Our* house." Garth watched her face. Along with a few other things, finesse wasn't one of his best traits. "It's a few miles west of Dodge and comes fully furnished." Jud Wiley's son had tried to take away the one thing that meant more to him than anything else, but by firing that gun, shooting Bridgette, the boy had made Garth take a good hard look at what his life would be like without her. Of what he'd be like. He'd be in worse shape than the entire Wiley family. That was a fact. And he wasn't going to wait any longer to make all her dreams come true, or his. "Living here seems fitting considering you've made quite a name for yourself, and you have more friends than a bartender on Saturday night."

"Here? You bought a house here? You want to live here?"

"Yes. Dodge has a good school for Bat to attend, and JoJo's agreed to stay on as a cook for the ranch hands.

Several of my cowboys have said they wouldn't mind hanging their hat in the same place every night. It'll also keep you close to your family."

She was shaking her head. "Bat. JoJo. My family?"

"Yes, Dr. Rodgers, his wife and daughter, as well as Ellen arrived last night. You slept through his examination."

"I did?"

"Yes, you did."

"How did—"

"I wired them." He cupped her face with both hands. Yesterday, while waiting through her surgery, his mind had traveled up and down many roads, and every single road had led to Bridgette. And he was more than fine with that. "I'm done walking away, Bridgette. I love you. I have loved you for years, and I want to make that promise we made to each other back at the orphanage real with a preacher and a ceremony."

Her eyes grew wide. "You do?"

"I'll never leave you again, Bridgette, ever, I swear." He shrugged. "You can be a midwife here if you want. Or just a wife."

"A wife? Oh, Garth, I—I don't know what to say."

"How about yes?"

She laughed, and nodded, and said, "Yes."

"You'll marry me?" he asked, just for clarity. This was Bridgette.

"Yes, I'll marry you."

"And live in a house west of town?"

"Yes, and live in a house west of town."

He kissed her then, and she kissed him back, but then stopped and pushed at his chest with the hand not bandaged to keep her shoulder from moving.

"Sorry," he said, checking that he hadn't squished the arm in the sling. "I didn't mean to hurt you."

"You didn't," she said, yet a frown marred her face. Whispering, she added, "Everyone, the entire town, thinks we're already married."

"Which is why I have to go do those things I mentioned earlier. Put on a clean shirt and let the others in the room." He kissed her briefly. "Dr. Austin didn't go to get you soup. Your father, Dr. Rodgers, has already fetched the preacher, as I asked him to." Kissing her once more, he whispered, "You may be the first woman to get married in her nightgown."

Bridgette hadn't known her heart could be so full, or that she could be so happy. Just as she'd always dreamed, Garth was giving her the world. Her world. And his.

She cupped Garth's cheek and kissed him thoroughly. He was the most amazing kisser. The most amazing man. Life with him would be an adventure every day, which was exactly what she wanted. Yet, she had to ask, "You're sure about this? That you want to marry me?"

"Would the Garth McCain you know marry you a second time if he wasn't sure?"

She laughed. "No, he wouldn't. He wouldn't have married me the first time, either."

"You're right. I wouldn't have." He kissed her. "This was my plan all along."

* * * * *

If you enjoyed this story,
make sure you check out these other
great reads from Lauri Robinson

UNWRAPPING THE RANCHER'S SECRET
HER CHEYENNE WARRIOR
SAVING MARINA
A FORTUNE FOR THE OUTLAW'S
DAUGHTER

COMING NEXT MONTH FROM

H HARLEQUIN®

ℋISTORICAL

Available May 23, 2017

MAIL-ORDER BRIDES OF OAK GROVE (Western)
by Lauri Robinson and Kathryn Albright
Follow the adventures of twin heroines from reluctant mail-order brides to Wild West wives!

THE DEBUTANTE'S DARING PROPOSAL (Regency)
by Annie Burrows
Miss Georgiana Wickford has a plan to escape the marriage mart—she'll propose a marriage of convenience to her estranged childhood friend, the Earl of Ashenden!

MARRYING THE REBELLIOUS MISS (Regency)
Wallflowers to Wives • by Bronwyn Scott
When Beatrice Penrose's and her baby's lives are threatened, Preston Worth makes Bea an offer of protection she can't refuse—as his wife!

CLAIMING HIS HIGHLAND BRIDE (Medieval)
A Highland Feuding • by Terri Brisbin
Alan Cameron was sent to track runaway Sorcha MacMillan down, but he can't overcome his instinct to protect her—by claiming her as his bride!

Available via Reader Service and online:

AN UNEXPECTED COUNTESS (Regency)
Secret Lives of the Ton • by Laurie Benson
The Earl of Hartwick may be Miss Sarah Forrester's rival in the hunt for a diamond, but soon she longs for another treasure—becoming his countess!

THE CONVENIENT FELSTONE MARRIAGE (Victorian)
by Jenni Fletcher
Respectable governess Ianthe Holt receives an unexpected proposal from a stranger! And soon Robert Felstone shows her there can be more to their convenient marriage than vows...

SPECIAL EXCERPT FROM

◆ HARLEQUIN®

ℋISTORICAL

When aristocrat's daughter May Worth's life is endangered, only one man can protect her: government agent Liam Casek…the man whose sinfully seductive touch she's never forgotten!

Read on for a sneak preview of
CLAIMING HIS DEFIANT MISS,
the third book in **Bronwyn Scott's**
captivating quartet **WALLFLOWERS TO WIVES**.

Liam wasn't willing to chance letting May roam free and unprotected. It infuriated him she was willing to take that chance. She had blatantly chosen to ignore him and vanished this morning just for spite. He knew very well why she'd done it—to prove to him she didn't need him, had never needed him, that he hadn't hurt her, that indeed, he had been nothing more than a speck of dust on her noble sleeve, easily brushed off and forgotten. But that wasn't quite the truth. He had hurt her, just as she had hurt him. They were both realizing the past wasn't buried as deeply as either of them hoped.

To get through the next few weeks or months, they would have to confront that past and find a way to truly put it behind them if they were to have any chance at an objective association. The task would not be an easy one. Their minds might wish it, but their bodies had other ideas. He'd seen the stunned response in her eyes yesterday when she'd recognized him, the leap of her pulse at her neck even as she demanded he take his hand off her. Not, perhaps, because he repulsed her, but because he didn't.

Goodness knew his body had reacted, too. His body hadn't forgotten what it was to touch her, to feel her. Standing behind her in the yard had been enlightening in that regard. He wasn't immune. He hadn't thought he was. He had known how difficult this assignment would be. His anger this morning at finding her gone proved it.

Anger. Lust. Want. These emotions couldn't last. A bodyguard, a man who did dirty things for the Crown, couldn't afford feelings. Emotions would ruin him. Once he started to care, deeply and personally, it would all be over.

Make sure to read…
CLAIMING HIS DEFIANT MISS by Bronwyn Scott.
Available May 2017 wherever
Harlequin® Historical books and ebooks are sold.

www.Harlequin.com

HARLEQUIN®

A *Romance* FOR EVERY MOOD™

JUST CAN'T GET ENOUGH?

Join our social communities
and talk to us online.

You will have access to the latest
news on upcoming titles and special
promotions, but most importantly,
you can talk to other fans about your
favorite Harlequin reads.

Harlequin.com/Community

Facebook.com/HarlequinBooks

Twitter.com/HarlequinBooks

Pinterest.com/HarlequinBooks